Little Gidding Girl

by
Vivienne Tuffnell

Author's Note

Little Gidding Girl was written in 2004 and reflects the technology (phones and computers) of the first years of the new millennium as well as the way people related to that technology. It's sometimes hard to remember that the internet, search engines and smartphones have not been with us forever, or that there were once other ways to find out stuff other than asking Google. I considered rewriting the novel to reflect the changes but concluded that I would spend my life playing catch-up as technology moves far faster than literature.

When I wrote the novel, I made up a whole batch of therapies that did not exist at the time (with the exception of Reiki which is a well-known and generally well-respected system). Some of those therapies now appear to exist. Genuine practitioners of complementary and alternative therapies are aware that there are many who work without their level of integrity and professionalism.

Chapter 1

It was at the Autumn Equinox, poetically enough, that still point between dark and light when they are held in almost perfect balance, that Verity first noticed that her life seemed oddly awry. She had rushed home from work, cycling fast enough to raise a faint red tinge in her pale face, to get that short time alone in the house that she sometimes so craved; that half hour of personal space, to do with as she liked which had saved her many hours of self-recrimination for being snappy and irritable with her family. A simple puncture had deleted fifteen of those priceless minutes, and she had been desperately trying to do up the zip of her new jeans when her son had burst into the bedroom without knocking.

"Mum, mum, can Matthew stay for tea?" Tom demanded breathlessly.

His hair was tousled and seemed to be full of fragments of grass and twig; his school uniform was already crumpled and dirty, and if she wasn't much mistaken, there was a hole coming at the right knee of the trousers. There was no easy way of getting a child to understand the implications of this to an already over stretched family budget and therefore no point in telling him off simply for being a child and being hard on his clothes.

"I don't know if I've got enough for an extra mouth," Verity said.

Tom could sulk for England and he was already starting his warm-ups; the trembling lower lip, the shining of eyes filling up with what Verity knew were really crocodile tears, were all warning signs, and she was too flustered at being caught trying to somehow smooth her spare tyre into her bra while hauling on the zip with a coat hanger, all while holding her breath, to try and do more than head him off.

"I'll go and see what we've got," she said. "But don't do this to me again, Tom. You need to ask me before you ask your friends home. Does Matthew need to ring his mum?"

"No need," Tom said. "His mum's never there anyway."

"Well, he should at least try," Verity said. "Show him where the phone is while I see what we've got for tea. Go on, out. I've also told you about knocking on doors first."

She was trying to sound stern but it never seemed to work. He ran from the room, yelling downstairs to his friend that, "Yes, it's all right: you can stay for tea."

"That isn't what I said," Verity said, uselessly and sighed.

She must have been an absurd sight, the coat hanger dangling at a weird angle to her belly, and her shirt pulled down to hide the straining waistband, but she knew her son hadn't noticed a thing. He might scarcely have noticed even if she'd been stark naked with a carnation between her teeth; he'd have noticed if she'd got a new bike, or if his father had bought a car, but really, sometimes, she felt she was simply wall-paper to his vivid and all-encompassing life. Wall-paper that cooked, cleaned and magically delivered clean laundry, but wall-paper nonetheless. She sighed again and began trying to extricate herself from the denim that gripped much tighter than she liked. Another month then, she thought, another half a stone, and I'll be able to wear them without fainting.

She dragged on her comfy old jeans, now half a size too big, and padded barefoot down the stairs and into the kitchen, trying to remember what she'd excavated from the freezer than morning to defrost. There was a packet of supermarket pork chops lying on the work surface, and she groaned inwardly. These things always came in awkward numbers, too many or too few and she peeled the plastic away from the pallid meat with distaste.

Tom came running through the kitchen with his pal close on his heels, a nondescript child of the same size and age as Tom, but with none of his vibrancy.

"Going to play in the garden," he announced tersely and pushed past her to get out the back door, banging it behind him. Why are boys so noisy, she asked herself and then returned to counting the chops? Damn, only three, she thought; I shall have to do something else for me.

"What are you doing Mum?"

The voice behind her made her jump very slightly; her daughter Rose was standing there, her school bag still distorting her posture by its weight, but even as she turned to look at her Rose dumped the bag in the big armchair near the boiler. Verity gave her head a slight shake, feeling suddenly inexplicably confused, as though something somewhere were wrong but she couldn't quite place it.

"I'm seeing if we have enough pork chops for tea," Verity said. "I think we're one short."

Rose came over and peered at the chops and began to laugh.

"I don't know how you ever got a GCSE in Maths, Mum," she said.

"They were O levels then," Verity said. "And I got a B. What do you mean, Rosie?"

Rose scowled as only a new teenager can at being reminded of her baby name. She put on her patient I'm-talking-to-my-mum-so-it's-the-same-as-talking-to-an-idiot voice.

"OK," she said. "Let's take it nice and simply; there's three chops, that means one each. Was that so very hard?"

She spun round, yanking off her tie which joined the bag, and sauntered out the kitchen leaving Verity feeling abruptly, and rather horribly confused and angry with her daughter for forgetting her brother's existence.

"Mum?" Rose called from the door. "Can we have apple sauce with them? Please, please, please?" She was suddenly a small child again, pleading for a treat, all pretence at teenage cool forgotten.

Verity shrugged, had been about to say they had no apples and then remembered that this house had a small orchard that was currently groaning with apples. They'd moved here over the summer and she was still unused to some aspects of the house despite the fact that for some of her youth it had been her home. She opened the back door, felt the wash of sweet air, picked up the bleaching wicker basket that waited there and began walking up the lawn towards the stand of mixed trees at the end of the long walled garden. Here, where the grass was shaved so close and the ground beneath so dry, she didn't expect to see the footprints of her son and his friend, but when she reached the long grass of the orchard there was no trace of their passing. The knee length grass should have shown the trampling and slashing they usually made, filling the air with the green scent of the bruised blades but all she could smell was the rich cidery smell of the fermenting windfalls of both apple and pear, and no children ran and laughed ahead of her.

7

As the wind blew through the trees and shook the leaves and swayed the branches, Verity felt herself go cold all over as she remembered that she had no son, that she had never had a son.

She didn't collapse, not as such, but she did sink slowly to her knees amid the wasp-covered apples and sat very still, hearing only her own heart for a few minutes, until she was composed enough to reach out and begin to retrieve today's offerings from the ancient trees. The windfalls were riper than those still on the tree, and if she found them the day they fell, they were perfect for cooking. Her grandfather had known all the names of these venerable trees, which were all-but extinct elsewhere, but she had never thought to ask such questions until now. This tree held eaters, but of such size that they were more use for cooking; they were sweeter than the Bramleys and needed almost no sugar and broke down to a soft velvety paste with only a short time on the stove. She filled her basket with the best of the fallen apples and tried to get to her feet. Her knees were shaking, showing her that while her mind was doing its very best to ignore whatever it was that had just happened, her body had no such plans. She crawled a little way from the base of the tree, close to the bole of the dwarf cherry that never bore fruit for people though it fed plenty of birds with its ripening fruit, leaned her back against the comforting bark, and took a long slow deep breath to calm herself.

The light was slanting through the leaves, and out of the breeze you could still pretend it was summer yet the light had that curious colour and texture of warmed golden syrup, and the air while full of the rich scents of garden and orchard held the faint ominous chill of the coming of winter, still far off but waiting patiently beyond this time of fruit and plenty.

"Seasons of mist and mellow fruitfulness," she whispered. "Close bosom friend of the oh, what was it again?"

She put the thought away, because it made her think of things she didn't want to think about, and with the aid of the tree, managed to get to her feet and, hauling the basket to her hip like an ungainly baby, she meandered her way back up the garden. When she got back to the lawn, she stopped and glanced back at the deserted orchard. The higher branches were swaying and trembling much as if there were children hidden amid the leaves, giggling and laughing; she could almost hear them, Tom and

8

Matthew, playing at being outlaws or something. At that thought, she trembled again, and made herself turn away, refusing to analyse what had happened, even to think about it much beyond saying to herself with false cheeriness, "Well, that is what comes of a vivid imagination," even though she knew she could never, never, never have imagined something as vibrant and alive as that.

Back in the sunny kitchen she sorted and washed the apples, knowing she had collected far too many just for an accompaniment to pork chops, but then Rose would happily eat the leftover cold cooked apple for her breakfast. Upstairs, she could hear the raucous music Rose chose to do her homework to and thought rather sadly of Mozart and Beethoven, imprisoned in CDs gathering dust in the rack by the stereo. She'd played them endlessly when Rose had been Rosie, but secondary school had put an end to that. No other parents played that sort of music to their children and Rose had refused to listen to it any more, for fear it would irretrievably contaminate her, mark her out as different and therefore a target. Verity later discovered that her sort of parenting was only practised by the sorts of mothers who chose to devote themselves utterly to their offspring, putting their names down for expensive and exclusive schools almost from birth and thereafter immolating themselves on the domestic altar; she'd met a few of them in recent years. They were a proud bunch in the main, but the bitterness of their sacrifices was beginning to show at the edges; those with teenagers had passed beyond the bitter-sweet moments of loving their kids despite everything and had moved into a cold disdain of them instead. The refrain was simply, "After all I've done for them!" and the chilled, growing knowledge of the complete indifference of their children to them went a long way to souring what had once been love of sorts.

It had been a shock to realise this was what parenthood for some was about; Verity's response was to allow Rose to buy the trashy pop music her friends liked and hope that one day Rose would allow herself to choose her own tastes. There were still moments of it, such as her liking for home-made apple sauce, but in the main it had gone underground around age eleven. Verity hoped it would re-emerge, blinking owlishly in the light, in a few years' time.

"Mum had a real blonde moment when I got home from school," Rose said conversationally at dinner.

David looked at her, quizzically.

"What do you mean?" he asked, spearing a piece of pork.

"Did she really get a B at O level Maths?" Rose asked.

David put the meat in his mouth and began to chew.

"I'll show you the certificate if you don't believe me," Verity said, moving her meat around the plate without enthusiasm.

David swallowed.

"What are you on about?" he said.

Rose smirked, a new talent and an unwelcome one.

"Mum couldn't get her head round how many chops makes three," she said. "There were three in the packet and she wasn't sure it was enough."

Verity glanced at her husband, her face blank.

"Were you expecting company or something?" he said.

She put her knife and fork down.

"No," she said. "I don't feel terribly well. I think I might be coming down with something. I wasn't thinking straight, that was all. The chops were stuck together."

She poked listlessly at a boiled potato.

"Mum can't count, mum can't count," Rose sang in a low giggly voice.

Verity said nothing, but David pointed his fork at his daughter.

"Pack that in right now, young lady," he said, but without rancour.

Rose shut up and carried on eating. David looked at his wife with some concern.

"Were you thinking about your granddad again?" he asked, in a lower voice.

"Maybe," she said, guardedly. If he thought she'd got caught up in a moment of grief, maybe he'd not push it any further. Whatever had happened today she didn't know, but she also had no intention of talking about it; a hallucination that vivid, that real wasn't something she wanted anyone even her husband to know about. It had to be a one-off, a single aberration, never to be repeated, didn't it?

"Does either of you want my chop?" she said. "I just don't feel like it now I've cooked it."

10

After they'd eaten, David and Rose washed the dishes, Rose grumbling the whole time that she was missing something vitally important on the television, but when she was released from servitude, as she put it, the programme turned out to be a lacklustre episode of a soap that she had previously declared that she hated anyway. The advantage of this house was that they didn't all have to sit in the same room on an evening; their old house had been so small and cramped that other than the main living room there was nowhere else to sit if one person elected not to watch TV. It had also been so poorly built that, unless you kept the volume very low, the TV could be heard too clearly upstairs. This had meant that until the move here, she and David had watched films with their chairs pulled uncomfortably near the set so that the sound wouldn't disturb Rose's sleep. It had also meant that when Rose was a baby, there had been nowhere in the house you couldn't hear her crying. It had saved on buying one of those baby monitor things, David had quipped at the time, but that had been the only even vaguely silver lining of such a house. This house seemed vast and sparsely furnished even with all their possessions that had previously crammed the old house, plus the remnants of her grandfather's stuff. David even had a decent sized study that didn't have to double as an occasional guest bedroom; he could leave his marking or lesson planning all over the desk and not have to clear it until he had to bring it back to school.

Verity sat in the corner of the study, huddling in the old wing-back armchair that had been her grandfather's favourite chair, a book open but unread, the electric light casting its yellowish light and making her look almost jaundiced.

"You don't look terribly well," David said as he came in, detergent bubbles still clinging to his sleeves. "Are you going to be all right for work tomorrow, do you think?"

"Probably," she said. "It's not as if it's demanding work, after all. I'll slap on some blusher if I look rough in the morning. If I look too pale, Juliet might offer me a treatment, at a discount of course, and I'd never have the courage to refuse again."

David giggled.

"You must be running out of excuses," he said.

"Quite," Verity said. "A vote of no-confidence is a sure way to get fired, even after this long working for her."

"Do you really think so?"

"She's never forgiven me for getting better O levels than she did," Verity said.

She managed a smile.

"I think I might have a hot bath and get to bed early," she said.

"It's not eight yet," he remarked, surprised.

Verity glanced out at the dark sky.

"It seems later," she said. "OK, maybe I'll hold off for a while and watch rubbish with Rose."

"That sounds like a children's programme: Rubbish with Rosie, recycling for the under-fives made easy," he said, opening the first book in his pile of marking. "Let's hope this week's offering is better than last week's." He was already engrossed in his task.

Only the light of the TV illuminated the living room, where Rose lay slumped watching something that seemed to involve a lot of cars chasing each other. Verity sat down at the other end of the sofa and tried to follow the story but found herself glancing continuously at the empty chairs around the room, as if she expected other people to be sitting there with them. At ten, David came back through and ordered Rose off to bed.

"Dad!" Rose said. "It's only ten!"

"It's a school day tomorrow," he said. "Now, kiss good night?"

Rose might have pushed it if it had been Verity alone but she knew there was no point arguing with her father and sloped off upstairs, returning a few minute later smelling of soap and peppermint toothpaste for a bedtime cuddle that she would not have admitted to her school friends that she couldn't settle to sleep without. Verity unconsciously waited for the other child, the one that didn't exist, had never existed, to appear at the top of the stairs complaining of monsters under the bed, but when Rose had stomped back upstairs, the house seemed silent.

"Do you still want that bath?" David said.

"Not really," she said and followed him through to the kitchen where he began making a hot drink, wishing beyond almost anything she could bring herself to tell him of her vision, if that's what you might call it, so that she could hear him explain it away, and reassure her that she wasn't mad, or even unstable and temperamental and over-imaginative. But she knew she couldn't say anything; the thought of seeing his face fall, shadows grow in his eyes at the realisation that perhaps she wasn't sane, made her shiver. It wasn't worth that, when it was just a one off, an aberration that would never be repeated.

David made a herbal tea for both of them and they sat and watched the rest of the news together before his yawns became so frequent that she had, as usual to say to him, "Shall we go to bed then?" He was sometimes as bad as Rose for not admitting when he was tired, but unlike Verity, he fell asleep usually within minutes of lying down. She often used to lie awake for hours, aching for sleep but unable to drop off however tired she had been. It wasn't as if she was actually worrying or anything; it was as though falling asleep was a huge fence she just couldn't scale.

Now in the comfortable darkness of their bedroom, she lay and listened as her husband's gentle breathing deepened and sometimes lapsed into the rasps of the occasional snore. She could hear traffic far off, quieting now as the night drew on, and the occasional cat yowling forlornly beyond the garden, but other than the tick of their clocks and David's breathing the house seemed silent. The face of the little boy she'd seen today flashed across her mind and it occurred to her with some shock that while he was dark haired, he didn't look in the slightest like David, nor like her own father, or grandfather or any relative of either of them. In fact, with that pale, somewhat pointed face, that dark curly hair and the dark chocolate brown eyes, he was the dead spit of Nick.

She sat up abruptly, and David stirred uneasily next to her. With an effort, she kept totally still until both David and her heart had settled again. That was absurd, she told herself; you haven't thought of Nick for years and years, why did he just pop up again like that? You can't let yourself think of that, you can't.

But in the darkness, his face seemed to float in front of her, that odd little boy from today's waking dream, suddenly so familiar and yet so strange.

This isn't fair; this is wrong, she told herself fiercely. I won't think about this.

Very carefully, she eased her legs out of the bed and taking care to make almost no noise, she crept down to the kitchen that still smelled vaguely of herbs and honey, and with a vast guilt, retrieved the big bar of dark chocolate she kept hidden in case of pre-menstrual emergencies and ate half of it almost without tasting it, swallowing down huge chunks with the least possible chewing so that the lumps hurt her gullet like stones as they passed. She ate the second half more slowly, savouring the bitter-sweet and powdery texture as if it was an unfamiliar thing. In the unlit kitchen, she could see the trees at the end of the garden swaying in the night wind, the moonlight gleaming on the leaves and apples, and as she chewed and swallowed the last of the chocolate, she felt suddenly sick, craving something more wholesome to take away the sickly taste that coated her tongue and teeth.

The garden felt colder than she'd thought, and her nightdress seemed suddenly inadequate as the wind whipped it around her and flattened it to her body. She padded over the moist lawn and into the longer grass of the orchard. At the foot of the apple tree that held the huge eaters, she stopped and reached out to touch the rough bark as a leafy twig brushed her face. There was no sense now of the children ever having been here; the vision was broken utterly, and she plucked a nearby apple and carried back to the kitchen to rinse and eat. It seemed to ease the sickliness of the chocolate as well as cleaning her mouth, so she went back to bed, chilled but feeling a bit better. As long as she didn't let herself think about Nick she'd be fine, she'd sleep and it would all be all right. But even as she slid into sleep, she knew her mind had got a hold of both the name and the face again and that her dreams would not be light and pleasant ones.

Verity looked pale enough the next morning for David to comment on it, but since her colouring was only about two shades away from being an albino, being pale was very much a relative thing. Actually she looked very slightly green as if she was standing in the light streaming through spring leaves and there were greenish blue shadows under her eyes.

"Are you sure you're up to going to work?" he asked, knotting his tie in front of the hall mirror.

14

"I think so," she said. "It's not as if it's a hard job, physically. I'm sure I'll look better when I get there. All the fresh air and exercise should do the trick. I... just didn't sleep terribly well."

He'd noticed both the chocolate wrapper and the apple core when he'd made tea but he'd not commented on it.

"Right, that's me ready," he said, straightening the knot. "Shall I get a take-away on the way home, seeing as it's Friday? Saves cooking and washing up and the hassle of thinking what to have."

She nodded and he kissed her on the cheek before he grabbed his briefcase and the stack of marking that wouldn't fit in it and left. Those moments when everyone else was gone were the hardest moments for her; that sudden stillness after the hurried routines of morning held a silence that she somehow expected to be filled by other voices. Living in a house she'd lived in, well, not as a child as such, but as a teenager, was unsettling her still. Despite a new kitchen and redecoration throughout, it felt unchanged, untouched since she'd lived here last and it wasn't just her grandfather she expected to appear at any time.

Once she'd done the morning's accumulation of dishes, she grabbed her jacket, locked the house and retrieved her bicycle from the shed, and began her journey to work. Where they'd lived before, she'd had to drive but now she could cycle it. It was much cheaper all round and she was considering whether she really needed her own car any more, but at least once a week she still used it for shopping and ferrying Rose to and from various activities. It wasn't as if they were still struggling financially; this house was theirs outright, and the money from the sale of their last house meant they actually had money in the bank for the first time in their married life rather than that nice big albatross of an overdraft. Yet she felt guilty about having her own car when she could easily manage without one now.

"That's silly," David had said robustly when she'd hinted as much. "We've struggled so much in the past, why shouldn't we have it a bit easier now? You probably don't really need to work at that daft shop of Juliet's now. You could stay home or start your PGCE again."

The thought of going back to college wasn't a comfortable one; she'd given up less than halfway through her teaching qualification because she was expecting Rose but even so she had already had second thoughts about being a teacher. David was a born teacher, keeping control of a class as well as keeping their interest with about as much apparent effort as a fish swimming, but Verity knew she would never be like that. She'd struggled to maintain discipline with her own child; the idea of a class of thirty was deeply frightening.

"I'll think about it," she'd said and hadn't.

As she pedalled smoothly along, she wondered idly what she could do apart from what she already was doing. Not a lot, she concluded, as she usually did. Her job wasn't well paid but she had the flexible hours she liked, and effectively no surprises. The customers were sometimes interesting, Juliet was a familiar thorn that she had learned to deal with, and the job didn't ask much of her. Saturdays were sometimes uncomfortable since that was when she was likely to get teenagers in the shop, who could sometimes be rowdy and rude, but the really troublesome ones had been banned and she quite enjoyed hearing their comments about some of the things they sold or about the therapies that Juliet offered in her treatment rooms upstairs above the shop.

Verity had been at school with Juliet but they hadn't been close friends. There are people whom you can go to school with every day from the age of eleven to the age of sixteen and while you hold them no enmity, never become friends. There are some whom you can sit next to in lessons for five years and yet five years after you leave, you would be hard pressed to remember their name and ten years on, to remember their face. For Verity, Juliet was one of these people. They'd sat together for the first two years of secondary school, before classes were setted for ability and thereafter had only been together for form time and PE and the one or two subjects that had never been divided into ability-based sets. Juliet had left school at sixteen to work in an aunt's shop and apart from passing her in the street occasionally for a year or two after Juliet left school, Verity had totally and quite naturally lost touch with her. They had never had more than proximity in common, so she might have passed her in the street and barely registered her presence had Juliet not been so tenacious on one crucial day. It had been a few days into Rosie's first term at school and Verity had been wandering aimlessly in town. When Rosie had been born, David had done the sums and unless Verity had a job that earned enough to cover childcare and a few other essentials, there had been little point in her working. It wasn't as if she had a job to go back to, she used to say, when people asked her when she was going back to work, so she had been a full-time stay-at-home mother. It had not been easy, both financially and emotionally. David was a devoted teacher, the kind that people remember with gratitude and often fondness, but he was still on a fairly low salary, being newly qualified, and they had nothing, not a bean, behind them to act as a buffer when things got tight. Verity's mother had said once, bitterly, on one of her very rare visits, that Rose truly was Second-Hand Rose; all her clothes, all the baby equipment, most of the household furniture even, had been accumulated that way or worse. Verity never told her how one chair she'd nicked off a skip when the house belonging to an elderly neighbour had been cleared when the old lady had died. She also never told her mother what David often threatened to, that they'd never have been put in such straits had it not been for her father's lack of skill with finance, years ago. There are some things you just can't say, after all, and still remain on speaking terms. She had therefore been somewhat vulnerable when Juliet had greeted her in the street like some long lost best friend.

"Goodness gracious, it's never Verity Fairfax is it?" she exclaimed in a loud voice that made Verity cringe inwardly. Juliet had never had a loud voice at school, being a mousy sort who never had much to say out loud, though she often seemed to be whispering and giggling with a few friends.

"How have you been?" Juliet went on, without waiting for Verity to answer, and enveloped her in an uncomfortably tight hug.

"Fine," Verity said, trying to get her breath back.

"It must be years," Juliet said. "What have you been doing? All the right things, obviously; you don't look a day over seventeen."

It wasn't true, but Verity hadn't changed much. In fact, now she thought about it, she didn't think she'd changed her hairstyle much since she was sixteen. Juliet couldn't have been more different; from a plump girl with mousy hair that straggled in wisps once it got below shoulder length, she'd become whippet thin, with hair so closely cropped it might have been growing back from being shaved off altogether and dyed a purplish red colour.

"I got married and I have a daughter who's just started school," Verity said.

"You and Nick did get married, then? I always thought you would, you were so obviously right for each other, even at that age," Juliet gushed and Verity shuddered.

"No," she said. "I didn't marry Nick. I met someone at university. His name's David."

Juliet was instantly contrite and apologetic.

"I am so sorry," she said. "What on earth happened? We all thought you and Nick were the business, thought you'd make it. Did you break up before or after university? Long distance relationships can be so tough."

"Don't you remember?" Verity said, frozen with sudden misery. "He died. Surely you remember?"

Juliet looked stunned for a moment.

"I left, you know, when I was sixteen," she said. "I didn't stay on at sixth form with you lot, so I didn't hear. I am so sorry. What on earth happened?"

Verity wasn't sure she could speak; she was certain that Juliet would have known, should have known but it obviously hadn't hardly registered long enough for her to remember it now.

"Let me buy you a coffee," Juliet was saying, taking her arm and steering her towards a coffee shop and settling her in a corner seat, where Verity sat numbly while Juliet ordered coffee.

"He drowned," she said eventually, once all the fussing about milk and sugar was done with. "He'd gone on one of these outward-bound Operation Raleigh things and he fell off the boat one night and drowned."

"That's terrible," Juliet said, her eyes wide with apparent sincerity. "How awful for you. How awful for his family."

"It's a long time ago," Verity said, wanting to change the subject, and Juliet was more than happy to oblige.

"Time heals almost anything," she said, folding her hands almost in prayer. "So what are you doing with yourself these days?"

"Not a lot," Verity admitted. "I'm trying to think what to do now Rosie is at school. It isn't as if I have a job to go back to. And there isn't much around here I can do. I never finished my teacher training after all."

Juliet was looking at her with a speculative gaze.

"You've got a degree though, after all," she said thoughtfully.

"A degree in English Literature, yes," Verity admitted. "It doesn't qualify me for much, really. If you want a critique of some poetry or a novel, I'm your woman, but beyond that it doesn't go anywhere."

There was a gleam of something very like satisfaction in Juliet's eyes, as if she had just had something confirmed for her that she had long suspected.

"There's nothing like practical experience," she said. "I worked for my aunt until she died and left me her shop. The last few years I've been revamping it and now I need someone to work in it part time so I can expand my horizons and do some study myself. What about it?"

The offer came as a bit of a shock to Verity.

"I'd need to be off in time to pick Rosie up from school," she said, tentatively.

"That's why I said part time," Juliet said. "I don't need someone full time yet, but maybe later, when your daughter is older…" She let the sentence trail off into an unspoken question.

So Verity had ended up working for Juliet, an arrangement that suited Juliet in ways Verity would have found hard to explain. In effect, Juliet took a not-quite secret delight in the fact that one of the clever girls from school, who'd swanned off to higher things, was now working for herself, who had left school at sixteen with poor qualifications and just as poor prospects working in the rather dull gift shop her aunt had run and owned for the last thirty years. It wasn't as if she bossed Verity around overtly very often but there was always that unspoken feeling that she could do so if she chose to, and she had a way of making her authority felt without apparently giving orders. She would explain how she wanted things done, even how she expected Verity to dress and do her hair for the shop, and it left no room for queries. Not that Verity would have queried anything then; she was too glad to be out of the house and earning some much needed cash. Even with the expense of running a small and rather elderly car, it had been bliss to have a little extra money and ease some of that nail biting worry at the end of the month when there were more days left than there was money in the bank. It didn't pay well, but it was steady and she could finish at half past two in time to go and collect Rosie from school; Juliet also seemed quite good about those odd days when Rosie was ill and Verity then was unable to come to work.

Juliet was already behind the counter when Verity got to the shop; she was setting up the oil burner for the morning.

"I've got a few clients this morning," she said. "But I've got to be gone by noon to get to this place in time for five o'clock enrolment. Will you be OK to shut up for me at five?"

Verity nodded and pulled on the Indian print blouse she wore for work; she kept it folded up under the counter and never wore it home. On her first day here, Juliet had instructed her to wear something in keeping with the ambiance of the shop; she pronounce it to rhyme with ambulance and had produced a rack of shirts and blouses from which she picked out one that suited Verity's colouring the least.

"And you could do a bit more with the make-up," she'd said, idly. "A bit of kohl around the eyes and some blusher maybe. Oh and let your hair down. Up in a bun like that is too middle-aged and frumpy; we want the hippy, flower-power mystical look and you always did have such nice floaty hair. Let it hang free."

Verity put on her make-up before leaving the house these days, but usually after David had gone; he really didn't like her with it. She didn't like it either, feeling it made her look almost clown-like. She undid her hair from the ponytail she'd put it in to keep it from tangling under her cycle helmet, and shook it out. Every working day, she felt as though she were putting on a mask, another persona and she'd never quite got used to it.

Juliet was busy measuring out drops of essential oil into the water in the little crucible part of the burner; Verity could see her lips moving as she counted them out carefully. She had strict instructions on how much oil to put on and which ones; Juliet kept a careful eye on the level of the bottles and didn't like to see any being wasted.

"All you need are a few drops and it should last all morning," she'd explained, when she'd noticed how much the levels had been dropping. "You don't need to keep topping it up every few minutes. It only needs a very small amount to maintain the ambiance. And remember, one joss stick in the morning and one in the afternoon. There's no sense in burning money."

After a few weeks, Verity had realised that Juliet ran a very tight ship and for someone who had been less than promising at school, she'd turned into quite a shrewd and effective businesswoman. Every detail was carefully thought-out, from the name of the shop to every item of stock; even her appointing of Verity as her assistant had been based on some cunning thinking. Verity's appearance and educated manner only enhanced the shop's atmosphere and it had not been simply a matter of kindness in giving her the job. It meant that Juliet could go off on courses at weekends knowing that the shop was in good hands. It also meant that as the therapy side of the business expanded, Juliet could have less and less to do with the sheer nitty-gritty reality of running the day-to-day side of the business. When there were no customers in the shop, Verity was expected to dust and sort things on the shelves, check stock levels, maintain Juliet's expectations of "ambiance", keep the CD player constantly fed with the New-Age music Juliet wanted playing softly in the background all day. She was also expected to man the phone and act as receptionist for the therapy room upstairs.

"What course are you doing this weekend?" Verity asked, when Juliet had finished putting rosemary oil in the burner.

"Mayan Heart Retrieval," Juliet said, briefly.

Verity said nothing, knowing that if Juliet were going to explain, she'd do so without prompting, and sure enough, once she'd lit the morning's joss stick, she turned to Verity.

"Apparently there are a lot of people being reincarnated who were human sacrifices in a past life in Mayan times and had their hearts ripped out as an offering to the Sun God," she said. "But their etheric hearts aren't being fully incarnated and so people feel empty and have trouble forming full-heart relationships. This therapy is designed to call back the etheric heart and restore it to the whole etheric body. It should be really interesting. I'll be back Monday afternoon. If you can put the takings for today and tomorrow in the safe, I can go to the bank when I get back. I've got to get ready for my ten o'clock Reiki appointment. I'd like coffee at ten past eleven, so if you'd put the kettle on when it turns eleven, I should be finished up there by ten past. But you'll know that when you see the client out."

Verity nodded, inwardly shrugging at the whole menial nature of her job.

"Oh, and could you run the vacuum over this floor before we open? There's ash all over the floor," Juliet said, gesturing to the spill of soft grey ash from the joss stick ash-catcher. Every few days, Juliet would clean the ash catcher simply by blowing away the powder-fine ash and she never seemed to register that the ash on the floor was only there because she'd blown it there. Verity tried to remember to empty it daily but since she went home at three these days, Juliet was at the counter from then till five and usually burned another incense stick and never emptied the ash into the bin.

"It doesn't give a good impression, you know, muck all over the floor," Juliet said, but Verity just blinked, her face impassive.

"I'll do it now," she said and went to the small back room that served as stock room and storage for the vacuum cleaner.

When she got back, Juliet had gone upstairs to "prepare" for her first client of the day, and Verity was aware of a heaviness lifting. She knew she didn't much like her employer but she was seldom conscious of quite how oppressive she found her presence. Knowing she was upstairs putting her feet up while Verity skivvied away didn't worry her as much as it might have done; she was out of Verity's space and that was what counted. It also meant that Verity had first choice of music for the stereo system and that meant her day could start with something less irritating that the mock native American chants that bore as much resemblance to the real thing as strawberry fragrance oils had to real strawberries; there was a kind of synthetic grubbiness about some of the CDs that Juliet liked the most that really grated on Verity's nerves. This morning she chose a natural sound recording of birdsong.

The day got slowly better as Juliet finished her Reiki session, drank her coffee and left for her weekend course, asking Verity to run the vacuum over the therapy room before she finished for the day. Another woman would have said no, told Juliet to hire a cleaner but Verity just nodded and Juliet left with a smug look on her face. Once she'd really gone, Verity relaxed enough to drop the duster she seemed to clutch the whole time Juliet was around and perch on the high stool behind the counter and let her mind wander. Friday was usually a quiet day, except near Christmas, so apart from the occasional customer and a few phone calls, she was undisturbed. If Juliet had been alone, she would have shut the shop to deal with any clients who could only make a Friday afternoon, but she wouldn't have put up with Verity shutting up early just so she could be home in time for her daughter. After all, Rose was thirteen now, had her own key and didn't need the kind of attention Verity gave her; in fact Juliet couldn't understand why Verity still refused to work the full afternoon when she'd have earned more for it. There had been a brief experiment earlier that year with a school leaver filling in those two hours at the end of the day before going off to start a shift at Tesco's; it had lasted just over a week and ended with the girl flinging her Indian blouse at Juliet and yelling, "'oo do you think you are anyway, ordering me around like that. I got rights, I have. Stuff this stupid job where the sun don't shine and take this 'orrible dishcloth and shove it there'n'all." Juliet had gone back to either minding the shop herself those two hours or shutting it if more profitable opportunities arose, like paying clients. After all, even near Christmas, it wasn't guaranteed that the takings for those two hours would be noticeably greater than the fee she charged for whatever therapy she was currently pushing hardest.

Verity shut the shop for half an hour at lunchtime and bought a sandwich at a shop nearby and ate it in the poky kitchen upstairs, with a cup of instant coffee with powdered milk that made her crave a decent cup of Italian coffee with frothy milk. Juliet's aunt had lived up here, but Juliet had a flat somewhere not far away and had had the rooms revamped so that she had two therapy rooms, this kitchen and a surprisingly decent sized bathroom that doubled as a changing room. Verity found it a bit creepy up here, knowing that the aunt had died here, but it was an old building and the chances are that in a house over fifty years old someone, some time, had died there. People have to die somewhere, after all; at least the aunt was found the following day and had a decent funeral. If she were totally truthful, she found the therapy rooms a bit creepy too; one was plain enough, with little to draw the eye but a few statues of angels. This one Juliet used for her Reiki, and also as a sort of living room when she was waiting for clients or just relaxing. The other was a strange room though, painted a shade of deep terracotta that reminded Verity of uncooked meat, and Juliet had had a framework of copper pipes built into the form of a pyramid, hung with small crystals and housing a pallet mattress covered with silk covered cushions in shades and prints that matched the walls, with a few cloth of gold ones thrown in. This was for the Egyptian Rejuvenation Therapy. Statues and sheets of painted papyrus lined the walls and a great Eye of Horus was emblazoned on the ceiling right over the head end of the mattress. Remembering their lessons together in the first two years of secondary school, Verity knew that back then at least Juliet had both a poor grasp of history and a very low level of interest, so it had puzzled her hugely that she had picked an Egyptian theme for this room when she knew very little about either Egypt or about its medicine. David had managed to explain it.

"It's not real," he'd said, when she'd first mentioned it. "None of it is real; it isn't based on either any real facts about either Egyptian religion or Egyptian medical knowledge. It's invented to fool a credulous public; anything that claims to reduce ageing is always suspect in my opinion. What exactly does she do to her victims, sorry, clients?"

"I've no idea," Verity had said. "But one of them said to me when she came out it was better than Botox."

"Cheaper at any rate," David said cynically.

Since then, Verity had managed to find out exactly what happened to Juliet's clients during their hour of treatment and she'd ended up agreeing with David's opinion. Reading between Juliet's personal endorsements of it, it seemed that the face was massaged with oils scented with myrrh and frankincense while an incense called Kyphi was burned, that Juliet claimed was based on a real Egyptian recipe. The client lay in the pyramid and key points on the body were anointed with the same scented oils painted into hieroglyphs honouring Isis, and then were allowed to rest with tiny crystal pyramids placed at stress points on the face while music played and Juliet invoked various gods and goddesses and waved a crystal over the body.

"An expensive way to relax," David had said. "But hope is a powerful thing and even that hour of relaxation is of some benefit. At least she isn't likely to do any real harm except to wallets."

This new therapy that Juliet was trying this weekend sounded even more kooky and outrageous, and quite frankly, utterly creepy, but Verity had no intention of saying so. Just as long as she got her wages every month, she had long ago decided that Juliet could get on with whatever she wanted.

At just after half four, she decided that it wasn't worth keeping the shop open any longer and went to turn over the sign in the doorway to, "The Enchanted Kingdom is closed, even to angels," and as she lifted the placard to turn it, a man hurried past and she felt a heavy lurch in her chest at the sight of him. He was gone in under a second, rushing past the door to escape the rain that had begun to tip down in torrents. It was Nick.

Not Nick at eighteen, when she'd last seen him, but Nick as he would be now, at thirty-six. She had the shop keys in her hand and she wrenched open the door, dropping the keys and dived out into the rain, turning her head to stare up and down the street, but there was no sign of the figure she'd seen. He'd vanished utterly.

She was panting, hyperventilating, and she could feel her skin prickle with the insects that heralded a major panic attack, those invisible ants that told her she would faint if she didn't do something quickly, so with her hands shaking, she retreated into the shop and locked the door behind her and lurched to the stairs and crawled up them. She lay on the smoky-smelling off-white leather sofa in the Reiki room until her heart seemed to beat normally and her skin no longer crawled with unseen insects, and when she felt she could stand again reliably, she made tea and drank it black and with a lot of sugar. It was now after five and with an effort she emptied the till and locked the takings in the safe, but she drew the line at vacuuming up here. She'd do that Monday morning, before Juliet got back; now all she wanted was to get home. David would be home after six with the usual greasy bag full of prawn crackers and char sui and sweet and sour chicken, and probably a bottle of white wine bought ready chilled from the off-license, and she could enjoy that and a hot bath and maybe a film and get away from these horrid fantasies that seemed so real at the time.

But all the time as she fought the rain and wind as she cycled home, she could see those dark curls being blown by the wild wind, touched now by a few strands of grey, and she was unable to stop the few hot tears that forced her way from her stinging eyes and mingled with the cold rain, and washed away some of the awful kohl that Juliet insisted she wear to work.

"You look like a panda, Mum," Rose said when she staggered in having stabled her bike.

"I'm soaked," Verity said. "I'll go and wash and change. Much homework?"

"Done it," Rose said tersely. "What's for tea?"

"Daddy's doing his famous trip to the takeaway," Verity said, sliding off her shoes with relief and padding upstairs in her socks to try and get clean.

In the bathroom, she saw the unmistakeable signs of tears as well as rain damage to her eye make-up and she wiped it all away before splashing her face with cool water to try and erase the tell-tale swelling and redness that could never be explained away by rain. Dry jeans and shirt and then, her old Guernsey sweater, faded and worn but still untouched by the moths that so loved real wool. She hauled on thick fisherman's socks instead of the dainty slippers she wore if they had company and hurried downstairs; she'd heard David's car pull in to their short drive and she wanted to look busy warming plates before he got in. If they could launch straight into supper, he probably wouldn't notice she'd been crying, and by the time they'd eaten, the signs would have gone. It was only a very few tears after all.

"Good day?" she asked as he came in.

"Friday's are always a bit manic," he said, briefcase under one arm, stack of marking under the other. "Half the kids seem to think the weekend has already started. We had an incident with some of the sixth formers who'd spent lunchtime in the pub and came back drunk. I was supposed to get a takeaway wasn't I? I'll go back out now. I forgot."

He dumped his marking and briefcase in the study and then went back out again, giving her more time to get the table set and plates warmed. By the time they were sat down to eat, Verity was so hungry she forgot entirely about her tears and tucked in with relish; that meagre lunchtime sandwich seemed days ago.

"This cycling thing seems to have given you a better appetite," David remarked when she'd finished up the remnants of the sweet and sour chicken. "You usually pick at Chinese."

"That's because it's so high in calories," she said. "But it's Friday and I need to pig out sometimes. I heard Juliet saying to someone on the phone the other day how much weight she's noticed I've lost; I think she's annoyed about it. She was one of the tubby ones at school and I was thin, so she's been a bit smug about the reversal of roles."

"I don't know how she stays quite so thin," David said.

Verity did.

"I used to wonder," she said. "But the other day she bought in Danish pastries and cappuccinos from the coffee shop up the road. She ate three pastries. I asked her how she stayed so slim eating stuff like that and she said it was down to a strict regime of exercise and meditation; she said she'd raised her vibrations to such a high level she actually required more calories to stop herself becoming too thin."

David raised his eyebrows with a quirky look she recognised as scepticism.

"Oh yeah?" he said. Verity smiled.

"Half an hour later, she goes to use the loo," she said. "I went to wash the plates and heard her being sick. I asked her if she was all right and she said that she'd raised her vibrations so high that high sugar food sometimes disagreed with her."

David grinned in satisfaction.

"High vibrations my left foot," he said. "She just eats what she wants and then sicks it all up again! Don't you dare ever try that! I'd rather have you plump that have you treat yourself like that."

Verity said nothing. She had tried it once, many years ago, when her grandfather had tried desperately to comfort her with food, knowing no other way to try and ease her pain, but she'd felt so wretched that she'd never done it again, but she'd never told David about that, nor about that time in her life and she didn't want to now. It was so long ago; what would be the use of it now? Gone is gone.

That night she dreamed of the sea and when she woke, she could for a moment smell the salt tang and the seaweed washed up with the tangle of bleaching debris above the tide line by the storms of winter and tears stung her eyes.

Chapter 2

As the evenings got darker and longer over the weeks that followed, Verity found that the memory of the visions or whatever they had been faded and she began to forget they had ever happened. She had concluded they were a result of a mishmash of stresses, that included both losing her grandfather and moving to this house. After all, were these not somewhere right at the top of the list for life stresses? That was the sort of thing Juliet might say; she had returned from her training course enthused beyond reason by the possibilities for the new therapy. She had booked all the three remaining weekend sessions to complete the course; this first had been merely the taster.

"They wanted to make sure we were all the right sort of people for the therapy," she said. "The therapy needs sensitive practitioners who are in tune with higher vibrations. I've been accepted for the rest of the training. Once I've completed it, I'm eligible for the discount on all their products."

Verity nodded and said nothing, and just let Juliet continue unhindered by questions or comments.

"There were so many sacrificed," she was saying. "They think the current explosion in divorce rates is entirely due to the fact that so many people are being reincarnated this century without their true hearts; people want to love but can't quite manage it."

Privately Verity thought that if this were so, why were all these people coming back to be reborn in the West when they died in South America, and why did their hearts not reincarnate with them if the rest of their organs did? But she said nothing and carried on dusting the Tibetan singing bowl arrangement while Juliet carried on regardless of her employee's negative thinking. It looked like the Egyptian paraphernalia might be part of the New Year sale that Juliet used each year to sell off the stock she'd been unable to sell full price; Verity idly wonder what props would replace it. In fact, she knew Juliet would probably phase it out gradually, if the new therapy proved to be enough of an earner, so maybe it would be the following year's sale that played host to the Egyptian bits and bobs, if it didn't end up as Verity's Christmas present instead. She'd had some very weird Christmas presents from her employer over the years and some even weirder birthday presents but a collapsible copper pyramid was likely to be the biggest white elephant of all.

After each weekend session, Juliet came back bubbling over with the things she'd learned and Verity listened without comment and shuddered inwardly at it all. Juliet had also taken to returning, only to head straight home after she had checked up on the shop, claiming exhaustion, but Verity had a sneaking feeling that it was more than tiredness that drove Juliet home. She'd glanced out of the window just after Juliet had left to go to her car, and there had been a figure waiting for her in the passenger seat, but she had about as much intention of commenting on the apparently buoyant state of Juliet's love life as she had of commenting on her therapies. It was peaceful in the shop without her and she could relax and get on with things without this constant sense of being somehow in the wrong all the time, and also of being in some subtle way utterly inferior to Juliet.

The weather sharpened abruptly as November flicked over into December and the first of the Christmas cards began to arrive. The season to be jolly filled Verity with anything but jollity and she left opening any post till she got home in the evening so that she could immediately write out a reciprocal card, make a note of it and then post it as soon as possible so that the recipient might think their cards had crossed in the post. She had a list of people she usually sent to, and by the twentieth of December of most years, anyone who hadn't already sent them a card had one scribbled out and sent. There was no joy in it; it was simply a duty and a boring one at that. Sometimes she wondered why it was she ended up doing it and not David.

"As far as I'm concerned, if they haven't been in touch all year, why should I bother just because it's Christmas?" he said. "I've got more important things to worry about."

He usually ended up phoning anyone he considered worth staying in contact with in the lull between presents and lunch on Christmas day itself, or in the days that followed, but Verity continued every year to slave away writing a short note to old school friends, distant relatives and the few friends they had retained from university.

They were waiting for the beef casserole to finish cooking one evening and Verity was opening her handful of envelopes.

"One from my mum and dad," she said, unfolding the letter that went with it. "They won't be coming over this year."

"Halle-bloody-luyah," David said. "First time we've had a house big enough to hold them without constant moaning about us living in a shoebox and they aren't coming? Why not?"

"Mum says Dad couldn't face it with Granddad gone and us living in his old house," Verity said.

"Translation: they're still sulking that he left this place to you," David said. "Even if your Dad didn't get on well enough with Granddad to stay there for Christmas instead of cramming in with us, he still thought he ought to get everything."

Verity said nothing but she knew it was probably true.

"They'd have run through the money this place would make in next to no time," he continued. "Let's face it, the only reason they keep that bar in Spain going is because your mum holds the purse-strings. Give any money to your dad and it's gone, just like that. Anyway, I'm relieved they aren't coming; we never manage to make them happy or even comfortable. There's always something for them to moan about. It'll be nice to have Christmas to ourselves for once."

Verity nodded and opened the next card. After a moment, David glanced at her.

"Are you all right?" he said. "I've never seen a jaw drop and stay dropped before. Who's it from?"

"Carla," Verity said in faint voice.

"You get one from her every year," he remarked. "What's so special about this one?"

"She wants to meet up," Verity said.

"That's nice," David said, vaguely. "You were at school with her, weren't you? She's the one who became a model, I seem to recall."

"That's right," Verity said. "She managed to make the switch to acting about five years ago; she always said she intended to once she'd reached her sell-by date as a model. I haven't seen her since Rosie was tiny. It used to get me down, seeing her so glossy and smart and me in charity shop rejects."

"Why do you think she wants to meet up; surely she's got enough friends to enjoy herself with in the run up to Christmas without making you feel inadequate again?" David asked,

31

somewhat aggressively. As far as he was concerned, clothes didn't make the woman and this model-turned actress was pushing her luck upsetting Verity.

"It's not like that," Verity said, defensively. "It isn't her fault she's beautiful. Or that she's used to a very different world to mine. We go back a long way and that's what counts. She says her mum has had to go into sheltered accommodation and she's been helping her sort the house and she's found some things she thinks I'd be interested in. It's probably some photos or something like that, from when we were at school. I was just a bit shocked at being asked to meet up like this; last time we met up was a long time back."

Inwardly she was shaking but she was pleased with the fact that little of it showed.

"Well," said David. "As long as she won't make you feel inferior or shabby or something, great. Why don't you buy yourself a new dress or something, just in case?"

"I will," she said.

"Just not from Juliet's hippy rail, though?"

Verity snorted in suppressed amusement.

"Not a chance," she said. "Anyway, Juliet will probably give me last year's unsold clothes as a Christmas present again this year so I won't have to buy any more work wear for some time. I wish she'd at least pick colours that don't make me look like a week-old lettuce or something that usually lives under a rock. I thought I might try Monsoon; I'm now just about within their size range again. Maybe Carla will have put on some weight finally too and then I can have cream in my coffee without feeling guilty because she can't."

"Are you sure about this? I don't want you feeling miserable about it," David said.

"I'll be fine," she said. "I'll get a new outfit anyway; something I can wear for Christmas too. She wants to meet up in town; afternoon coffee at the posh place that opened a few months back, you know the one that does all the really fancy coffee and eggnog and stuff like that or so Juliet tells me anyway."

"Nice," he said with studied insincerity. "Do you think dinner is ready yet?"

She sniffed; the air had a rich smell of hot meat and wine sauce.

"I think so," she said. "Give Rose a call will you and I'll serve up?"

A week or so later, Carla Raphael, born Carla Braithwaite, was putting the finishing touches to deliberately subdued make-up while her boyfriend lay back in their tousled bed and watched her. After a while, he raised himself on his elbow and said speculatively,

"Not expecting the paparazzi today then?"

It was a bit of a gibe; Carla had been a moderate success as a model and was a moderate success as an actress but she was still a very long way from the kind of celebrity status she'd once craved. Johnny had realised that hers was not a shooting star some time ago and really didn't mind, but once in a while he liked to have a pop at her, just to remind her she wasn't really as important as she seemed to think.

"As I explained to you earlier," Carla said patiently. "I'm meeting an old school friend. The last time we met she had baby sick on her collar and didn't notice but I think I made her feel a bit scruffy so I am being a bit more sensitive this time."

"How long ago was that then?"

"About twelve and a half years, I think."

"So maybe the baby sick will be gone then?"

She gave him a withering look and he rolled over giggling.

"What makes you want to meet such a loser again now?" he asked, rolling back again.

"I told you that before too."

"Tell me again; I was too drunk last night to remember anything," he said.

"She was my brother's girlfriend, that's why," Carla said.

"I didn't know you even had a brother!" Johnny said, sitting up in surprise.

"I don't any more," Carla said. "And I did tell you about it, years ago. I'd cut down on the booze if I were you; your memory is going."

"So how come you're meeting up with the loser ex-girlfriend of your dead brother when she's clearly not someone you want

Hello! Magazine seeing you with unless you can claim you do charity work?"

She stared at him with irritation.

"When I was helping Mum clear her old place, we found stuff that I think Verity should have," she said. "I'm not sure how she's going to take it but I thought I'd try one or two items first and then if that goes OK, I'll meet her again and pass on the other things."

"You do do charity work!" he grinned.

"She was a good mate to me back then," Carla said. "I'm still fond of her. I stopped seeing her because I was sure I was doing more harm than good. She took Nick's death harder than I did, to be honest."

"But that must be years ago. How old were you then?"

"Verity and I were both seventeen; Nick was eighteen," Carla said. "It's a lifetime ago; but when Nick died, it did something to her that it didn't do to me. The lights went out."

"What was he like, then?"

"Nick? He was an idiot," Carla said dismissively. "Right, how do I look?"

He looked her up and down; and then grinned.

"Good enough to eat," he said.

"Later," she said, and glanced critically in the mirror again. Smart, but not too smart, and certainly not smart enough to make poor scruffy Verity feel too inferior.

"Right, I'll see you later," she said, leaning over Johnny and kissing the air above his head to avoid smearing supposedly smear-proof lipstick. She'd been obliged to advertise the stuff but she knew that it was only really smear-proof if you avoided any contact with anything for the next four hours. She had so many free samples she was tempted to pass on a few to Verity but wasn't sure there would be shade that wouldn't make her look like either a clown or a vampire. Still, hot red lipstick was a must for the festive season and she slipped a spare sample of Holly Berry Red into her handbag in case Verity admired hers. Generosity had always been her watchword, after all.

"Right, how do I look?" Verity asked her reflection. "Fine, you just go and enjoy yourself. You've rarely looked better."

She glared at herself.

"Some comfort you are!" she said, sticking her tongue out.

She had enjoyed herself finding and buying this new dress but somehow it seemed to be a bit over the top for an afternoon coffee with an old friend now she had actually put it on and done her hair and make-up. Still, Carla was bound to be light years smarter than her and anything was better than last time they'd met. She'd been drowning in the baby blues and hadn't washed her hair in a week and all her clothes seemed to have shrunk so the only thing that fitted comfortably was something she'd bought in a charity shop when the size of a brick outhouse at eight months gone; she'd looked down later only to discover that Rosie had dribbled milk on the collar. She'd also been embarrassed by the state of the house; it had been not just untidy and cramped but really rather grubby. At least Carla had found the tact this time to meet her somewhere on utterly neutral territory.

She drove to the coffee shop; blue silk dresses don't go well with bicycles after all. She'd managed to get the day off from Juliet's slavery, having worked late the last few Fridays to cover for Juliet's training, but she'd managed to lie about why she needed the day off. If she'd told her who she was meeting, Juliet would have hijacked the whole afternoon; after all, she'd been at school with Carla too and if there was any chance of there being a new contact there, she'd have been there, drooling over her. Carla wasn't exactly a household name, but hers was a face that was probably very familiar to most people both from her modelling career and now from her acting, and if there were any possibility of there being a photographer around, Juliet wouldn't be shy about being snapped with her. The last time Verity had foolishly mentioned Carla, she had regretted it; Juliet had nagged her for weeks about arranging a meeting.

The coffee shop was a bit of a shock to her when she walked in. Here, coffee had become some sort of God to be worshipped in his multiple forms. She was used to the national and international chains of coffee shops that homogenized coffee drinking so that wherever you were in the country or indeed in some cases, the world, you knew what you were getting. This was something different again; somehow more genteel, more exclusive. Soft classical music was playing and the air was thick with the scents of burnt sugar, vanilla and roasted coffee beans, and the subtler fragrances of the cakes and pastries that gleamed like holy treasures behind the glass of the dessert cabinet. Today's special was written in gloriously Gothic letters on a wooden board by the till. The woman at the counter stared at her, rather pointedly.

"I'm meeting a friend, we'll order when she gets here," Verity said and scuttled away to a cosy leather armchair near the window so that she could watch the door but stay inconspicuous. As she passed her, she heard the woman sniff in disdain as if Verity were a bag lady who had obviously come in here to shelter from the cold; Verity ducked her head so her hair swung forward to hide her face as it reddened. She couldn't imagine ever coming in here either in her work clothes, which made her look like a New Age traveller, or her home clothes which were just comfy and nothing more. It was no comfort that when Carla arrived five minutes late, she was wearing carefully ripped jeans and a faded denim shirt. On Carla, this had the look of the highest fashion and that coupled with her air of a celebrity slumming and her tantalisingly familiar face got them such service from the previously frosty and unwelcoming staff that Verity felt slightly sickened by it.

"You look marvellous!" Carla declared, kissing her and holding her by both hands. "You don't seem to have aged at all."

"You've lost so much weight, too. You must tell me how," she went on. "Now I don't have to ease myself into tiny clothes I seem to have lost control. I must have put on easily four pounds since I stopped modelling full time."

"Try cycling to work every day," Verity said, quietly.

"Oh, I have a static cycle at home and a rowing machine but I never seem to have the time," Carla said. "I don't think I told you but I've got a part in one of the big soaps. Only a small part so far but they said they'll expand the character over time, but it's a great start. I've done so many ads I'm sick of them. I want something I can get my teeth into properly. How have you been? Are you still working for Juliet? How's your Granddad these days? He must be nearly ninety now."

"He died in the spring," Verity said. "He was eighty six. We were just discussing whether we should come and live with him and he got pneumonia and died."

"Oh I am so sorry," Carla said, wringing her hands in a thoroughly theatrical gesture. "How stupid of me. I haven't upset you, have I?"

Verity shrugged.

"As you said, he was getting on for ninety," she said. "But you get used to thinking someone like him is somehow going to go on forever and then he didn't. I'm not upset but I do miss him sometimes. We've moved into the old house; he left it to me. I assume you still have that address; your card went to our old house and got forwarded on, but the forwarding service will be over by next year so…" She tailed off.

"Of course I remember that address," Carla said. "That must be a nice change for you, living there."

"We rattle around a bit," Verity said. "There's four bedrooms and even the smallest is bigger than the so-called master bedroom at the old place."

"I thought there were more bedrooms than that," Carla said.

"There are two attic rooms but they're too cold to sleep in during the winter; they don't have any heating up there," Verity said. "We used them as junk-rooms when I lived there before."

"I remember now," Carla said. "There were all sorts of old boxes and things up there and we could play music as loud as we wanted. But you haven't told me how you're doing."

Verity just shrugged again.

"Great," she said. "Still working for Juliet, who incidentally would give her eye teeth to meet you again and wangle you into giving some star endorsement of her therapy business. Still married to David, still mother to Rose. David was made head of department a year or so back; I think I mentioned it in my Christmas letter last year or maybe it was the year before. Rose is doing well at her new school; she had to change school when we moved but that was a good thing, and it was well before she started doing any exam work so that was fine. Mum and Dad are still out in Spain but I think they wanted to move back home, but Granddad leaving the house to me put paid to that."

"Did you know he was going to do that?"

"Oh yes," Verity said. "That's why he wanted us to move in with him. If he got infirm he reckoned that if we were dependants living in his house no one could make him sell the house to pay for care. As it turned out it wasn't an issue. Mum and Dad were furious but after all, he gave them the cash to buy the bar and everything so I think they'd had all they were going to get back them. But I think Dad sort of conveniently forgot about that; he doesn't like being reminded of how he once went bankrupt and had to be rescued by Granddad."

"I bet!" Carla said with some genuine feeling.

"They were pretty cross about it," Verity said. "I think Spain has lost its charms. Not that I ever thought it had any."

Carla threw back her head and laughed, making heads turn in the room. She'd once had dark curls like her brother but today her hair was a very natural-looking shade of auburn and all the curls had been flattened away by straighteners, but her eyes were the same deep chocolate brown as Nick's had been and it gave Verity a real shock to see them again.

"Do you never go out and see them then?" Carla asked. "Nice cheap holiday in the sun, you know, that sort of thing."

"Once and never again," Verity said. "Anything we saved on accommodation was spent on sun-cream for me. I spent the whole fortnight ducking and diving from one spot of shade to another, and I still got burned when I ventured out to go swimming."

"I'd forgotten how easily you burn," Carla said. Her own skin was kept to the same shade all year round with the aid of sun beds and occasional bursts of instant tan, and now she was looking at her friend's lack of lines and wondering whether Verity's aversion to the sun was maybe a factor in that very lack of wrinkling.

"Anyway, I said never again and David said the same," Verity continued. "He was pretty fed up of them by the end of it; Rose was quite small at the time and they were always going on about how we should be saving to put her into a decent school when she was older. All this and we struggled every month to pay the mortgage; I don't know how they thought we could possibly save anything. It wasn't as if they ever offered to help. Poor David's mum and dad did try and help but they've never been exactly well off themselves so it's never run to much. I prefer to holiday in this country if we holiday at all now."

"Too wet and too cold for me," Carla said carelessly. "I had a week in India last month but that was work too so it doesn't count. I was filming a commercial."

"I shall look forward to it," Verity said with a dryness Carla missed entirely.

The waitress came over with a tray with a mug of something each and some rather wonderful looking chocolate brownies that Carla had ordered, much to Verity's surprise.

"I ordered their cinnamon eggnog for us both; so Christmassy," Carla said, taking a big bite out of one of the brownies and chewing with gusto.

Verity sipped the drink set before her and found it rather sickly and artificial. She wished she had the courage to say she didn't like it and ask for an espresso instead, and to tell Carla that she wasn't so overawed by this place that she needed someone else to choose for her. I might be a hick from the sticks but I do know what coffee I'd like, she thought mutinously, but said nothing and nibbled at her brownie. It was no wonder Carla had finally begun to put on weight if she was now indulging in this sort of thing but perhaps, and the thought was a scary one, perhaps Carla had seen how much weight Verity had lost and was simply trying to tempt her into bad eating habits again. She shook her head to that and managed to smile at Carla.

"And how's your mum?" she asked. "You said she's moved into sheltered accommodation."

"Yeah, it seems like a nice place, but boy did we have a time of it going through everything," Carla said. "Mum was always a bit of hoarder, but I never realised how bad it was. It was like one of those programmes where some human pack-rat gets help sorting their life out. Anyway, we found a few bits that she didn't even know she still had, and this," here she rummaged in the canvas bag she'd put under the table, "This is something I think you should have."

She put on the table an old box still wrapped in brown paper and with ancient tape peeling off like shredded skin. Verity stared at her and picked it up cautiously. It was a parcel of sorts, that had been undone and then partially done up again, and when she turned it over to read the address written on it in sprawling exotic-looking handwriting, she felt herself lurch much as if the floor beneath her had bucked like a living thing, like an unbroken horse with an unwelcome rider. It had been originally sent to Nick.

"It's been opened," she said stupidly, as if Carla wouldn't have noticed this fact.

"Yes," Carla said simply. "It's from our barmy Aunt Charlotte. We didn't have a clue where she was so we couldn't let her know about Nick when it happened. Mum hoped there would be an address in the parcel but there wasn't, so it wasn't until after Christmas that she got in touch with us again. This was supposed to be a Christmas present to him, but he'd been dead for months when she sent it. She was a buyer for a company that sold antiques and curios and she was hardly ever in this country; this was sent from somewhere in South America, I think, but I don't think that was where she found it. Go on, open it."

Carla's face seemed childishly eager, and Verity sighed. She didn't really want to open it here, not with Carla watching but she turned it back over and peeled away the dry tape and unwrapped the parcel carefully. It was surprisingly heavy and when she'd got the layers of brown paper open, there was a lump wrapped in yellowed and brittle tissue paper, heavy and intriguing. She unrolled the paper, feeling it disintegrate as she did so, revealing a small bronze figurine, greening in places, of a woman, about four inches high, very stylised. She had her arms raised above her head almost in triumph or greeting; the face was blank and smooth and the curves of her body generous.

"It looks like some sort of goddess figure," Carla said, filling the long silence. "I think it may be valuable."

Verity said nothing, and turned the figure over and over in her fingers, feeling the cold metal under her skin.

"It's quite lovely," she said finally.

"There's a letter too," Carla said. "I did read it when Mum showed me it."

"I'll read it later," Verity said, shrouding the figurine in decaying tissue again and then enclosing it in the other wrappings. "Now, tell me about this new part. Do you think this'll be a real breakthrough or is it just going to pay the bills?"

Carla hesitated; she'd hoped she'd get more of a response to the parcel than this, and frankly, the drama queen part of her was disappointed. She'd imagined Verity's eyes filling with tears, maybe breaking down even, but she didn't seem bothered at all, merely slightly disconcerted. But now her favourite topic of conversation had been restored she couldn't resist, and she snuggled down in her comfy chair and began to tell Verity all about the auditions and who she'd seen and what they'd said. Verity was always such a good listener, after all.

When Verity got home, David was still out; he'd taken Rose to their nearest major city centre to go Christmas shopping now school was over for the term. The house felt appallingly quiet and she crept up the stairs to her and David's room and sat down on the bed. Her handbag felt like it was filled with lead; the statuette had taken on a greater and greater heaviness the closer she got to home. She had no idea what she should do with it and she didn't want to read a letter sent more than eighteen years ago by Nick's loving aunt.

Slowly she undressed, hanging her new dress up carefully and peeling off tights like a snake shedding its skin, before pulling on jeans and the old Guernsey sweater. The parcel lay on the bed and she knew she couldn't look at it in here. The attic stairs were dusty; it had been weeks since anyone had been up there and they creaked now as she padded up them in thick socks. She'd show David the statue later but she needed to read the letter alone and somehow up here, above the rest of the humdrum reality of the rest of the house, up here among the boxes and trunks and relics of so many lives where she'd hung out with Carla and Nick and other friends all now dispersed and gone, it seemed the right place to read what Aunt Charlotte had written to her nephew all those years ago.

The paper crackled as she unfolded it; the ink was surprisingly dark still and the handwriting sprawling and individual. The date was blurred as if she'd smeared the ink while it was wet, but she could make out the word November. Nick had been dead since August at this point; his aunt hadn't known and that somehow seemed to make this even more poignant than ever.

"Dearest Nick," Verity read it aloud, feeling her throat constrict as she did so. "I found this and thought it would be better to send it to you than to have it go to some rich Philistine who wouldn't know its beauty but only its price. I know you have your own goddess now, and I hope it won't be too long before you tell the world what you told me in your last letter. Ignore anyone who says you're both too young to marry; grab happiness by both hands while you can. I'm just a silly romantic but maybe that's why we've always got on so well. I hope this year will go quickly for you both and then you can be together again. Have a beautiful Christmas, love Aunt Charlotte."

In the bright glare of the bare light bulb, Verity felt darkness all around her; she was suddenly seventeen again and stricken. There was a cold place in the centre of her chest that seemed to hurt in a vague, unfocussed way. She tucked the letter and the wrappings into a shoebox where she kept the odd old letter and made her way down to the kitchen where she put the statue on the windowsill and stared out into the dark garden. Please God, let David be home soon, she thought, as the silence seemed to grow deafening, I don't think I can stand being alone just now.

"How was it?" Johnny asked from the rowing machine. He was glistening with sweat and very slightly out of breath. "How was your loser friend then?"

"Surprisingly well," Carla said. "I was surprised. She's lost a lot of weight since I saw her last. Mind you, she really needed to. She's still a bit fat but not too awful. She really let herself go when Nick died and again when she had the baby. Comfort eating I guess. I'd eat like a pig if I had her life; dull as ditch-water."

"I'm told that if you look at ditch-water under a microscope, there's a lot going on," Johnny said mildly.

Carla said nothing but snorted in irritation and went through to the bathroom to swallow some laxatives; she had no intention of hanging onto the calories from the coffee shop. This way wasn't glamorous but at least it worked without stripping away all the enamel off the teeth. And since Johnny was out at rehearsals or something this evening, it wasn't likely to be a problem. She'd be clear of it all before he got home.

"It gave me a bit of a turn, to tell the truth," Carla said as she came back through and her tone of voice made Johnny pause at the rowing.

"What do you mean?" he said, puzzled. A reflective Carla was a new one on him.

"Well, when I came in and saw her, it was like time had stood still, sort of," she said. "She'd got this blue dress on and I remember she had one that exact same colour when we were seventeen, and I suddenly thought, she hasn't changed a bit since then. I swear she hasn't changed her hair or anything, and she's hardly aged at all, or much less than you'd expect. And even when I got closer and I could see she had aged a bit, she still seemed seventeen in some way. Very odd indeed. It wasn't mutton dressed as lamb either; I can't really explain it. Anyway, I gave her the present Aunt Charlotte sent Nick the Christmas after he died and she wasn't fazed by it at all, so I guess I'll pass on the other bits when I remember. Funny though."

"What was?"

"She made me feel old," Carla said and frowned.

"How was it?" David asked.

Verity was curled up on the sofa with the gas fire lit and an empty mug next to her on the floor that had clearly contained hot chocolate. There were carols playing on the stereo and everything seemed very calm and quiet.

"All right," she said. "She's a bit full of herself, but that's just Carla. It must be hard to be yourself when all your working life you have to be someone or something you aren't."

"What did she have for you then?" he asked, sitting next to her.

"Something an aunt sent them years back," she said. "I think she thought I'd like it what with Granddad being into archaeology. I think it's probably valuable but it may be a fake or a reproduction or something, but it's rather lovely anyway. I've left it in the kitchen."

She seemed rather distant.

"Are you very tired?" he asked. "Is she very exhausting to be with?"

She nodded.

43

"Draining, really," she said. "Everything always has to come back to her. But she tried to be kind, I suppose. The coffee place was posh and horrible; give me Starbucks any day!"

"I hope she paid!" David said.

She smiled.

"She did," she said. "I felt a bit sick when I got home, though. Did you get what you wanted today?"

"I think so," he said. "Rosie had fun though, trying to find you a present. I think you'll like it. She's gone to hide it, I think."

"I hate Christmas!" Verity said suddenly with such venom that it startled David.

"I didn't know you felt like that," he said, concerned.

"I didn't used to," she said. "It's just it seems the one time of year we end up remembering those who aren't with us for it, and I hate that."

He was silent for a moment.

"I know," he said finally. "But your Granddad wouldn't have wanted you to be sad. It's just another day, after all. Come on, let's get some supper on, unless you're too full from cake, that is?"

Christmas with all its extravagant promises of happiness and family harmony had always seemed a mocking reminder to Verity of what she'd never really had until she had her own family; but now Rose was no longer young enough to be enchanted simply with the atmosphere and the glitter and glamour, it got harder year by year to make that one day special for all of them. This year, with the welcome absence of her parents and the not-so welcome absence of her grandfather, she was hoping that at least they would have a day free from the obligatory post-luncheon row. The morning had gone beautifully; Rose still got up at about six, as excited about presents as she'd been at four years old and that meant Verity was sure to get the turkey on early enough for them to have a lunch rather than that late afternoon meal spoiled by a day's worth of nibbling at sweets and chocolates, which is what always seemed to happen in the past when her parents had been for Christmas. This time, things were looking up, as after breakfast David offered to set up Rose's new computer for her, and so Verity had the kitchen to herself to get on with all the cooking. In previous years she'd usually been worn thin with her mother's unasked advice and unhelpful help, and with the tiny kitchen of the last house, her own appetite had usually vanished by the time she served up a dinner she'd been inhaling for hours. But even though this kitchen was much bigger, it had become desperately hot and she was beginning to be uncomfortable. She decided she could take a break and cool off in the garden for ten minutes or so, so she abandoned her apron and stepped out into the cool air.

The grass was moist with thawed frost but beneath it the ground was hard as concrete. A few apples still clung to the tips of branches but most had either fallen or been picked. There were shelves and shelves of them laid out in the shed, none quite touching each other and inspected weekly for rot. As she walked among the bare trees, she noticed something unusual at the end of the garden, something that hadn't been there yesterday. A great mound of earth, some twelve feet long by maybe three or four feet high cut across the garden down at the far end near the high wall.

"What the-?" she said, walking rapidly towards it.

Where the trees ended and there was a gap between them and the wall, a huge trench had appeared, and the scent of damp sour earth filled her nostrils as she got closer to it. The trench must have been four or more feet deep, cut sharply from the compacted soil. There was a scraping noise from inside the trench and as she neared, she could see there was a figure kneeling in the bottom of the trench, carefully excavating away the hard mud and stones with a trowel.

"Granddad?" she said, breathlessly. "What on earth are you doing out here? It's freezing; you'll catch pneumonia."

He glanced up at her and threw her one of his breathtaking smiles, all teeth and ice blue eyes flashing.

"Nonsense, girl," he said. "Once you get working, it's warm enough."

He was dressed in a ragged pair of shorts and filthy sandals and nothing else: his digging outfit, worn every summer he helped out on various digs even after he'd officially retired. His indifference to weather conditions had been legendary, his skin tanned like an old kipper at the end of each season. He was so thin she could see every rib bone and every vertebra along his spine, and his cheekbones stuck out like those of a famine victim.

"Lunch will be ready in about half an hour," Verity said. "That'll be enough for you to get clean enough to sit down to the table with us, won't it."

"Is that layabout husband of yours there?" he asked and Verity shuddered.

"Yes, he's upstairs setting up the new computer," she said.

"Then I'll have mine when he's gone," the old man declared. "I've said I didn't want him in my house. I'll make the exception since it's Christmas day and I'd not spoil it for the kiddie by making a scene but I want him out by dusk."

There was a pulse beating in Verity's temple; a tightness in her mind as she tried to grasp what was happening.

"Don't be unreasonable, Granddad; it's Christmas Day after all," she said.

"So bloody what? That changes nothing for me," he said heatedly. He never swore, never! She was shocked.

Change the subject, that's what I should do, she thought.

"What exactly are you doing down here anyway?" she asked and he looked up at her, the thunderous look being wiped away by a smile as sweet as a baby's.

"I think," he said. "I think I've found the site of the century; the decade at the very least. There's everything here from Bronze Age right through to the medieval. Best site I've ever dug."

"In our back garden?" she asked. "May I step in?"

He sat back on his heels and waved her in. She carefully jumped down into the trench, feeling the hardness of the ground under her thin-soled slippers as she landed.

"I can hardly believe it myself," he said. "All these years I've lived here, all my life and I never knew what was here. A week's work and I've found stuff that'll change the face of archaeology forever in this country. There can't be many places in Europe or even the world that have evidence of such a long occupation. As I get deeper, I may even find Neolithic finds too. Maybe even further back."

"That's amazing, Granddad," she said, her heart thumping unevenly. "Will you be getting funding for it?"

His face darkened again.

"No," he said. "Bloody department said they don't have the budget for another speculative dig especially now I'm retired. So I'll have to do it all myself. I've got all my evidence ready and they won't even give me a hearing."

"That's a shame," she said neutrally.

"Silly fools, they'll look like total morons when I set up my own exhibition," he said, chuckling. "Still, all the glory will be mine alone; no one can steal this from me the way they've always done before, prattling about team work and modern techniques and sharing the credit."

The trench seemed devoid of anything of interest; but then she wasn't an archaeologist so perhaps she didn't know what she was looking for anyway.

"I'm excavating a post hole, right now," he said, gesturing for her to come and look. "Probably an Iron Age round house but we'll see when we find others."

The mud where he was scraping did look very slightly darker than the mud surrounding it.

"There's a hearth further over, but I dug that over to see what was under it," he said and Verity frowned. This wasn't how she knew it should go; any finds like that were carefully photographed and recorded and only if there was no other way did they then dig through. And if he'd only been at this a week, he'd shifted a hell of a lot of earth; he must have dug straight through layers of important stuff just to get to the bottom of the trench.

"Are you all right, Granddad?" she asked nervously and he bared his teeth at her in a mirthless grin, more like a snarl than a smile.

"Of course I'm all right," he snapped. "Don't you go all concerned on me too girl. I know you only put up with me because I've given you a home."

This doesn't make sense she thought desperately, but I can't seem to-

"Show me the finds, Granddad," she said suddenly, her mind seeming to finally latch onto something it could hold onto.

He scrambled to his feet with some creaking and swearing.

"Over there," he said, and gestured to a makeshift row of shelves made from old planks and bricks set up at the edge of the trench off to one end and she stepped carefully over the uneven surface of the trench bottom.

She stared at the row of items, slowly going colder and colder inside as she looked at them.

"Would you talk me through them, please, Granddad. You know I'm not the expert you are," she said carefully and he beamed at her.

He picked up the first, some reddish looking ceramic shard.

"Samian ware, second century Roman import," he said. "It suggests we have a high status villa here somewhere. This isn't just any old pottery; this was the Crown Derby of its day and had to be imported. Very expensive."

It's a bit of old terracotta flower pot, she thought; it might be Victorian since it's so crumbly but it might just be the cheap stuff from the garden centre up the road. He was watching her, grinning like a shark, and looking very pleased with himself.

"This is a votive statuette, probably a bit later, maybe even a Lares from the household shrine," he explained holding up the mangled remains of an old Barbie doll, hairless and partially melted from a bonfire."

She nodded, saying nothing, just getting colder and more and more scared.

"This," he was saying, "Is a very fine piece, a dagger of the late Bronze Age; missing its handle but still very fine. Excellent condition though. You wouldn't think it had been in the ground over three millennia, would you?"

He was showing her an old kitchen knife, its bone handle sheared off long ago and lost.

She said nothing and began to examine the other items on the makeshift finds shelf; there were a lot of old bones, meat bones she guessed discarded when the household rubbish had been mostly burned and buried in the days before refuse collections. The Barbie had probably been thrown over the wall at some stage; she was pretty certain she'd never had one when she'd lived here. There were lots of pieces of glass, some quite old, maybe from the days when a small greenhouse and cold frames had sheltered the tender plants and vegetables from the frosts long ago, but none of it very old, or old enough to be thought Roman or even medieval. The house itself was Georgian but even her own inexpert knowledge told her that none of this rubbish was older than the house.

Dear God, he's gone mad, senile even. What am I going to do?

He was watching her, his eyes filled with something she didn't understand or like. This wasn't the man she knew and loved at all.

"What do you think then, girl?" he asked, his voice strangely low and harsh.

"It's all very interesting," she said. "But I need to go and carve the turkey. Shall I bring you some out on a tray if you won't come in."

"Do you agree it's the site of the century?" he said, prodding at her with his trowel, hurting her ribs, and making her feel suddenly annoyed.

"It's just rubbish," she snapped. "I don't know what you're thinking but this isn't archaeology. No wonder you couldn't get funding. They must all be laughing at you."

He stared at her, his face flushing.

"It's jealousy from them, but from you, it's just ignorance," he said. "Always thought you were such a little clever clogs didn't you but you haven't got the brains to get anywhere in this world; always got to cling to someone haven't you, you spineless wonder."

She couldn't move as he poured out more and worse insults, until she could stand it no longer.

"You're crazy," she said. "You need a doctor."

She turned away, still holding a piece of bone and as she crossed the trench, he roared at her to come back.

"No one steals my finds," he yelled, and she turned in time to see him grab his heavy shovel and swing it at her head in a wild, Berserker movement that would have looked rather fine and elegant had he been holding a broad sword and not a mud-encrusted Spear and Jackson spade. But sword or spade, she went down just the same and dropped to the cold earth like a sack of potatoes.

David had become aware of a beeping that wasn't coming from the computer game he was playing with his daughter and had decided to investigate. He knew his wife much preferred to be left alone to get on with a meal like this one; other people in the kitchen tended to flummox her and divert her from her own routines, so he kept out of the way but within earshot in case he were needed for something. The beeping proved to be coming from the oven timer; it was patiently telling whoever might listen that the turkey was probably ready. He took a quick look in the oven, saw nothing was about to burn, and turned the temperature down a bit just to be sure nothing would over-cook while he tried to work out where Verity had gone. He'd not heard her come up, but he'd been quite engrossed in the game, so he shouted for her at the bottom of the stairs. Rose appeared instead.

"Is your Mum up there?" he asked.

Rose gave an extravagant shrug, another mannerism acquired at school.

"Is lunch ready then?" she asked.

"Not just yet. Can you have a look in our room, see if she's gone in there?"

Rose was back in a few seconds.

"Nope, not in the bathroom either unless she's hiding behind the door," she said.

David glanced in all the downstairs room and then decided he'd better have a look in the garden. The kitchen had got very hot so maybe she was standing outside to get some cooler air. He stepped outside, leaving the back door open to cool the kitchen and stared at the empty garden. No Verity. He was about to go inside again when his eye was caught by a patch of blue down at the end of the garden and began to stride rapidly down towards it; Verity's dress was a blue just that shade.

She was lying half on her side, half on her back, her eyes just flickering open as he reached her.

"Are you OK? What happened?" he asked, trying to help her sit up, all over fingers and thumbs with the anxiety and not really being much help.

She rubbed her eyes; her head was pounding like a set of hammers on either side of her temples.

"I think I fainted," she said, her voice sounding full of gravel. "I came out to cool down, and then I think I just fainted."

David was near to panic as he tried to get her to her feet; he had no idea how long the timer had been beeping and so no idea how long she'd been lying out here in the cold grass and icy air in this lovely but thin silk dress.

"I'll get the car," he said as he got her into the living room and onto the sofa. "You really should see a doctor and the only ones available on Christmas day are all at the hospital."

"I'm OK, I just fainted," she said and he stopped trying to find his car keys. "I just got over-heated, and then the shock of the cold air made me faint."

Rose had come in and was trying not to look worried.

"Maybe it's The Change," she said, and David glared at her.

"Not helpful," he said. "What shall I do?" he asked Verity, helplessly.

"Nothing," she said. "I'll be OK in a minute. A cup of tea and an aspirin will have me right. Is the oven still on as high?"

"I turned it down," he said. "Are you sure you're OK?"

She nodded.

"Fine, just got a horrible headache, that's all," she said, and because they were both watching her with pinched, worried faces, she made herself smile to make them relax. "It happens sometimes; don't worry. Every woman faints once in a while and most men too, under the right circumstances. And maybe Rosie is right; maybe it is the start of the change. I'm a bit young but some women do go through it at my age or even younger. Let's just get lunch sorted, eh?"

They ended up doing the unthinkable and ate Christmas dinner off trays in front of the television and the afternoon film, and David didn't bother doing any sprouts and no one minded and the sky didn't fall because they pulled crackers after the meal and not before because Rose suddenly remembered them. They ate the pudding with vanilla ice cream because Verity hadn't begun making the brandy butter when she'd gone out into the garden, and it was a revelation that it tasted much nicer with the ice cream than it ever did with the brandy butter.

After lunch, she took off the blue silk dress and reverted to jeans and the old Guernsey sweater and sat and watched the sky darken to midnight blue from the study window while Rose and David washed the dishes, and tried to make some sense of what she'd experienced and found that it just made her head hurt more and made that cold spot inside her become so icy it was almost painful. She wished she could talk to someone about it but who would believe her, who wouldn't assume she was barmy and needed locking up?

"It wasn't a ghost," she said aloud. But what was it? What was happening to her? Was she going mad, as her Grandfather seemed to have done in the vision?

David came through, his hands wrinkled from washing up.

"Do you want some coffee?" he said.

"Please," she said and as he turned to go, she said, "David?"

He stopped at the door.

"Are you OK?" he asked, his concern back to the fore again.

"I'm fine," she said. "My head's a lot better. I just wanted to ask something. The last weeks before Granddad died, did he seem OK to you? Or did he seem a bit more forgetful or a bit moody?"

He stood in silence, thinking for a moment.

"A bit, yes," he said. "But you know what he was like; I was never sure how much of the absent minded professor stuff was an act and how much of it was real. And moods, well, we all have the odd mood swing. Why?"

"I was just wondering if he might have been going, well, you know, a bit senile," she said. "I mean, I know he was physically OK, but when he had that fall, and then he got ill, I was wondering if maybe his age was catching him up in more ways than just wear and tear on the joints."

"I don't think so," David said. "He had that fall because he tripped on a stick; maybe if someone had got him in sooner, he wouldn't have got as chilled and then gotten ill. But you know how he prided himself on how tough he was; it was his own silly fault he didn't get warmed up properly or called someone for some help. He was the sort who digs bullets out of his own leg and then marches twenty miles to do something heroic. They don't make them like that any more; he just didn't accept that he couldn't do what he'd done when he was younger and that he did need a bit of caring for."

"Maybe I should have made him accept that," she said, thoughtfully.

"He was a stubborn old git and you couldn't have made him do something he didn't want to do except maybe at gunpoint. You know how he wouldn't retire properly, kept on working even after they asked him not to," David said patiently. "Don't blame yourself for anything. He made his choices and in the end he passed on very peacefully."

He made coffee and brought it through and Verity sipped hers, her eyes still pensive.

"It's been a good day, though," David said presently. "No rows with your parents, no rows with Rosie; lovely food, nice presents."

She smiled.

"Except one," she said. "I didn't tell you what Juliet gave me, did I? She gave me a gift voucher, for one of her therapies. Would you credit it? She even thinks she's doing me a huge favour, giving me a freebie. She charges an exorbitant sum for all of them. You should have seen her face when she gave me the envelope. She said, "Here's something you might find very useful indeed," and I thought, at last a Christmas cash bonus, since it was an envelope, or at the very least some M and S vouchers, instead of the usual bizarre gift. You'd have thought she was giving me the keys to the kingdom the smug look she had on her face. God knows how I'm going to get out of having one of the damned treatments without offending her."

He smiled.

"You don't need the job really any more," he said. "Let her sack you if she gets huffy."

"Maybe I will," she said, but thought in horror, and then what would I do? Hang around the house going crazy instead?

"There are loads of other jobs out there you can try for," he said.

Doing what? she thought miserably. I've a degree but I'm no real use for anything; I've no useful skills or experience.

"Or you could go and do your PGCE," he went on.

"Not the way schools are these days," she said, hastily. "Everyone wants to get out, not in. I'd be useless anyway."

"No, you wouldn't," he said and relented. "Don't worry, you don't have to do anything you aren't happy about. Stay working for Juliet if that's what you want."

What do I want? What do I want to do anyway? I just don't know, she thought hopelessly. It's all very well for him saying that but what do I want out of life? I just don't know. I don't know if I ever knew.

She smiled at him, hoping the pain inside wouldn't show if she at least tried to look happy.

"I'll think about it," she said.

Chapter 3

Christmas passed, as it does, leaving behind some pleasant memories, some not so pleasant ones and the expectation of some large bills in the New Year. David's parents came to stay in the lull between Christmas and New Year, having spent Christmas itself with his older brother and his family. Verity liked her in-laws but found them difficult to be with for more than a few hours; she had more than a sneaking feeling they did not understand her at all and while that was tempered by their obvious affection for her, she usually became uneasy with some of the questions they asked. It was usually along the same lines each time; why, when she had a good degree, was she working in a shop for someone else when she might be running her own business or at the very least teaching as she had planned to do when she and David had married? What was she going to do with her life? And when was she going to do it? Now Rosie was so much older, she didn't even need to worry about childcare, so why wasn't she even trying to find a better job or start a career?

Good bloody question, she thought, as she cycled to work, glad to get away from it even for the dubious pleasure of being with Juliet all day. Juliet shut the shop for Christmas Day and Boxing Day, as well as New Year's Day but had it open otherwise, and today she was fully booked with clients wanting to somehow offset their Christmas over-indulgences with one of her therapies.

"I've seen two more courses I want to go on," Juliet said, as Verity donned her work shirt over her tee-shirt, which was now slightly dampened with sweat. "Japanese Forest Therapy and Angelic Massage. They both have a taster weekend in January so you'll need to be available for Friday afternoons till five. I'll give you the dates later when I find my diary again. By the way, you'll need to book your session with me in good time. It looks like I'm going to be very busy for the next few weeks. Oh, and would you pick up the new flyers from the printers at lunchtime?"

She was buffing her nails as she spoke and running her eye down her booking list for today.

"Did you hear me?" she said sharply when Verity had said nothing.

"Yes," said Verity. "I'll let you know about the therapy when I've had a chance to think about it. And yes, I'll pick up the flyers at lunchtime."

She picked up a CD at random and put it in the stereo to cover the awkwardness. She had been very close to saying something she was sure to regret. But when it came down to it, she didn't have the courage for a row that was sure to be bruising, and going home minus a job while her in-laws were staying wasn't her choice for a peaceful life at all. She picked up the feather duster and began flicking it carefully round the interior of the big cabinet full of crystals.

"I'm booked solid for weeks, so don't expect me to put myself out," Juliet said, her voice full of reproach.

"I won't," Verity said, and then because she couldn't bear the hurt in Juliet's voice, however insincere and feigned, she said, "It was a kind thought. Thank you. I'm just not sure I'm ready for any of them; you've always said the therapies are most effective if the client is mentally and spiritually prepared and I don't think I am."

Juliet looked slightly mollified.

"Well, when you do feel ready, let me know," she said. "Right, I'm not going to have a chance for a coffee break at eleven as usual so either grab yours when there's a lull or leave it till lunchtime."

Another woman might have protested about employment rights, and so on; Verity said nothing and resolved that if she had to go out to collect these wretched advertising flyers, then she'd take half an hour extra and stop by at the Starbucks at that end of town and have her break there rather than in the dingy kitchen upstairs with instant coffee that tasted of the lime-scale in Juliet's kettle. The shop was shut for lunch anyway and Juliet's afternoon clients didn't start till two so it wasn't a problem. Her mouth suddenly watered at the thought of a nice big latte and a cake or something.

The shop was as quiet as she'd expected it to be; trade was always down between Christmas and New Year. Even when Juliet had started her sales the day after Boxing Day, they never sold a vast amount and it was really only the fact that Juliet was busy with her clients upstairs anyway that made it even half way worth bothering to open the shop at all. Most people had spent their available cash already on Christmas, so all she sold that morning were three packets of joss sticks, some green candles and a packet of white sage to one lady who intended to perform what she called a money spell on New Year's Eve, and some temporary tattoos to a teenager who had failed to persuade her parents to allow her to have a real tattoo and who was determined to appear at a party sporting one, even if it was one that would wash or peel off in a few days, maximum. Juliet's clients came and went, by and large consisting of women with too much spare cash, too much faith in Juliet and too few working brain cells to analyse what was really happening to them. As David said, there was nothing like being able to lie down and relax for an hour with someone taking their troubles seriously for making almost anyone feel better, and if there was even a very sketchy sort of massage thrown in for good measure, then the money was seen as well spent. For the first time, Verity saw the clients leave and wondered how much Juliet was earning by all this; it had never occurred to her before to even think about the money side of it.

At twelve, the last of the morning's clients left and Verity was free to go and collect the flyers from the printers; she had a fairly horrible feeling that she might well be the one who ended up carrying them around town and distributing them in shops and businesses that would have them. The boxes were heavy enough for her to wish she'd got the car with her, but there were only two so if she took her time she'd be able to carry them back to the shop without too much trouble. She ducked into Starbucks and dumped them by a chair near the stairs to the upstairs lounge and went to order herself a coffee and something sweet to compensate for the sourness of her mood. Why am I such a doormat, she asked herself as she gazed at the white froth in her mug? It isn't as if she'd really just sack me for disagreeing with her or refusing to do some of the things she asks me to do. She knows she'd have trouble finding someone who'd put up with her and with the low wages. She'd sulk for a while but she wouldn't really sack me, so why do I just take it?

She took a bite of the cinnamon swirl and savoured it and then nearly choked on it. A man had come down the stairs and headed out of the door. She swallowed hard and leapt out of her chair and ran across to the door. It had been Nick.

The street wasn't empty but he was gone, and short of running out and yelling his name as she searched the streets, there wasn't anything she could do, so she turned and returned to her table, her coffee and her bun.

"Are you all right?"

She jumped; it was the young man from behind the counter. Even though it was lunchtime, the café was quiet enough for her behaviour to have been noticed.

"I thought I knew the guy who just went out," she said. "But he'd gone when I got to the door. I haven't seen him in a long time so I hoped to catch him."

She was blushing; her whole body felt hot and clammy. It wasn't as if it might have looked like she was running out without paying; she'd already paid before she'd even got her coffee, but she felt suddenly so desperately visible.

"I didn't see him," said the young man. "I just thought you might have been taken ill; you did look very pale."

Verity snorted mirthlessly.

"I always look pale," she said.

He grinned at her.

"Well, relatively," he said. "You looked like you'd had a shock."

"I did," she said and then recklessly, "I thought he was dead, you see, the guy I saw."

He shrugged.

"I didn't see anyone," he said. "But everyone ends up at Starbucks eventually, so I don't see why ghosts don't too."

He turned away and went back to the counter but she could feel him shooting her the odd puzzled glance now and again as she drank her coffee. She left half the swirl, feeling strangely sickened and uneasy and unable to finish it, and when she left, struggling with the boxes, the young man from the counter ran and held the door for her.

"See you soon," he said and she felt the cold wind catch her hair as she stepped out into the street again, her arms already feeling the tug of the heavy boxes.

"You were a long time," Juliet said when she got back to the shop.

"These are heavy," Verity said, not choosing to explain her detour, and hoping Juliet couldn't smell the pungent sweet tang of the good coffee and the pastry clinging if not to her clothes, then to her breath. She felt a hysterical giggle welling up from somewhere, threatening to betray her, so she dumped the boxes on the counter, hauled off her coat and went to hang it up in the passage-way at the foot of the stairs, hiding her face briefly in the folds of the coat, trying to wipe away the guilty pleasure of fooling Juliet.

"You seem rather pleased with yourself," Juliet said suspiciously, when she got back a few seconds later.

"David's mother said she's cooking tonight," Verity said. "It's just nice to know for once I won't have to go home and start cooking."

Juliet grunted.

"I thought David was a bit of a whiz in the kitchen," she said.

"He is but in term time, I'm home first," Verity said. "It's nice having them with us. We don't see them very often."

Juliet said nothing and then said in a rush,

"You don't know you're born, sometimes, Verity. You've got a lovely husband and a fantastic home now, not to mention a daughter who does you both credit. Sometimes I don't think you know how lucky you are."

Verity was stunned and didn't have a clue what to say but Juliet just picked up her client books and went upstairs without another word, leaving Verity rather dumbfounded. Could it be that Juliet was envious of her, even after all the subtle and spiteful things she'd said over the years?

She didn't see her again except when she was showing clients in and out until five o'clock when Verity was shutting up the shop. She seemed her usual self again and didn't mention anything about what she'd said earlier.

"I'll finish up here," she said. "You get off home to your in-laws."

In truth, Verity was glad to get out and have the chance to think about what had happened at lunchtime, so she fetched her coat and her bike from round the back and began walking home, pushing the bike. Despite a whole afternoon in the shop, she still felt shaky and didn't trust herself on the bike in this sort of rush hour traffic if she was likely to wobble and maybe fall off. It had seemed utterly real, seeing Nick like that, but she knew it had to have been another vision or hallucination and that made her feel ill at the thought. If she was somehow conjuring up images of a man who had been dead all these years, someone she'd barely thought of for a long time, then she must really be sick. Maybe there was something growing inside her brain, making her see these things, things that had never been real, never could be real. If I think about it, it'll just get worse; you can't apply reason to madness, she told herself and as the traffic thinned, she decided that she would ride rather than walk after all. It's hard to brood when the sound of the wind whistling past your helmet fills your ears.

I won't think about it; it's nonsense anyway, she said fiercely to herself and began to pedal hard. If I am ill, I'd rather not know about it; it might just go away anyway. I don't want to end up in a mental hospital. If I give in to this, that's what'll happen.

But in bed that night, in one of those lucid moments before sleep rolls us into its arms, she let herself think the unthinkable, a thought far worse than the possibility of her losing her mind. What if it really had been Nick, what if he was alive after all?

Verity was an old hand at stuffing unwelcome and unwieldy emotions and fears back down into the glory hole under her metaphorical stairs and so even the thought of Nick somehow being still alive was rapidly erased from her active daily thoughts and lurked unheeded somewhere deep inside where it couldn't threaten her hard won serenity.

January blew in bitter and cold with a wind straight from Siberia, or that's what it felt like, and resolutions vanished almost as completely as the Christmas decorations on Twelfth Night. The new school year began, the credit card bill rolled in, and everything was back to normal. She stopped thinking about her visions and tried to stop thinking about her life and her future but found at quiet moments, those lulls between activities, that little worm of a thought crept in, whispering, "What are you going to do? What are you going to do?"

One icy bright and crystalline morning, she set off for work feeling unusually buoyant; maybe it was the weather, the feel of the air that was making her feel good. A brisk breeze herded the fluffy little clouds across the hard blue background of the sky, and made her skin redden as she cycled. She locked her bike in the staff car park, fixing it to a railing near the main entrance and made her way in to find what classes she'd be taking today; supply teaching paid better than regular teaching but the drawback was that she had to be prepared for just about any class.

First lesson proved to be a year eight science lesson; not exactly her forte but she was effectively only babysitting the class as their regular teacher had rung in sick. All she was required to do was supervise them copying up some notes from text books, and keep order, it wasn't going to be as horrendous as it might be. The science department smelled of gas from the Bunsen burners and a chemical tang that made her mouth dry and her eyes itch, just as it had when she'd been at school. She sometimes wondered how David, the head of department, endured his job; not just the children he taught but the environment in which he was obliged to teach. He assured her there was no evidence of any effects long-term on health, but his lab coat smelt as powerfully of the aroma of gas and chemicals as the vestments of a High Church priest tend to smell of incense.

The class was waiting for her, the usual suspects catcalling as she walked briskly along to the front desk.

"All right, sit down and be quiet." she said, her own quiet voice barely audible above the rising cacophony of childish voices. "Mrs Bruce is off sick today so-"

"She's up the duff," came a voice from the back.

Verity knew better than to engage this wag and ignored it and continued regardless,

"-So you are to turn to page 90 in the books I shall be handing out and you are to start copying out paragraphs seven to nine, and I want silence while you do it," her own voice was rising as she said it, becoming shrill and frankly lacking in any authority at all.

She handed out the books, walking up and down the benches as she did so, knowing that the instruction to take one and pass it along would result in mayhem and half the pupils claiming they hadn't got a book because so and so wouldn't give them one, and various books being either thrown or secreted under the benches to reduce the available numbers.

"Miss, I haven't got one," one child said. Verity knew she had already handed her one.

"Try looking under your desk where you put it," she said. "I will be giving out lunchtime detentions to anyone who fails to produce the required paragraphs before the bells goes, and that also includes those with illegible handwriting and botched diagrams, so take your time and don't rush it."

One boy was leaning his lab stool so far back she knew he'd fall.

"Get up," she snapped, standing close enough to break his fall if he let go of the edge of the bench. "You'll break your neck if you mess about like this. This is a lab, not an adventure playground."

The boy swung himself back up to upright.

"Mrs Bruce says it's all right," he said, his face surly.

"Do you see Mrs Bruce here? No, nor do I, so I say it isn't all right. Now, get writing," Verity said. "I mean it about detention. And less noise please."

With a very slight reduction in noise, some of the class began writing in their exercise books and Verity knew those who hadn't started would need more than subtle encouragement to do so. These were the ones for whom detention held no fears, since they probably wouldn't turn up unless they were only a short step away from exclusion anyway and had parents that sort of half way cared about it. The hard case ones scared the life out of her; some of them were already taller than her. Oddly enough, it was the girls that bothered her the most; the threat and the occasional close encounter with physical abuse from boys was nowhere near as demoralising as the personal insults and snide bitchy comments from the girls. They dissected her clothes, her hair, her accent, her figure; everything they could revile and scorn in the most disgusting language, they did. She dreaded getting even one small premenstrual spot because it would not escape the eyes of these monstrous children; being called Pizza-face or being asked if she had chickenpox were the mildest of the insults hurled at her. Smudged mascara and eye make-up made them jeer that she'd been crying; clothes that were less than bandbox fresh and fashionable got her called The Bag Lady. A cheerful face made them speculate out loud that she must have got her leg over the night before.

She approached each pupil who hadn't started and told them that if they hadn't started in ten seconds, she would be taking their names. Then she had to start taking names, not as easy as it sounds in a class full of Donald Ducks and Bart Simpsons. That was all she could do; anything worse got them sent to the head of year for discipline but so far no one had gone over that subtle and shifting line between acceptable bad behaviour and the unacceptable.

The noise level was rising and she could feel her temples beginning to pound with a tension headache. This wasn't unusual but this was early; usually it started just after lunch. She shut her eyes, squeezing them tight to try and force back the pain and recoiled suddenly as a hard edge struck her on the cheek with enough force to make her stagger back. A textbook clattered to the floor in front of her and the noise stopped abruptly, just for a moment. The whole class knew that line had been crossed and the chances were that they were all in more trouble than a simple detention was going to put right.

She put her hand to her cheek, and met wetness. The corner of the book had hit with such force that it had broken the skin and beneath it, the flesh throbbed with pain that radiated across her whole face.

"Who threw that?" she said, her voice trembling.

There was chorus of denials and accusations; her mind struggled to decide what she should do. This never happened to David, who ran his classes and the department with the efficiency of a military dictator and the apparent charm of a Pied Piper; she had never asked him his secret but she suspected it was simply that he loved his job.

A great rage and burning sense of injustice and injury threatened to take her over and she knew she was shaking with the shock of her assault.

"All of you, sit down and shut up," she shouted, her hand pressed to the trickling wound. "I am going to fetch Mr. Meadows. If anyone is out of their place when I return, for whatever reason, they will be facing exclusion along with whoever threw that book."

She left the lab, pulling the door closed behind her and saw the corridor blur as the tears began to spill down her face, making the cut sting as the salt filled it. Nothing is worth this sort of abuse, she thought fiercely, and opened the next classroom door at random. Mr. Meadows wasn't there, but another teacher with another class was.

"Need a little help here," Verity said, moving her hand to reveal the bleeding cut and the other teacher, a woman somewhat older than herself rushed to the door.

Outside in the corridor, the other teacher, whose name she didn't know, put a handkerchief to Verity's cheek.

"What happened?" she asked.

"Got a book thrown at me," Verity said.

"You'd better get down to the Casualty department," the other woman said. "That's quite a deep cut. You'll need it seeing to. I'll get someone to deal with your class but that needs attention quickly if you want to avoid scarring. Go on, don't worry, I'll tell David to sort out your class. Any idea who threw it?"

"I looked away just for a second," Verity said, miserably, her face hurting like mad now. "I didn't see who threw it, but I think it came from near the back."

The woman patted her on the shoulder.

"Go and get someone in the staff room to take you to the hospital," she said. "We'll sort this out."

Outside the staff room she paused, unwilling to go in suddenly and face whoever was in there. She'd cycle to the casualty department; then there was only one extra teacher needing to cover for her. Once she got back to her bike, she realised she couldn't cycle with the handkerchief padded against the cut and as she unlocked the security chain, she saw her hands were shaking. She wheeled the machine to outside the school gates and then as she tried to think what to do, she heard her mobile phone begin to ring deep inside her handbag. She leaned the bike against a wall and fumbled to find the phone as it seemed to become louder and more insistent.

"Verity, where the hell are you?" Juliet's voice, petulant and cross, filled her ears. "It's gone ten o'clock; I've had to shut the shop while I saw my first client. What the hell are you playing at? I've rung three times already."

Verity shut her eyes, and put her hand to her injured cheek. There was no blood now, no cut, and no handkerchief. She was standing outside the school still, the same school David taught at, the same school she'd been to herself years and years ago.

"Are you there?" Juliet's voice had become shrill with irritation.

Verity shook her head as though there were flies pestering her, trying to clear her mind. She was over an hour late for work and her mind was spinning.

"Sorry," she said, her voice hoarse. "Having trouble with the bike. I'll be with you shortly. Sorry."

She ended the call before Juliet could ask her anything else and then turned the phone off. She was feeling horribly sick and shaky; the events of the last hour and a half had been so real, and yet they hadn't been real at all. She'd never been a teacher, let alone a supply teacher. She remembered setting off for work, but somehow she'd ended up here. Had she been wandering round David's school for the last hour or so, or had she been standing here outside the school gates. She felt very cold and her skin was like marble to the touch, so maybe she'd been here all the time; there was no way of telling short of going to reception and asking if she'd been in and she wasn't going to do that.

In the end, she did the only thing she could do, and got back on her bike and cycled to the shop and the irate and indignant Juliet.

"That wretched bike of yours is always breaking down," Juliet said when Verity finally reached the shop, cold and shivering. "You should chuck it on a skip and buy a new one."

Verity said nothing and hauled on her work shirt over her tee shirt.

"I don't know why you bother anyway," Juliet went on. "It's quicker to drive."

Juliet had driven everywhere since she'd passed her driving test at seventeen, and hated walking.

"It keeps me fit," Verity said, but her voice was still very shaky and Juliet looked at her.

"Are you OK?" she asked. "You didn't get knocked off or something did you?"

"I sort of fell off," Verity said, desperate for some sort of excuse. "I'm a bit shaky but I wasn't hurt. I think I hit a patch of ice or something."

Juliet made her some coffee and made her take some sips of some flower essence she swore by for shock but didn't suggest she run her home. She had another client at eleven and she didn't want the shop shut again; concern only went so far, after all.

It was a surprisingly busy morning; the constant procession of people either coming to see Juliet or to browse among the sale items meant that the wind chimes that hung over the door seemed to be constantly jangling. The flat metallic sound had really begun to get on her nerves by the time lunch time came round and she considered taking them down altogether but then decided not to. Juliet liked them there as it alerted her when someone came into the shop; it gave her a limited window into how business was going downstairs when she was busy upstairs.

"I'm going out to get a sandwich," Verity said as soon as Juliet emerged at five to one from her twelve o'clock session, and made it out of the door before Juliet could ask her either to get her something or tell her to be back at a certain time.

Verity knew she'd pay for it later but all she wanted was a quiet corner of a café somewhere to eat and drink in peace, away from Juliet. She would have liked longer but half an hour was pushing it enough and when she came back, Juliet was scowling at her anyway.

"It hardly seems worth you bothering coming back at all when you'll be finishing at three," she said.

"It's only half one," Verity said. "There's another hour and a half. Did anyone come in while I was out?"

Juliet sometimes used to keep the shop open at lunchtime and drink her own coffee at the counter, if Verity was elsewhere.

"No," she admitted, reluctantly. "But I'd have liked a bite of lunch myself, you know."

"You could go now," Verity said. "You've got half an hour before anyone else comes."

Juliet was about to say that she hardly thought half an hour was enough for her to find, buy and then eat some lunch; she thought better of it, remembering she seldom gave Verity even that for her lunch and grabbed her handbag and rushed out of the shop without another word, though when she got back, she was still scowling at Verity.

"This late, all the sandwich shops have either sold out or else they've only got egg rolls," she said. "Next time, try and think of something other than your stomach and be a bit more considerate.

You could have got me something while you were out, but did you bother to stop and ask? No you didn't."

Verity had an urge to slap her; the amount of times Juliet had swanned out of the shop on an extended lunch break leaving Verity with the options of shutting the shop altogether while she went out to get something for her own meal, or going without altogether, were so numerous she was astounded that Juliet didn't remember them.

"After all," Juliet was saying, "It won't exactly do you any harm to miss lunch once in a while."

The heat was rising in Verity's blood; years of unacknowledged fury was bubbling there just under the surface, waiting for a final trigger to let it loose. The moment passed. Verity just nodded and said nothing, picked up the feather duster and began to run it carefully along the shelf that was packed with little statues of the Buddha. In her mind she'd wanted to ask Juliet what was the point was of her buying a lunch at all when she would probably stick her fingers down her throat later anyway; the comment stayed in her mind, unspoken but still gleaming like a polished knife blade.

She told David about it later and he was indignant on her behalf but it only renewed his questions about her doing something better, and it all came back to her doing her PGCE. Remembering the "incident" of the morning, Verity said irritably,

"I'd have been a useless teacher. I could hardly keep Rosie in order, let alone a class full of the little hooligans you get in state schools."

"Then go private," he said. "Do the PGCE and only apply to private schools."

"As if there's an abundance of them here," she said. "They only take the very best teachers anyway. I'd not stand a chance of getting a post at one."

"You're so negative," he said.

"That's what I get every day from Juliet, so please don't you start. I'm being realistic, David. Coming in as a mature student teacher, what does that say about my ability that I couldn't do it properly the first time around?"

"You were pregnant," he said. "You couldn't stop being sick. No one could reasonably expect you to study like that and Rosie was due when you would have started teaching practise. Otherwise you'd have done fine."

"Just because you're a born teacher doesn't make me one too," she said and bit her lip as he looked hurt and upset.

"That was what we agreed we'd do," he said. "It's what we both wanted, what we both felt was right."

Yes, and I made a botch of contraception and got pregnant instead, Verity thought miserably, but kept silent.

"Things have changed," she said. "I'm not who I was then. I know now I'd have been an awful teacher, and I don't want to take my bloody PGCE just to prove it to you."

"There's no talking to you when you're like this," he said turning away, annoyed.

She said nothing, wishing she'd kept silent about Juliet, which was what had started this row, and wishing she could tell him why she knew beyond reason why she would have been a terrible teacher and knowing she couldn't. She began chopping onions instead so that any of the traitorous tears that she knew were hovering there would be attributed to the onions and not to emotions. After a minute, he put his arms round her.

"I know you don't think you'd have been any good, but that's just how you are about things. You never think you'll be good at things," he said. "OK, don't take the PGCE. But you need to find something you want to do, otherwise one of these days you might just snap and take a swing at Juliet. She takes appalling advantage of you, you know, and she gets away with it because you're still behaving as if it'd be the worst disaster possible if you lose that job. But you don't have to put up with it or her if you don't want to. Look, I've got marking to do, so give me a shout when dinner is ready. Just think about it."

She nodded and he disengaged himself and left her to the cooking.

Juliet's training courses proved to be a mixed bag. After the taster sessions, she had returned alternately enraged and enthused.

"The Japanese forest therapy was a rip-off," she said and Verity nearly choked on her coffee.

"What do you mean?" she said. This was a bit rich coming from Juliet.

"Well, all it seems to involve is lying down among a whole load of bonsai trees and listening to Japanese music and birdsong recordings," Juliet explained. "To set up costs hundreds and hundreds of pounds just for the bonsai trees alone and even then it's a pain because you have to keep them outside and you can't do it in the depths of winter if they all lose their leaves. So you either have to have a whole load of conifer ones which aren't as nice as the other sort, or else you have all these pots with bare twigs in. And apparently the trees can be tricky to look after anyway and they want you to go on their bonsai maintenance course as well. And I can't see the benefit of the wretched thing anyway."

It wasn't what she'd said when she had first read about the course; she'd been waxing lyrically and inaccurately about Japanese spirituality and the power of the connection with nature. The Angelic Massage therapy course had hit the spot though.

"It was brilliant," she said, on the Monday after her weekend taster. "We all connected to our Angelic guide and to the Archangels Gabriel and Raphael. I felt a huge and beautiful presence filling the room and there was a wonderful fragrance."

Probably the air freshener, Verity thought cynically.

"I shall definitely be doing the rest of the course," Juliet went on happily. "I was told I had a real flair for it, and I can use my Reiki room for it. I won't need to do any decorating; just need a massage couch and a few other things. It was so soothing to be with so many people devoted to higher things."

As opposed to being with me, who only thinks of her stomach, Verity thought sourly. She'd been able to put on her newest jeans without the usual contortions and antics with a coat hanger, but it still hadn't made her happy or at ease with herself.

"And the Angelic massage therapy comes with a whole product range I can sell to my clients too," Juliet was saying. "Angelic products for a celestial beauty."

"You mean like face creams and bubble baths?" Verity asked, and Juliet glanced at her with distaste.

"Hardly," she said. "Face mists endowed with angelic flower essences, room enhancers. Aura-enhancers. Not just face cream."

"But they do a face cream, though?" Verity asked.

"I shall get a practitioner discount when I qualify," Juliet said. "I have some free samples to try out on myself. Perhaps you'd like to try one?"

Verity nodded; it was easier than refusing. Juliet rummaged in her goody bag and handed her a tiny plastic pot containing the palest pink cream that smelt of rose-scented air freshener.

"It only needs the tiniest amount to awaken our inner angelic nature and bring the beauty of our outer nature to life and shining loveliness," she said.

Needless to say, it brought Verity out in a rash.

Chapter 4

Carla called round at the house one damp Sunday afternoon in February; she had given no warning of her intention to visit and Verity was only pleased that she had bothered to have a good tidy up the previous afternoon and only the coffee cups left after lunch were left in the kitchen sink.

"You've done a lot with it," Carla said, glancing round the hall as she came in.

Verity noticed the blatant insincerity of the comment and put it down to Carla trying to put her at her ease; she had jumped in her chair when the doorbell had rung and had felt flustered when she'd seen who was at the door.

"Not really," she said. "Just fresh paint, stuff like that. It used to be rather gloomy with that dark paper in the hall here."

"This is much better," Carla said following her through to the kitchen, though privately she had preferred the dark and mysterious hallway to the light and airy one. It had seemed so much more atmospheric, rather like a film set. Maybe she could recommend a few interior designers to Verity; this was all too bland for words.

"Nice kitchen," she said as Verity made coffee.

"What brings you here?" Verity asked when she had brought her guest through to the living room. She knew Carla lived a good hundred or so miles away and Carla had never been over-dutiful over visiting her mother.

"I was over visiting Mum," Carla said. "She likes having a snooze in the afternoon so I thought I'd bring over a few bits that she turned up the other day when she was doing some more unpacking."

This was only partly true. Carla had a box of items she intended to pass on to Verity and nothing more remained in her mother's possession as far as she knew, but it was true that she had come to visit her mother for the weekend. It wasn't true about the nap; in fact, Carla and her mother had fallen out and Carla had made herself scarce for the rest of the afternoon to let the dust settle.

"Where's David?" Carla asked suddenly, realising that something wasn't as she'd expected it to be.

"He's taken Rosie to a swimming gala," Verity said. "Nothing serious, just a bit of fun. She likes swimming and she's quite good at it. I don't like to go."

"Oh right," Carla said, and then forgot about it. She had sort of hoped David would be there, so that he might ask questions but since he wasn't, she carried on anyway.

"I found some old photos," she explained. "You know, from the summer before Nick died. Your Granddad took them some of them for me with my camera and they ended up with our family photographs. Mum doesn't want them so I thought you might."

She passed an envelope across and gazed at Verity expectantly and with a silent, inward sigh, Verity opened it. The top photo showed all three of them in the back garden of this house, piled into the big hammock that they used to sling between the two biggest apple tree; Verity was in the middle, her mouth wide open in helpless laughter. The blurring of the focus showed that they had just flung themselves into the hammock and it was still moving when the photo was taken. She remembered that moment, remembered them counting backwards aloud before leaping into the hammock behind them in unison, herself sandwiched between Carla and Nick and her Granddad laughing almost as much as they were. It had been O level results day, late August, when she was sixteen. She and Nick and Carla had been inseparable that year, even though she and Nick hadn't been going out till the September. She flicked to the next one; they were out of sequence because this one had been taken the moment before they had leapt. Nick had turned and kissed her on the lips just as Granddad pressed the button and the moment was frozen in time. The next one was a second before this, all three of them grinning madly at the camera. The final photo was from a year later that she recalled Carla taking; herself and Nick standing by the apple trees, holding hands and oblivious of the camera, lost in their own private world; his hair was much shorter in this one. His father had made him have it cut really short before going off on his trip.

Verity could feel a lump in her throat.

"I'd forgotten we were ever as young as that," she said and took a sip of coffee to make the lump go away. "It seems like an age ago. You never realise time will go the way it does."

Carla nodded. It had made her feel strange, rather uncomfortable to see those pictures again, especially after reading that letter her aunt had sent to Nick. Her mother had opened it at the time, but until they had uncovered it again when they were clearing the house, Carla had never read the words Charlotte had written to Nick.

"I didn't know you and Nick had been planning to get married," she said, feeling suddenly rather unsure of herself.

"It was a long time ago," Verity said, lightly, wanting to pass over this. "I wondered: did you ever find Nick's poetry book? He had a book he wrote up all his poems in and I wondered if you'd found it, could I have it?"

Carla sighed theatrically.

"Dad burned it," she said. "He hated, it you know, Nick being so into poetry and all that arty stuff. When we were little, it was cute, and Dad didn't mind. It was something you did at school in those days but when Nick got a bit older, Dad wanted him to be a bit more "manly", macho, that sort of things and poetry docsn't really come across as macho. They fell out over it loads of times, if you remember."

Verity did; remembered her grandfather telling Nick about samurai warriors who had to do flower arranging and write poems as part of their training, not to mention the druids and others.

"Nick never managed to be the son he wanted," Carla said. "It all started going wrong when Nick was about twelve and he refused to go to scouts any more. Dad went ballistic when he said he'd rather go to guides with me! He was convinced Nick would turn out to be a poof! I think that's why he was so pleased about you and Nick; it was proof he wasn't a queer. Though what he'd have made of you two wittering on about getting married when Nick was only eighteen, I have no idea. By the time he knew, Nick was dead anyway so it didn't matter. But he'd already burned Nick's book of poems."

Verity was shocked; she shouldn't have been surprised. Nick and Carla's father had been a sergeant in the Royal Engineers or something of that sort before he had been invalided out and had no time for the things in life that Nick had held dear. He'd only tolerated the idea of Nick going to university because back then any degree, even one in something ostensibly as useless as

English literature, was seen as a passport to higher things. He'd agreed to fund Nick through university on the condition that he go on the trip that had ended in Nick's death; the idea was it would toughen him up and give him a taste for adventure that would mean he'd be queuing up to join up with one or other of the armed forces. But to burn the book that contained the essence of his son's thoughts and dreams, well, that was almost unbearable even now.

Carla had seen the pain and shock on her friend's face.

"I found a few," she said. "They were ones he'd copied out for something or other and left in his desk with his photos. I think he'd been meaning to send them to some magazine or competition and just never managed it before he left. I would have thought you'd have had some of his poems. You were very close."

"Nick could be very secretive about them," Verity said. "He'd sometimes read me stuff but he didn't used to let me keep anything. I wish he had now."

"The ones I found," Carla said. "Shall I post them to you? I didn't think to bring them. I sort of assumed you'd have a copy of everything he wrote."

"Please," Verity said. "Poor Nick; he'd have been so upset about that. He had another notebook too, the one he used for stuff he was working on but hadn't finished. Did that ever turn up?"

"I think he took that one to sea with him," Carla said. "He'd just started a newish one, hadn't he? I do recall the older one ending up on the bonfire with the proper book. I don't know what happened to the one he took with him. I suppose it must have been shipped back with his things after they cleared his bunk but I never saw it. I would have thought someone would have had a look in it during the enquiry."

"Why?" asked Verity, feeling cold.

"Well, he used it as a sort of journal, didn't he?" Carla said, patiently. "They'd have read it to see what sort of state of mind he was in."

"I don't understand," Verity said.

Carla's drama sensor had begun buzzing a warning and her eyes seemed to brighten.

"In case he'd done it on purpose," she said.

Verity said nothing but the room seemed to have become very dark as if night were arriving even earlier than it should.

"Why on earth would he have done that?" she said finally. "I know he didn't want to do the trip but it was the only way your Dad was going to finance him through university."

Carla was feeling enjoyably bad right now.

"Did he write to you from the boat?" she asked.

"I got a few letters," Verity said.

"Then you know he hated it, being on the boat I mean," Carla said. "He was getting picked on by the others, he hated the food, and he was seasick. He hated it."

Verity was silent. This she knew. He'd said as much in his few letters.

"There's a world of difference between just hating something and killing yourself over it," she said eventually, when Carla's bright gaze grew too much. "It wasn't going to be forever."

"It must have seemed like it to him," Carla said. "You know Nick; you know how soft he was. He didn't have a tough bone in his body; that was why Dad sent him. Dad didn't think you could go through life as Nick did. If anyone had a go at Nick, he didn't fight back; he'd cry. He was utterly miserable on that boat and he was desperate to come home."

"Desperate? Then why didn't he just leave? Surely the company wouldn't make him stay if he were that unhappy?" Verity asked.

"Money," Carla said, bluntly. "It'd cost a lot to ship home kids who were just a bit homesick, so they weren't going to do it unless he were actually ill. He rang, you know."

Verity shook her head.

"I didn't know," she said.

"He managed to find a phone when he was ashore one day," Carla said. "And he had enough money on him to ring Dad. I answered at first; he sounded terrible, as if he'd been crying for days. I got Dad and Dad started shouting at him, telling him to grow up, and be a man and all that sort of stuff, and no he wouldn't send him the money to come home, he'd have to put up with a bit of discomfort in his life and he might as well learn how right now. Then Dad slammed the phone down. About a week after that, we got the call saying Nick was missing. Put it together yourself: he can't go home, he can't endure it, so what would Nick do?"

"You think he killed himself?" Verity said, faintly.

"Makes sense to me," Carla said. "Nice and easy. Swim away from the boat when everyone else is asleep and just keep swimming till you can't swim back. It's supposed to be an easy death, drowning is. I don't think Nick would have had the guts for anything that wasn't easy and painless."

Verity was listening in horror.

"I don't believe he'd have done that," she said. "Not like that. Nick loved life."

Carla looked at her patiently.

"I loved my brother dearly," she said. "And that's blinded me for years to what he was really like. He was a wimp; he didn't have the courage and grit to survive without someone to hold his hand the whole time. I'm sorry, I know you idolised him but he was a dreamer and nothing else. I'll send you the poems if you want but that's all there was to him and I think Dad was right to burn the rest of them. It was all airy-fairy nonsense, dreams and moonshine. He'd never have made anything of himself you know; there wasn't anything to him. He was a man of straw if you like, except he was never really a man. I'd better go. Mum will be waking up now and I'm off as soon as she's up and about again. I've got a long drive ahead of me and I've a heavy schedule for rehearsals next week so I need to be home fairly early tonight. My face is my fortune still, after all, and I need my beauty sleep."

She got up and gave Verity the usual air-kissing routine at the door.

"I'll pop those bits of poems in the post first thing tomorrow," she said. "But you'll see what I mean. He wasn't in the best frame of mind even before he went on the trip. Don't fret about it, hun; you had a lucky escape. Your David has always managed to put a roof over your head and food on the table; I doubt Nick would have done that."

When Carla had gone, Verity sat down and tried not to cry. The sheer casual cruelty of Carla's comments took her far back to the time when they had been at school together and Carla had been the class wit, her comments quick and sharp and painful. She had always said she hadn't meant to upset people, that some people

76

were just too sensitive for words but now Verity wondered how much of it had been meant, how much had been worked out and measured and how much of it was down to Carla's own monumentally thick skin and egocentric outlook on the world.

When David got home, she'd managed to calm down but there was still a painful place in her chest again that felt like something hard and sharp had been bashed against it, bruising her deeply. When he came into the living room his nose was twitching like that of a Labrador scenting dinner.

"Smells like we've had a visitor," he said.

Verity had become immune to Carla's heavy expensive scent within a few moments of her entering the house but to someone just entering form the cold damp air of the miserable dusk, the fragrance must have been overwhelming.

"Carla came over," she said. "She'd been to see her mum and she came over here while her mum had a nap."

"What did she come over for?" he asked. "Other than to treat us to a mega dose of chemicals claiming to be perfume?"

"She'd found some photos of when we were at school," Verity said.

"Cool!" said Rose, coming in, her wet hair reeking of chlorine, and picked up the photos and began leafing through them. "God, the clothes you used to wear!" she shrieked. "Hey, that looks like Carla Raphael the model!"

"It is. But she was known as Carla Braithwaite then," Verity said. "How come you know about models? I didn't know you were interested in that sort of thing."

"She was in one of my magazines, a month or so back, advising about careers in modelling," Rose said. "Who's the guy? He's cute!"

"That was her brother, Nick," Verity said, her mouth suddenly and horribly dry.

"How come you were at school with a model, Mum?" Rose asked.

"She wasn't a model back then," Verity managed to say. "And she wasn't famous then either. I bet there are loads of people who were at school with famous people but I reckon not many of them still keep in touch."

"She must have been a few years below you then," Rose said. "She's only thirty two and you're thirty five, Mum."

David gave a dry and cynical laugh.

"She's the same age as your Mum, give or take month or two in either direction," he said. "All celebs lie about their age. That's why they drop all their old friends in case they give them away. At least your Mum doesn't move in circles where it might get out. What happened to her brother? He looks like he'd have done all right on the catwalk too."

David was now flicking through the photos; she saw his eyes flicker over the one where Nick was kissing her and the one Carla had snapped in the orchard the following year.

"He died," Verity answered, her voice sounding deceptively normal. "Not long after that photo was taken, actually."

There was a second where Rose looked appalled and then she said, in a horrified voice,

"Poor Carla, losing her brother like that."

Verity looked up and saw that David was watching her with an odd speculative look in his eyes.

"What about poor Mum, then?" David asked. "It looks to me like you were quite close to him too."

"Don't be silly Dad," Rose said. "Mum looks about sixteen, it can't have been serious."

"I was seventeen," Verity said. "We were the gang of three, back then, me and Carla and Nick. They were here nearly every day that summer; Granddad loved having them here. He was trying to persuade Nick to do archaeology."

"That sounds like Granddad," Rose said. "He wanted everyone to love archaeology as much as he did. What did this Nick want to do?"

"He wanted to be a poet," Verity said.

"Weird!" said Rose with feeling.

"Was he any good?" David asked, quietly.

Verity thought for a moment.

"Yes," she said. "Yes, he was good, as far as I can remember. But it takes more than talent to succeed and I don't think many poets ever make a living let alone a decent one. He was going to be a teacher."

David was looking very thoughtful and Verity was feeling less than happy about this.

"Anyway, it was a long time ago," she said. "Half a lifetime ago. Heaven only knows what would have happened if he hadn't died. I've no idea if he'd ever have been able to reach any of his dreams. Not many people do anyway. Right, are you both hungry? I put some potatoes in to bake a while back and there's some cold meat to go with them and some coleslaw."

"Starving," said Rose. "If Carla comes again, do you think she'd mind having a picture taken with me?"

"I'm sure she'd love it," said David, dryly. "Go and set the table, Rose and we can eat. You aren't the only one who's hungry."

Rose slouched out to put plates and cutlery on the table and David put out his hand to Verity.

"Are you OK?" he asked helping her to her feet as if she were an invalid.

"Fine, why shouldn't I be?" she asked.

"Just what with Carla raking up things from the past, I thought maybe you might be feeling a bit depressed by it," he said.

She felt her eyes fill up with tears and the cold spot in her chest seemed to thaw slightly.

"I'm OK," she said with gratitude. "It brings it all back though, the sadness of it. But I am all right, really."

"Good," he said, and they went through to the kitchen where the smell of baking potatoes made Verity's mouth water reluctantly.

A few days later, much to Verity's surprise, Carla kept her promise to send the poems. They arrived just as she was putting on her bike helmet, her bicycle leaning against the gate.

"Posh paper," said the postman, as he handed her the heavy crimson envelope. The address was written in gold ink and she found herself shivering. That had been one of Nick's affectations, writing letters in gold or silver ink on dark paper, but the writing on this was so different from his elegant, spiky script and she knew it was from Carla even before she opened it. The fragrance still clung to the envelope despite it having travelled miles and days since Carla had posted it.

There was no time to look at it now, so she stuffed it into the small rucksack she used for a handbag when she was at work, and tried to focus simply on getting to work safely. The morning traffic was always a challenge and she had to take evasive action more than once when a car or a truck squeezed her off the road simply by not noticing her.

"Am I not big enough to see?" she fumed, aloud when a car had whizzed past her, splattering her with mud from a huge puddle it could so easily have avoided. "What a great start to the day!"

She felt like going home and getting changed but at least once she took her waterproofs off, there was no mud visible on her clothes, even though she felt filthy. Juliet was in a bad mood but gave no clue about why and after making some comment about Verity needing to polish the crystal cabinet rather than just flick round with a feather duster, she disappeared upstairs to wait for her first client of the day, leaving Verity free to open her post.

There was a short note from Carla and several pieces of paper. They looked like old A4 notepaper from the standard student pad, but she could see the old familiar handwriting that made her shiver. She read the first poem. It was entitled, The Vampire, and she grinned when she'd read it.

I'm a vampire, you know.
No tricks with blood now,
That's so outdated.
I dress not to kill
But rather to smother
All questions, all enquiries.
Have you ever sat down,
Suddenly ambushed
By exhaustion in the street?
That was me,
Siphoning off your energy.
I eat garlic daily:
It's good for the heart.
I even wear a cross
And walk around in daylight.
Your best defence?
Knowing I am here.
I can see you now,

Glancing round uneasily.
I'd wave, but
You might spill your drink;
Such a waste.
You're not in any danger.
I just wanted you to know-
I'm watching you.

She wondered when he'd written it; it must have been after that first summer after he and Carla had joined the school, when they were all inseparable. After that, Carla had become clingy and impossible, hanging round them wanting things to be the way they had been before. Then she had latched onto other groups and left Verity and Nick alone. She wondered why he'd never shown her this one; it was so clearly Carla he was writing about. Perhaps he had felt guilty for comparing his sister to a vampire. She wondered also if Carla had recognised herself in the poem; perhaps that was why she had effectively written him off as having no talent. It would have surprised her if she had; Carla had never been that good at self-awareness if it came down to less than flattering aspects of herself. These days she seemed perhaps even more insecure than she had back then and just as unaware of it.

It made her feel strange, remembering Nick's funny side, his merriness and his refusal to take some things seriously. Somehow she had forgotten that side of him in the intervening years; she could just imagine him now, miming vampire fangs every time Carla came near.

The next one made her go cold inside; this was the side she had wanted to forget:

Just words

No one listens to me,
But then I have nothing to say
I have not said
A thousand times before.
I'm dying for someone to hear
My silent screams
And offer help.

I'm searching for the words:
The right words,
The magic words.
They're just words;
They hold no power
To save or damn me.
Just words: no more.

It was dated a week or so before he'd left for that trip.

The door chimes jangled and she hastily folded the paper back up, gathering up the pieces of paper together into the envelope and put it in her jeans pocket, hoping for time later to read them all without interruptions. It felt like she'd got a sudden glimpse into his state of mind even before he left on his trip and it was a dark world he had been inhabiting. And yet she had not known quite how bad he was feeling. Could Carla have been right, could he have drowned himself?

The day left no room for introspection and no time to read the rest of what Carla had sent, nor even any time for lunch. Juliet had taken herself out for lunch without asking if she could get Verity something and had stayed out till ten to two so there was no time for Verity even to nip to the sandwich bar and grab something she could eat at the shop; it was clear that she was being punished.

At three, Juliet made some comment about the state of the floor in the shop. It was a cold, wet and decidedly muddy sort of day so it wasn't surprising that the floor was filthy. Each customer had come in with dirty feet and since Juliet had always refused to buy a doormat, saying that it gave such a bourgeois impression, the floor was coated with a layer of ground-in dirt all the way across from the door to the counter. She was about to ask Verity to make a bit more of an effort with the cleaning, when Verity hauled off her work tunic and said,

"Have a look in the yellow pages for someone that clean carpets professionally. There's no way that lot will come up using just your old vacuum cleaner. Right, I'm off."

Juliet gaped at her as she pulled on her coat.

"You're not going, are you?" she demanded.

"It's gone three," Verity said. "I didn't have any lunch and I need to do some shopping before I go home. And as far as I can recall, I think my hours finish at three."

Juliet was irritated; she had intended to get Verity to at least give the floor a once-over before she left but this was obviously not going to happen.

"Go on then," she said as if she were making some huge concession. Her attempt at graciousness was distinctly sour, to say the least.

Verity pushed her bicycle into the main shopping area and picked up the few items she needed to get; some new pens for Rose, various household items and a French stick for dinner. As she passed Starbucks, her stomach rumbled and she felt suddenly weary much as if some New Age vampire were indeed lurking nearby, sampling her energy like a strawberry lolly. A quick cup of coffee and a muffin and she'd have the energy to cycle home. And it was a place out of the rain where she could read the remaining poem without the chance of either Juliet, or later on, David or Rose reading it over her shoulder. She found a convenient bit of railing to chain her bike to and went in, feeling the warm air and the scent of coffee surround her like a soft cloak.

The final poem was called Breathe.

I can't breathe.
Oh, my lungs work fine.
See: In, out, in, out.
But I still can't breathe.
I dream of mountain tops,
With air thin enough
To draw deep like wine,
Cold and sharp inside me.
I stand so high
I cannot see the ground.
I spread my wings,
Step forward, feel the rush
As I plummet, plunge and fall.
And then my wings support me.
I soar above the clouds,
The land below forgotten,
And just breathe.

She sipped her espresso warily and gazed at the faded ink and the worn paper. His writing seemed much the same as it usually had, maybe a bit untidy but nothing out of the ordinary. This one wasn't dated so she had no way of guessing when he had written it, or even what it had been about. Certainly the atmosphere at Nick and Carla's home had been suffocating at times; even at sixteen she could see how oppressive it was. Their father had insisted on military precision in everything; their rooms had to be tidy, and in the rest of the house something left out of place would provoke rages of which Verity had never seen the like. She had been horribly embarrassed by it but Nick had just shrugged and carried on as if it were the norm. No wonder they had preferred to hang round her house, with her eccentric grandfather and her largely absent parents, and the attics strewn with discards and treasures all mixed up together in a glorious Bohemian mess.

This one seemed less despairing but even so she felt uneasy about it; he had seemed so sunny natured most of the time they were together, only as the day for his unwilling departure came closer did he sometimes seem to be morose, taciturn and unhappy.

A shadow passed her table and she looked up without much interest. She put down her cup with a crash and spilt half of it in the saucer and tried to get to her feet but her bag had somehow tied her to her chair, the straps catching both her arm and the arm of the chair together. By the time she was on her feet, the door had slammed shut against the rain and Nick was gone.

She hurried to the door and leaned out into the intermittent drizzle, scanning the darkening street until someone shouted to her to shut the bloody door- she was letting all the cold air in. As she sat back down, there seemed to be a huge lump in her throat that she couldn't swallow.

"Do you know that guy then?"

She jumped; it was the young man she usually saw here, serving behind the counter. He was standing near her with a tray of empty cups and crumpled paper napkins.

"You saw him then?" she asked.

"Er, yes," he said, as if she had asked something absurd. "He comes in here fairly often. Do you know him then?"

"I haven't seen him for years. I thought he must be dead," she said.

"Shame you missed him," he said. "Next time he's in, shall I tell him you keep missing him? Or maybe you could leave me your mobile number and I'll give it to him?"

"That's very kind of you," she said. "There's no hurry, though. I'm sure we'll bump into each other sooner or later."

It wasn't until she was halfway home that she understood why his face had fallen; he hadn't been asking for her number just so he could play Good Samaritan and pass it on. She nearly fell off her bike at that point, overwhelmed with such a fit of giggling that she could hardly breathe, let alone pedal. She hadn't gone many more yards before she had to stop, pull over onto the pavement and try to control the shaking that had come over her as she realised that if the young man at Starbucks had been able to see Nick, then it had been real and not another vision.

"But that can't be so," she said aloud. "He's dead, I know he's dead. How could it be real?"

Unless the whole sequence of events from coming into the coffee shop until she left it had all been another vision; that was the only explanation. The coffee shop guy couldn't really have seen Nick too so the whole thing had to have been another of those awful visions. Her heart had settled into a more normal beat so she got back on the bike and tried to focus entirely on the task of cycling safely home while holding a French stick under her arm.

She slept poorly that night, tossing and turning so much that she even disturbed David who was a sound and resolute sleeper. He sat up and put the bedside light on.

"Are you all right?" he asked.

She sat up, rubbing her eyes in the brightness that pooled round the bed.

"Don't seem to be able to get to sleep properly," she said. "I keep thinking I'm going to drop off and then I wake again. Shall I go and sleep somewhere else?"

He obviously didn't want to say yes, but it was clear that he really didn't relish being kept from his sleep, so she got up, wrapping her dressing gown around her shoulders and went downstairs to the living room, and lit the gas fire and curled up on the sofa. There was a heavy woollen throw over the back on the sofa which she pulled over herself, and she lay there, perfectly comfortable but so wide awake she thought she would never sleep again. But sometime after one she did slip into sleep, and it was Rose rattling around the kitchen making toast and hot chocolate that woke her. She felt rotten, every limb aching and her eyes and throat were hurting. She could hear David come into the kitchen and fill the kettle but still she couldn't bring herself to ease herself into an upright position. A few minutes later, David came in with a mug of tea for her.

"You really don't look so well," he said, and put his hand across her forehead much as he would do if Rose were ill. "I think you have a fever. It might be a dose of the flu. Go on: go back up to bed. I'll bring you a hot water bottle and something to take, some paracetamol or something."

Verity was having trouble getting up so David managed to get her to her feet and helped her up the stairs and back into the bed. She burrowed under the duvet, trying to find some warmth; it must be very frosty out there for it to be so cold in the house.

"Has it frozen outside?" she asked when David came back with a hot water bottle.

"No, it's quite mild," he said. "That's just the fever; you always feel cold when you've got a temperature. Here, snuggle up with this."

It was Rose's Bagpuss hot-water bottle and she held the warm fur close to her chest; it was hurting rather a lot. David put some tablets into her hand and a glass of water.

"I'll phone Juliet to tell her to find another slave for a few days," he said. "Then I'll have to get going. I'll make sure you've got water by the bed. I'll pop home at lunchtime to see how you are."

Verity said nothing but swallowed the tablets and lay back and pulled the duvet round her, laying the hot water bottle across her chest. The heat was comforting and she seemed to lose her grip on waking life and slid into an uneasy sleep, only stirring a bit when the door banged as David left the house. Rose went to the other secondary school in the area and had left earlier, having said goodbye from the door rather than risk catching whatever her mother had got.

The morning passed drearily, and she began to feel worse rather than better as the day went by. Her joints were hurting as much as if she had just worked out for hours and hours, her chest was uncomfortably tight and she couldn't get warm however many blankets she heaped on the bed.

"Definitely flu," David said when he got home again that evening. He had stopped by at lunchtime long enough to help her to the bathroom, refill her water jug and hot water bottle, give her some more tablets and rearrange her pillows. "Juliet wasn't pleased when I called her; she took it very personally and was less than supportive about it."

Verity shrugged; she knew what Juliet thought of most illness. When anyone else got flu, it was only a cold as far as Juliet was concerned, but if Juliet got a cold, it was some new strain of flu. She could just imagine what Juliet would have said to David. The words, mind over matter would certainly come into it.

"I don't mind so you don't matter," she whispered aloud, and David looked at her.

"What was that?" he said.

"Juliet's mind over matter mantra," Verity said faintly. Speaking was a surprising effort.

"Can I get you anything to eat?" he asked but Verity felt sick at the thought of food, so he brought her some orange juice and sat with her while he did his marking later that evening while Rose watched TV downstairs.

Verity was too poorly to get out of bed for more than trips to the bathroom for more than a week, and spent most of her time in a restless, unrefreshing sleep, though when she woke it was usually during the dark lonely hours before dawn. During those endless hours she would lie as still as her aching body would allow and try to let her mind wander so she might slip back to sleep. David had put up a camp bed for himself, so that she could have the bed to herself but have him nearby. She might have worried whether he would sicken with whatever bug she was suffering from but neither he nor Rose caught it. By the time she had slowly begun to recover, she was horrified how weak it had made her; David had run her a bath one day but she'd needed his help to get out of it, and the simple effort of washing had worn her out so much she went back to bed. She had to get David or Rose to brush her hair for her as her arms seemed to lack the strength to hold the brush for more than a few moments; David had helped her wash it when it had reached the point of being so clogged with sweat and grease that she could endure it no more.

After a fortnight of illness she was well enough to come downstairs and spend most of the day on the sofa though like a four year old she needed to be in bed by seven each evening and slept till mid-morning. One Sunday morning, shortly after she had been tucked up on the sofa, the doorbell rang and David, who had been sorting laundry upstairs, hurried down to answer it. She could hear him speaking to someone and she wondered if it were Carla. She hoped he would tell her to come another time but after a moment, she heard him say, "She's through here."

"Well, you're looking better," said Juliet. "I thought I ought to come and see how you're doing."

Damn and double damn, thought Verity. This is really the last thing I need right now.

"A bit better," she said, unconsciously tugging her blanket closer to her chin as if to hide from Juliet.

She had dressed that morning but she hadn't had the energy to brush her hair so it still lay in a tatty plait, half of it escaping and tickling her face with odd tendrils. She saw the tiny half hidden look of satisfaction on Juliet's face when she glanced at her; she was clearly pleased to see her looking so dreadful. The house was surprisingly tidy; Rose and David had spruced it all up the previous day. Only Verity looked a mess.

"Some sort of flu, wasn't it?" Juliet asked, though she knew this already. David had kept her informed of how things were going simply to stop her ringing the house daily to try and find out when she would be coming back to work.

"The doctor said there's been a lot going round but I got it very badly," Verity said.

"You must have been very run down to go down so badly with it," Juliet said. "I almost never get ill. I put it down to my good diet and my regime of meditation and exercise. Yoga is so good for the health."

Maybe, but never as good as a brisk bike ride, Verity thought mutinously, and then felt guilty. How could she be so narrow-minded? She'd never tried yoga; loads of people said how good it was for their health. Was it just because it was Juliet that was advocating it that she immediately wrote it off?

"Lucky you," she said lamely, because she couldn't think of anything else to say.

David came through with two mugs.

"I've made you both some coffee," he said. "I haven't put any milk in yours, Juliet, but I can go and get some if you take it."

"Do you have any rice milk?" she asked. "Or soya milk?"

"Sorry," said David. "Just the stuff from a cow, semi skimmed and pasteurised."

She gave him a brief smile that never reached her eyes.

"I'll stick with black then," she said.

Verity was irritated; Juliet had her coffee with ordinary milk at work, so why this charade? Unless, in the intervening weeks, she really had moved away from dairy products, this was just another of her little dances to try and show how advanced, how evolved, how enlightened she was. Verity sipped her coffee gratefully. David had come back in, his coat pulled on and jingling his car keys.

"Right," he said. "I'm off to take Rosie swimming. She missed it last week. Is there anything I can get you before I go?"

Verity looked at him, her eyes full of mute appeal for him to get rid of Juliet but David made a hidden movement with his hands that somehow managed to convey helplessness.

"Don't worry, I shall look after her," Juliet said, her voice saccharine.

That's what I'm afraid of, Verity thought, and David kissed her and went. There was a long silence, filled only by the clicking of the radiators.

"Well!" said Juliet, settling herself into the cushions of the armchair opposite Verity.

Verity's heart seemed to sink. It was clear that Juliet meant to stay some time; this was not a fleeting visit but one with some sort of purpose. She was looking both comfortable and crafty.

"I was thinking, you know, a day or two back, that you haven't yet redeemed your Christmas present," Juliet started. She carried on before Verity could think of something innocuous to say. "So I thought that since you've been so very poorly, now would be a really good time to do something about it. I do wonder you know whether in fact this illness has been a heaven-sent warning for you. You've obviously got a lot wrong in your life for you to have been quite so ill just from the flu."

Verity wanted to shout at her but the rising spark of anger died from lack of energy.

"So I though, for the sake of your health, I should come over and see what I can do for you now myself," Juliet said, and smiled.

What the hell do I say? Verity was near to panic.

"I'm really not sure about this," she said, trying to shrink even further under her blanket. "Don't you need stuff from the treatment rooms?"

"All that isn't strictly necessary, you know," Juliet said in a tone that was meant to be confiding. "It helps people relax, sets the scene, the atmosphere, that sort of thing. Apart from a few tools, I have all I need here." She placed her hands over her heart in a gesture that looked very ritualised. "My hands and my heart, they are all I really need."

Verity felt sick but any energy for revolt or protest just seemed to be vanishing by the second.

"Now I thought that since the Mayan Heart Retrieval therapy has been going so well, and I've had so much superb feedback- some lives have been changed utterly, for the good you understand- I thought I could do that for you," Juliet said. "I don't need all my props here. After all, how long have we known each other?"

Too bloody long, Verity thought, but the words died unspoken.

"So it won't matter if I don't wear my costume or my Mayan headdress," Juliet said. "You know me, I like things simple but most people like a bit of the exotic with their healing. They feel it's better value for money that just some woman in a tunic. So I give way and have a few props, a few simple costumes. But we don't need it for you; it wouldn't make a jot of difference to you since you've known me so long."

Oh God please let there be an earthquake or something, just get rid of her, please.

Juliet sat there, untouched by acts of God, her hands still pressed together over her heart like a particularly pious praying mantis.

"Can't you just do some Reiki?" Verity said helplessly. "I know how busy you must be. There's no need to spend so much time with me."

Juliet looked at her with the look of a fond teacher with a disappointing pupil.

"Oh Verity, Verity," she said, shaking her head. "I don't think Reiki is the answer. I don't think that would solve things. Things go much deeper for you, so much deeper. Your heart is missing, sacrificed and lost so long ago. How can you lead a normal healthy life without it?"

How did I manage so long, then, if I can't manage without it? How come I have been married forever and you seem to have just a string of failed relationships? How come... the questions died unspoken and she tried to make herself invisible under the blanket as the tears of frustration and rage spilled over.

Juliet was next to her the moment she saw the tears, her arm around her shoulders, rummaging in her bag with her free hand. She brought out a small bottle and sprayed freely round Verity; there seemed to be hardly any scent, as if the bottle contained just water.

"This will clear your aura of negativity," Juliet said. "It has the essence of the Mayan Gods channelled into pure spring water."

So it's Evian with a smidgeon of prayer? Wonderful! And I haven't even said yes to this, either.

"Where is your stereo? Ah there it is!" said Juliet getting up and pulling a CD out of her capacious bag. "I'll just put this on. Some gentle appropriate music often helps people relax and get into the mood for the healing and I can tell you are just so tense."

She hit the play button and the room was filled with the sound of panpipes.

"I think we can skip the incense," Juliet said, once she had checked there was no heatproof dish for her charcoal. Things were being extracted from the bag at the rate of a desperate magician pulling rabbits from a hat. "Maybe I can pass you some appropriate joss sticks when you're back at work. I hate to say it but this house, this room, has such a heavy oppressive atmosphere I am genuinely not surprised you have stayed ill for so long though it did lighten a bit when David went out. You really need to do some serious cleansing. This was your grandfather's house wasn't it? I thought I remembered it from when we were at school. I can feel his energies still around, you know, very heavy, very dark. Perhaps you need to think about calling me in to help free him, help him move into the light. I sense he's stuck somewhere dark. Anyway, I shall certainly give you some incense to help clear the atmosphere here a bit but... Long term I am not sure what good it would do. Shall we start?"

Verity was shaking now, with such a mixture of emotions that she would have had trouble separating them enough to identify them but somewhere in the mix, there was something that tasted very like fear.

"Just lie back on the sofa," said Juliet. "Let me slip that blanket off. You don't need that right now. Put a cushion under your head. That's it. Now just close your eyes and relax."

It was pretty hard to close her eyes, let alone relax, when she really didn't trust Juliet at all, but there was no way she could think of to stop this without it causing such a breach between them that she'd be job hunting as soon as she had fully recovered. Best to let her get on with whatever mumbo-jumbo she wanted to do and not interfere.

The sound of the music almost drowned out Juliet's soft incantations and,through her eyelids, Verity could sense Juliet's hands moving around over her head and torso. Verity's eyes snapped open, alarmed. Juliet had her eyes shut and she held a dark coloured pendulum over Verity's chest; her eyes fluttered open like those of a stage medium coming out of trance, and met Verity's gaze.

"I have been looking deep into the past," she said in a voice unlike her usual one. "Your heart is indeed gone. And I have seen who holds it: a dark man, a little older than you. He is linked to you in this life by love but not true love. It is servitude, bondage, slavery, but you think it is love. He took your heart long ago and he holds it still, and while he holds it you will never be free to love truly and freely. You must take action soon or he will destroy your heart again and again on his altar."

Bollocks, thought Verity, a word she would never have said aloud, but a tiny thread of fear like ice seemed to run down her spine. What if Juliet had seen Nick in her visions of the past? Don't be silly, she isn't seeing anything beyond what she invents.

Juliet had moved back to her armchair and was shaking her head with sadness.

"I'm sorry," she said. "I can't do anything for you. Usually, with most people I help, I can call back the etheric heart because it isn't being held by anyone. In your past life, the man who cut out your heart kept it, and keeps it still. You were drawn to him in this life because he holds your heart still but he has no intention of freeing it and letting you have it back because it serves him well to have you his slave as you were in the ancient past. You must take it back and I can show you how."

Verity sat up and dragged her blanket off the floor and over herself, right up to the chin.

"I'm very tired," she said faintly. "Do you think you could go now? I am too tired for anything else."

"Of course," said Juliet. "It is exhausting, isn't it? I know when I had my first retrieval, I felt washed out and good for nothing for hours afterwards. But it is a simple matter to get your heart back, even in a case like yours. You just have to leave David, that's all, break the bond between you somehow. If you're financially dependent on him, you don't have to leave literally. If you break the bonds other ways, you can continue to live with him and be married still. Breaking off the old bonds in the other life means breaking them in this one; release yourself from any vows you have made to him in this life and you will free yourself in the past and your heart will return to you like a homing bird. A nice easy and totally pleasurable way is to have a little fling with someone; you're still nice enough to look at. I don't think you would find a problem finding a willing partner to help you break your bonds."

"Just go," said Verity, from under her blanket.

"Of course. You just rest and think about it," said Juliet, and Verity could feel a pressure over her head that might have been a kiss or just a pat and after a moment she heard her go out and shut the front door with a hefty bang. Verity burst into tears.

This was so unfair; her first and only visitor since she'd been ill and it had to be Juliet. For the first time, she asked herself what had happened to her friends from where they had lived before, the women she had waited at the school gate with from the time Rosie turned five, the people she had socialised with at the school fête and the Christmas bazaar, the friends she had sometimes had coffee with or sometimes gone shopping with, the couples she and David had entertained to dinner or to the odd barbecue. There had been Christmas cards but in most cases that had been the first contact she'd had with them since they had moved here. A distance of a little over twenty miles and suddenly she was friendless; her only friends were Carla, who had always been an egocentric bitch who felt that if the world didn't revolve around her, then it ought to, and Juliet, whom she had discovered she actually disliked quite a few years ago. That was the sum total of her existing friends; all the others had been friendly acquaintances and nothing more. She had phoned the few she had been closest to, and there had been vague talk of meeting up, of visiting, of staying in touch, but nothing had happened, and life had swept on. Now she wept with the sheer shock of loneliness.

She wept quietly, mopping her eyes and nose methodically until she ran out of tissues and then went upstairs to see if there were another box in the bathroom cabinet. The sight of her own face in the mirror over the basin made her recoil. If David came back and found her looking like this, he'd want, quite naturally to know why, and she hardly knew why herself; explaining it to him was likely to be a stumbling affair at best and he'd probably conclude silently it was just hormones. Very carefully, she washed her face, bathing her eyes with cold water until it looked like she had maybe had a sneezing fit, rather than weeping till she was almost sick with it. She returned to her blanket and the sofa and curled up miserably and tried to doze, tried to let the whole thing drift away, but couldn't. Surely that wasn't what Juliet was telling all her clients? Could anyone be that irresponsible, recommending such an appalling course of action as a necessary step on a road to healing?

Or was it simpler than that? She had recently begun to suspect that Juliet was jealous of her settled life, her home and her husband. After all, she had more or less said as much to her. This was too much though! To try to persuade her to wreck her own marriage, her own life simply on the strength of this kooky therapy, well, Juliet must think her stupid. Could it really be that Juliet really had managed to convince herself that Verity had less intelligence than she did, that she was so gullible and easily led?

94

They had been at school together; surely all those supposedly worthless bits of paper that said that Verity had achieved such and such a grade, surely they stood for something? The more she thought about it, the more she realised that for Juliet, the evidence of exams success meant less than nothing, that all these years of Verity's passive serving in the shop simply meant that of the two of them, the one who owned the shop must be the brighter by far than the one who ran errands, pushed a hoover around and worked at the till taking the money and the orders. Juliet saw herself as a spiritual entrepreneur, a healer who saw market opportunities and took them; she clearly saw Verity as a drone, a servant and despised her for it. Otherwise how could she treat her the way she had just done?

It was a horrible, sickening thought, but there was a worse one, born of her own debilitated state, and her own anxiety. What if it were actually true? What if you took Juliet out of the equation, was there any chance that any of the mumbo-jumbo about past lives and etheric hearts could actually be true? If she had not been so unwell still, the thought would never have crossed her mind at all; logically she knew that if Juliet believed in it, the chances were it was at best mistaken, at worst an outright fraud and a damaging one at that. She wondered if there were any way of checking whether what she had told her about David having been the priest who had sacrificed her in the distant past and was still to this day holding her heart, was something she told every married or otherwise spoken-for client, or whether she had just singled her out for it. Verity found it difficult to imagine that her boss could despise her so much that she would try to break up her marriage with this absurd suggestion; this was someone she had worked with every day for years. Could someone conceal such strong dislike for so long, so completely?

A little traitorous voice inside her asked, why not? You have for years. Only David knows how hard you find working for her; even Granddad hadn't guessed, had only thought you might do better financially working somewhere else.

Verity pulled the blanket up over her head and closed her eyes to squeeze back the tears that were stinging them. In the warm darkness of the improvised tent, she began to feel both sleepy and suffocated so she drew it back a little and felt the cooler air on her face with some relief. After a while, she began to doze, but her dreams were filled with horrible images and she was glad when David got back with Rose, both breezing in, their hair and clothes filled with cold sweet air from outside. It made her feel fusty and stale; she'd not been outside except to drag herself to the doctor and then it had only been from house to car, leaning heavily on David's arm.

"Would you give me a hand out into the garden?" she asked. "I could do with some fresh air."

"Juliet has that effect on me," he said with a grin. "I don't know how you stand her all day. Sorry about abandoning you but I had to go and I didn't think she'd hang around for long. How long did she stay?"

"Too long," Verity said. "However, it did mean I no longer have a therapy session to go to as she very kindly did me one here."

Her tone was as dry as it might have been sour, and David laughed as he helped her up.

"I wish I'd been here to see it," he said.

Out in the garden, she could see spring had arrived while she had been in bed, the daffodils in full bloom and the snowdrops drooping and rusting to nothing, and the buds on the fruit trees were furry as they started to unravel slowly. David brought a chair and a coat out for her but she didn't stay long; the wind was still cold and the light was almost gone, but at least when she came inside again she felt almost clean.

Chapter 5

It was after Easter before Verity returned to work; even then, the ride to work left her so puffed out she had to sit for ten minutes before she could do more than wheeze hopelessly like a broken accordion. While she had been ill, Juliet had found a replacement for her, a twenty-something blonde called Martine, who was less than pleased by Verity's return to what she had taken to be a permanent arrangement. Verity wondered what on earth Juliet had said to give this girl the impression that Verity's illness had been somehow terminal. Martine was given the job of taking over when Verity's hours finished, even though Juliet still maintained that really, Rose was plenty old enough to take care of herself for a few hours when she got home from school. Verity didn't actually want to work till five or six in the evening but she maintained that even though her daughter was a teenager, she still needed her mother at home.

"You can't expect a teenager to cook herself a decent balanced meal," she said. "I don't mind her doing beans on toast once in a while if I have to be late in but every day? No, it isn't fair. She has homework to do, too. I'd rather be around most of the time so she can ask for help."

"My mother was never around for me, and I still did fine," Juliet said, irritated. "But have it your own way. Martine is happy to do the hours you don't want. She can do alternate Saturdays if you want, too."

In fact Martine usually turned up not long after lunch. She was married to some executive and was clearly bored with her life and found working for Juliet such a thrill that Verity was slightly sickened by it. When Juliet spoke, Martine listened with a rapt expression of such interest and respect that you might have thought Juliet was some sort of infinitely wise guru holding forth on the mysteries of the universe. Verity was certain this couldn't be good for Juliet, whose ego had seemed to grow significantly over the years; she wondered if Martine would ever believe her if she explained how, once upon a time in the dim and distant past of their school days, Juliet had hardly a word to say out loud and mainly specialised in whispering inane and usually inaudible comments to her pals, and when asked something by a teacher almost always responded with a nasal, "I dunno!" O tempore, O mores, thought Verity. You'd never guess now I was the clever one.

Martine certainly hadn't.

"You went to university?" she said incredulously one afternoon. She had arrived more than an hour before her shift and had been making idle conversation with Verity rather than have that ogre Silence appear and Verity had mentioned something about her university days without thinking it would provoke such a reaction.

"I mean, nowadays nearly everyone goes to something or other for further education of some kind," Martine went on. "But back then, it wasn't nearly so common. What did you do?"

"English Literature," Verity said and Martine goggled at her.

"Really?" she said. "All those books and poetry and such like? What did Juliet do?"

"She didn't go," Verity said, shortly, unsure what Juliet had actually told Martine and unwilling to create a row should she inadvertently give a different version of events to the one Juliet may have given.

"I thought she would have done," Martine said, puzzled. "I mean, she's so clever, isn't she? I should have thought she'd have done something really intellectual like Psychology. She's so clever about people."

She thought about it some more and continued,

"But I guess back then, girls weren't encouraged to pursue the really intellectual stuff. Or go at all for that matter."

Verity was torn between amusement and irritation.

"How long ago do you think it was? The Dark Ages?" she said. "You're, what, twenty five? Well, I'm coming up thirty-six. Juliet was in the same year as me at school. It isn't that long ago. It might have been before mobile phones and PCs on every desk but it's only a short while. Anyone would think it was the Palaeolithic to hear you talking. Juliet didn't stay on for A levels; her aunt wanted her to work here so she left school at sixteen."

Martine nodded, trying to look intelligent and failing.

"I guess there wasn't much encouragement at home for her to want to push for something more, back then," she said, as if Verity hadn't already explained. "I'm sure she would have done if she'd had the chance. She said your Grandfather was an archaeologist; I expect he helped you get into university."

Verity felt her irritation growing to monster proportions.

"No," she said. "For a start, I did a different subject; for seconds I got four As in my A levels. And universities don't work like that."

She wanted to slap this stupid, harmless bimbo till she was pink in the face, but more than anything, she wanted to beat Juliet to a bloody pulp for hiring her.

"Anyway," she said seeing the bafflement on the girl's pretty but somehow vacant face. "How did you meet Juliet?"

"I came for one of her marvellous therapies," Martine said, her face clearing. "Surely you remember me? You let me in often enough."

"Sorry, of course," Verity said. "I've been off so long I've forgotten things."

"I came for the Egyptian rejuvenation therapy at first, which is so good. I'd been thinking about Botox for these awful lines that were starting round my eyes. Two treatments with Juliet and they were going so fast I thought, I'll come weekly. Then she did the Mayan Heart Retrieval therapy course and when she told me about it, I thought, hey, that's me, that's what I feel like. My heart was missing."

It isn't your heart you need retrieving, love, it's your brains, if you ever had any, Verity thought, but what she said was,

"And have you got it back then?"

"Oh yes!" Martine said enthusiastically. "It took a few sessions to get things sorted but yes, it's back and I feel fantastic. I've been going for the Angelic massage every week too, as well as the Egyptian therapy. Oh and she let me have one of the Mayan heart bells for trade price too. It was only thirty five quid."

She reeled out a thong from under her tight top and held up a small silvery heart that chimed softly as she moved it.

"Very pretty," Verity said. "Does it do anything?"

"Well, it makes a lovely sound when it moves," Martine said.

Well, duh, thought Verity, I'd never have guessed that if I hadn't already heard that.

"It also helps stabilise the returned heart in the etheric body, and it reminds me to take care of myself, to value my heart more,"

Martine continued. "She said I'm still in danger of losing it again if I'm not very careful. I thought she did a retrieval for you too, to help you get better."

Yep, thought Verity, and a load of old codswallop it was too.

"Yes she did," she said. "But she didn't mention the heart bell, though."

"Maybe," said Martine, lowering her voice even though there was no chance of anyone hearing, "Maybe she's saving it as a present for you. She's so kind, isn't she?"

Verity grinned, but the lack of real mirth passed over Martine's head.

"She has a heart of gold," she said and to her herself she added, yeah, small, yellow and very hard to find.

"Oh she really does, doesn't she," Martine said with such obvious sincerity that Verity felt suddenly rather sorry for her. "She's been so good to me, you wouldn't believe. It's an honour to work for her, it really is. I've changed so much for knowing her, my whole existence has changed and I feel so marvellous. I was so down before; so miserable. Now I feel as light as a feather. An angel feather of course."

"Of course," said Verity, wondering if she could leave early before she threw up.

"And it's so nice, you two having been friends all these years, right since you were little girls," Martine said.

"We were eleven when we met," Verity said, as neutrally as she could. "Little girls" was hardly a fitting description of pre-adolescent girls, all straining double A-cups and mint-flavoured lip-gloss.

"Twenty five years!" exclaimed Martine clasping her hands together in rapture. Verity had seen Juliet use that self-same gesture but this was unconscious and genuine. "That has to be such an omen: I'm twenty five! You met when I was born. It has to be a sign."

A sign of what? That sometimes numbers collide?

"Not quite," Verity said. "Not till the autumn. Sorry."

Martine looked disappointed that the fates weren't leaving her clues, and she picked up her duster and began polishing the display of crystals nearest the desk.

"Do you know, Juliet's must be the only shop that cleanses all the crystals it sells before they're sold," she said, rubbing a piece of polished amethyst. "Oh, I don't mean the dusting. I mean properly cleansing. Every time she gets a new consignment of crystals she soaks them in salt water to remove any negativity. She says that way they are free to draw their new keepers to them sooner. She showed me how and I'll tell you something amazing! I put them all in the big cut glass bowl she told me to use, and put in the sea salt and I put in the new crystals and when I got in the next morning, do you know, one of them had utterly vanished. Juliet says it happens sometimes and that crystal has apported to where it's really needed, to someone who really needs it and can't afford to buy it."

"Let me guess," said Verity. "Was it the halite that vanished?"

Martine's eyes went round with surprise and sudden awe.

"How did you guess that?" she said, her voice hushed.

"Just one of those hunches," Verity said, wickedly, but didn't add that halite is a salt crystal that dissolves completely in water. It didn't seem fair to destroy such dearly held illusions and irritating as Martine was, she was also rather sweet. Disclosing such information would be like kicking a puppy. It also seemed to win her an entirely undeserved reputation for extreme wisdom that a degree had entirely failed to elicit.

"I've got a headache," said Verity, abruptly. It had seemed to materialise out of nowhere.

"Why don't you ask Juliet for an angelic massage, when she finishes her next client. I'm sure she won't mind fitting you in just for a quickie. It eases my migraines in no time at all," Martine suggested.

"I think I need a decent coffee," Verity said but Martine didn't seem to hear that.

"Here, use this," she said passing her the stone she had been rubbing. "That'll ease it. Amethyst is good for headaches."

The stone was cool and smooth against her forehead and after a minute or two she did feel a bit better but she was counting down to three o'clock when she could escape: a quick stop at Starbucks and then off home. That way she would get home roughly the same time Rose did, and she'd have enough energy to get on with cooking something for them all. She was still exhausted by the end of the day but the terrible weariness was easing; for some time after the worst symptoms had left her, she felt much as if she was living on a planet with far heftier gravity and everything was a huge effort. When she had finally stood on the bathroom scales, she had been shocked to discover she had lost almost a stone in weight over the course of her illness. The jeans that had been uncomfortably tight were now loose.

Juliet appeared at three and Martine scampered up the stairs to make her some coffee while she checked the day's takings in the till. This had been Verity's job at the end of her day, but it appeared that Juliet didn't quite trust Martine to add it up right. Juliet was always checking things like that, making frequent trips to the bank to pay in money both from the shop and the therapy rooms.

"I don't like having too much money hanging round the shop," she'd say. "It's not good. It isn't earning me interest, and it's a risk to have here even in the safe. You never know when someone is going to break in or rob us."

This had never happened. They did get the odd item that vanished, not just halite in the cleansing bowl, but any shop with easily portable stock is subject to shoplifters. For a while they had a sign on the counter that read, "Shoplifters deserve all the Karma they will certainly get!!!!" but it, too vanished. Verity had had a silent chuckle when that went; she had herself removed the sign that had read, "Lovely to look at, lovely to hold but if you should drop it, consider it SOLD!" She knew and had explained repeatedly to Juliet that this had no basis in law at all and that charging people for genuine accidents was immoral and illegal, but this had fallen on such deaf ears that she had quietly binned the sign in the industrial bin out the back. It always appalled her how willing people were to pay up when something got broken. She was always as careful as she could when dusting since she wouldn't have put it past Juliet to dock it off her wages; so far she hadn't broken anything.

"Are you off home then?" Juliet said, rather absently as Verity came through with her coat. "Have you thought about what I said about how to get your heart back?"

"I'm not doing that," Verity said quietly.

Juliet shook her head in apparent sadness.

"Then you'll go through the rest of your life without ever knowing what it feels like to love and be loved and you'll be reincarnated again without it, too," she said.

Not know love? You stupid, stupid bitch! But she didn't say it and left without comment. In her warm corner of Starbucks she felt her headache recede with each sip of coffee.

I've got to do something; I can't go on like this, she thought and drained the cup to the gritty dregs and got up to go.

She didn't go straight home but made a detour to the flat, being sure to lock her bike to the railings on the main road. She'd had one bike stolen when she'd decided she didn't need to lock it up just for a quick visit; that had been an expensive mistake she wasn't making again. The dirty stairs felt like they were covered with dried coffee grounds that crunched unpleasantly underfoot as she made her way cautiously up them in the shadowy late afternoon quiet. The carpet was so worn and frayed it was frankly a danger but the landlord had ignored all appeals to have it replaced or removed at the very least and since she wasn't a tenant, her word counted for nothing. There was a strong mousy smell and a hint of vomit, though it was stale and probably days or weeks old. The lack of light both on the stairs and on the sordid landing was probably a blessing; what she couldn't see she couldn't be disgusted by quite as much. She tended to breathe through her mouth when she visited, for obvious reasons. The door was shut and when she knocked, there was no answer. She had frequently asked for a key but he had always forgotten about it by the next time she came.

"I'm your wife, damn it, even if I can't live with you," she had fumed once. "I should at least have a key. What if you were ill, how would I be able to help if I can't even get in?"

He'd shrugged, feigning indifference.

"I'll get one cut, babe," he'd said. "But can I have one for your house? You know since we're equals and that sort of thing. What's yours is mine, what's mine is yours and all that."

"Granddad won't like it if he ever found you there," she said.

"Don't worry about me; I can handle Granddad," he'd said.

In the dark of the filthy landing she felt such sorrow at this memory, knowing how much he and Granddad had liked each other once. How could things have soured so badly, how could life have gone so wrong when it had started so well?

"He went out over an hour ago," came a voice from a nearby doorway, startling her. "Maybe I'll do instead?"

The man who lived over the landing was a vile piece of humanity that she found hard to pity; he still seemed to assume he was as attractive as he might have been at twenty, before years of hard drinking and smoking had changed both his shape and his temperament. Or perhaps he'd always been a foul-mouthed thug with a belly the size of Belgium and a perpetual cigarette glued to his lip.

"I don't think so," she said, turning away and beginning the precarious descent with greater speed than might have been safe.

"Snooty cow," he called. "Think you're too good for me do you?"

"I don't think so," she said. "I know so."

She was almost at the bottom now so she knew she could get out before he reached her and made her feel twice as filthy as she already did, as his obscene suggestions oozed down the stairs after her, too grimy to move any faster. He had groped her once before and it wasn't something she wanted a repeat performance of. She'd been hard pressed first to get away safely without worse happening and then equally hard pressed to prevent a fight when she admitted in tears what had happened. Men!

Back on her bicycle, with the clean cold wind blowing away the staleness and the oppressive sense of failure, she pedalled home with a sense of relief that at least she had this place to come home to. In the hall she stood shocked to see the pale walls, the soft off-white of rich cream rather than the heavy dark red flock paper she remembered.

"Wotcha Mum!" said Rose cheerfully from the living room. "What's for tea?" and Verity knew she'd had another vision, had become so lost in its reality that she had not at first recognised her own home.

She leaned against the smooth wall and tried to take a deep breath but found she felt much as she had at eight when she had fallen out of a tree and landed so hard she had been winded.

"Mum?"

It was Rose, standing at the living room door watching her. "Are you all right? You look as if you've seen a ghost."

"Horribly tired, that's all," she said, finding she could breathe after all, and even speak quite normally. "I just need to sit down for a bit before I start tea. Is that OK?"

"I've had some biscuits to keep me going," Rose said. "I'll be OK for a while. I just wondered what was for tea."

"I don't know," Verity said and staggered through to the living room and flopped inelegantly down onto the sofa.

"Do you want me to ring Dad and say you're not well again?" Rose asked, and Verity felt tears of gratitude tickled her eyes. How could Juliet say she had no love in her life when she was so palpably surrounded by it?

"No, I shall be fine, but if you could make me a cup of tea...." she said.

Rose made her a mug of tea and even found her a few biscuits that had escaped her own quest for post-school snacking. After a half hour spent with the mindless chatter of children's television surrounding her reeling mind with comforting white noise, she felt ready to resume life, but as she bustled around the kitchen she found herself trying to analyse what had happened.

The location of the flat had seemed not dissimilar to the one she and David had lived in when they had first married, so utterly penniless that one room with a tiny bathroom and kitchenette had seemed to stretch that first month's money to twanging point but never quite to breaking point. So many people had told them they were being silly marrying with nothing behind them that it had been a matter of pride to manage on their pittance and even hold the odd cramped and imaginative dinner party in their tiny home.

But love in a garret is fun when you know it won't be forever, that it is a staging post onto better things. Tough as it had been managing then, they had managed to save enough for a deposit for their tiny house; even before they knew Rosie was on the way, they had been busy making plans for better things. There had been no feeling of the flat in the vision being a staging post on the way to greater things; it had the feeling of an end in itself and a sad end at that.

She recoiled as she caught the edge of her thumb with the vegetable knife as she chopped onions. Blood began to drip onto the chopping board and she grabbed a bit of kitchen roll to stem the bleeding. I must concentrate, she told herself severely, and tried to fix a plaster to her cut thumb. What worried her most was that she had no idea if she had actually gone somewhere, knocked on the door of a seedy flat somewhere in the less salubrious end of town or had she simply cycled home in a waking dream, negotiating traffic as if driven by an inner autopilot and the time she had spent at the flat had not had a parallel in her waking world. The thought that she might really have been wandering round that place in a kind of state of somnambulism made her feel quite sick with fear; what might have really happened that she would have no memory of now?

Somehow she managed to cook a reasonably pleasant meal, though it wasn't easy with a thumb wrapped in a series of plasters, and by the time David got home she'd managed to put the vision into the back of her mind, but by the time he was snoring softly, she was still lying, watching the darkness and wondered what was happening to her and why. She fell asleep with as few answers as before and the next morning the daily scramble to get all of them up and out of the house on schedule wiped the urgency of the memory from her mind.

It occurred to Verity that Martine must have almost nothing to do at home and have even less of a circle of friends than she herself did for her to spend so much time hanging round the shop. As they talked, a picture emerged of Martine's life that filled Verity with reluctant pity. Martine had married someone older than herself- "He's about your age," she said carelessly, and who had more than enough money for her not to need to work but not quite enough for Martine to play as much as she would have liked. Verity baulked at paying more than about ten pounds for a pot of skin cream but Martine thought little of spending ten times that amount, and her idea of a brilliant day involved a lot of shopping, a trip to some sort of beauty parlour and at least one pair of new shoes. Threatened with the confiscation of her store cards and her credit cards, Martine had been obliged to look for work.

"And here I am!" she said brightly. "It's done me so much good, getting back to work. Sometimes I think Will only married me for my looks; I think he'd begun to forget I'm more than that. It's hardly fair for him to treat me like some sort of accessory and not be willing to pay for my maintenance. It takes a lot to look this good, you know."

I wouldn't know, I've never tried, Verity thought, vaguely amused.

"You must tell me who does your hair," Martine said. "I've tried to get my hairdresser to get mine that shade but it never quite works. I bet it's that fantastic new place on the high street; I've been meaning to try them anyway."

"The last time I went to a hairdresser was about a year ago," Verity said. "And that was only for a trim."

Martine stared at her, the mental cogs rotating so obviously Verity could almost hear them creaking.

"You mean that's your natural colour?" she asked finally when she'd finally worked it out. "You lucky, lucky girl! That's so unfair!"

She looked almost aggrieved that such a shade was wasted on someone of Verity's age, looks and obvious lack of fashion sense.

"You try avoiding sunburn through the summer," Verity said. "I'd burn under a daylight lamp."

Martine wasn't listening but was inspecting Verity's hair with such intense scrutiny she appeared to be looking for head-lice. Verity said nothing but she guessed Martine was trying to see how many of her hairs were actually white from her advanced age and how many were really blonde. After a while the mathematical and observational skills overwhelmed her and she gave up with a small frown showing how aggrieved she was.

Verity shrugged and moved away to get on with something useful in the limited context of the shop, while Martine sat on the high stool behind the counter, inspecting her nails.

"What does your husband do?" she asked, suddenly.

"He's a secondary school teacher," Verity said. "He's head of science, actually."

She wondered where this was leading but apparently it was simply another means of staving off silence and boredom.

"What's he like?" Martine asked.

"What do you mean, what's he like? Do you mean to look at or what?" Verity asked.

"No, just... what's he like?" Martine said, puzzled by her reply.

"You mean, as a person? OK, well, he's always been my best friend, since we met," Verity said and Martine goggled at her.

"You're not serious? Friends with a bloke?" she said incredulously.

"Why not? I've always had male friends, haven't you?"

By the look of horror on Martine's face it was clear the concept of being friends with a man was not a pleasant one. Over the course of the next half an hour it became clear that for Martine men didn't come from Mars but rather from a galaxy far, far away. They were for flirting with, going to bed with, paying for drinks and meals, taking money from and so on but never, ever to be friends with. The only time her husband had seen her without make-up, it had been when she'd been so ill with a stomach bug that she'd hardly had the energy to wash let alone spend half an hour painting her face and the smell of her lipstick had caused her to start retching again. Her view of men hadn't altered from the time she'd been at school; they were another species and an enemy one at that. All her energies went on keeping her husband ignorant of her own activities as far as possible; he wasn't nearly wealthy enough not to notice significant sums vanishing every month on things he considered a waste of money. One of the things he considered a waste was Martine's visits to Juliet.

I'm right with you there, buddy, Verity thought.

"He swears he can't see the difference the Egyptian therapy has made to my skin," she said, pouting. "But the lines have gone away from my eyes already so it is working! And as for the others, well, maybe you can't see the difference it's made to me inside but I know and that's what counts. I have to stay beautiful for him and that costs and Juliet says beauty always comes from within, real beauty that is."

Verity felt profoundly sorry both for Martine and her husband, locked into this mutual lack of understanding, and wondered how long they would last together like this. When she got home that evening she felt a sense of renewed horror at what Juliet had so lightly proposed she do, all in the name of a therapy that had no basis in either logic nor in history, let alone in a therapeutic context. It seemed no more than the most absurd madness, maybe dragged out by Juliet's jealousy and cloaked in concern for her health. If I tell David, he'll only tell me to resign, she thought and put the memory aside with all the other things she had promised she would think about one day and forgot it.

During the evening, after Rose had gone up to play on her computer, she snuggled up to David who was finally finished with his load of marking and let the sounds of the television be washed away by the gurgles of his digestion and the steady beat of his heart as she lay her head on his chest. I am lucky, she said to herself, and closed her eyes.

"You OK?" he asked after a while.

"Why?" she replied sleepily. "Don't I look it?"

"I didn't mean just now. I meant generally," he said. "You did have the flu very badly and you've seemed rather... distant, distracted I guess lately."

"Fine, just permanently tired," she said. "I think I'll head for bed, now, since there's nothing on worth watching."

"Do you think you maybe ought to see the doctor again, just in case?" he said.

She eased herself to an upright position and glanced at him.

"What, just because I'm a bit tired?" she said. "That'd be a waste of time. The best I'd get is the advice to rest and maybe think about a vitamin supplement. Not a lot of point with that. I'm sure it'll pass off given time."

But as she got up, she saw he was still looking slightly worried.

"If you're sure," he said. "I'll be up a bit later. I want to watch something on BBC2; just one of those popular science programmes. Someone is bound to ask me about it if I don't watch it."

She went up to bed alone and was fast asleep when he came to bed.

The next few days at work passed drearily; sometimes it felt like being trapped in a nightmare, not one of those that are full of monsters and running and blood and screaming but rather the dull sort where time passes maddeningly slowly and nothing ever happens but you still wake feeling bereft without ever knowing quite why. Nobody else can ever quite understand why the nightmare had been so awful since the events sound neither horrifying nor even disturbing; simply the mood, the atmosphere had been so strangely destructive, so life-denying. Imagine a world of tedious Sunday afternoons where evening never comes, the boring visitors never stop talking but never manage to say anything worth hearing, and there is a persistent smell of boiled cabbage and overheated fat even when such things have never been cooked and always, always there is a single blue-bottle that buzzes away at a window upstairs, never loud enough for someone to be bothered getting up and either swatting it or opening the window and letting it out, but the persistent drone on the very edge of hearing is going to drive you over the brink and into insanity. Martine's constant chatter felt much like the sound of the blue-bottle; she could never quite ignore her because once in a while she needed to give an answer to something that had some minimal importance in the scheme of the shop. Juliet came down between clients and held forth to an awestruck Martine and a very blank Verity, and time just simply crawled by.

Each afternoon as she began pedalling home Verity felt a good ten years older than she had that morning, and she began wondering if she might go grey just from the sheer tedium of her life. She had not given any thought lately to the visions and had even begun to wonder if they were simply the memories of dreams that she had half forgotten when she woke but which occupied her mind when her daily life let her go into automatic pilot for hours on end.

It isn't as if I ever use my mind much these days, so perhaps it deserves to just go off and play by itself once in a while, she thought as she was putting on her coat one afternoon. I don't miss it really; a trained ape could do what I do after all. Maybe this is what it would be like after a lobotomy.

She shuddered and left the shop in Martine's willing but probably not terribly capable hands and began to make her way home, instinctively dodging traffic and pedestrians. She hit one large puddle left over from the previous day's rain and covered the lower part of her jeans in muddy water, so by the time she got back home, she was keen to get into something dry and clean. She put her bike away in the shed and went to unlock the front door. Her key wouldn't turn.

She extracted the key, to check it was the right one but it was the only Yale key on the bunch, saw that it was the right key and tried again. It wouldn't even turn, so perhaps the snick had fallen; it was a fairly old lock after all. She rattled it in the lock, trying to make it turn. A voice came from an upstairs window, startling her.

"I wouldn't bother doing that," said Granddad, his voice rough with emotion. "I've just had the locksmith change it for me."

"For goodness sake, Granddad, what on earth for?" she demanded, stepping back so she could look up.

His foreshortened face was deep red and gaunt and his eyes seemed to be red-rimmed and staring.

"Just let me in," she said. "Tom will be home soon and I need to get tea on for us all."

"No he won't be," Granddad said, harshly.

"Oh God, what have you done?" she demanded, her heart beating faster and faster. He'd been so erratic lately; heaven only knows what he'd done. He'd sworn blind that when he'd hit her with that shovel on Christmas day it had been an accident, that he hadn't meant to hit her and he'd been starting a new trench and she'd moved in his way, and her memory of the moment had been so hazy she'd not argued about it when she came to. Oh God, please let Tom be all right; I'll be such a good person if only Tom is all right.

"Me, I haven't done anything. It's that worthless husband of yours," Granddad said. "He came here just as Tom was off to school and he's taken him. I was busy digging so I only found out when I came in at lunchtime and found all Tom's stuff gone and a note. So that's me clear. You can just get lost now, young lady. I only gave you a home for Tom's sake; you betrayed my trust by giving that useless lout a key to my house. Just go or I'll call the police. Thieving bitch, you've been leeching off me long enough. Go and earn a living."

I do earn a living, just not enough.

"But what about my stuff?" she asked, close to panic.

"I've just lit a nice big bonfire," he said and indeed she could smell wood-smoke faintly.

111

"You can't just burn my things," she protested. "Granddad, you're not well. You need help. Just let me in and I shall sort everything out. He's probably just taken Tom for a little holiday."

"On what? Magic beans? Don't be absurd; he hasn't earned a penny in his life, so how do you think he'd pay for a holiday? No one but morons like you will accept moonshine and promises as payment. Go on, get lost. I don't want you here, just like my stupid son and your stupid bitch of a mother didn't want you either. No one wants you. Why not go and see if the fishes in the river want you? I despise you, I hate you," he snarled and she leapt back as he spat a great gobbet of stringy saliva at her.

"What am I to do?" she shouted back, pleading, oblivious of the eyes behind windows along the street.

"I don't care!" he shouted and slammed down the window.

She hammered on the door till her hands hurt and she'd even broken a nail and she shouted till her throat hurt too but there was no response beyond stony silence. Then she thought, he'll be at the flat, he'll have taken Tom to the flat. Now they could all be together, even if it was cramped and grubby. It'd be a new start to their life. Maybe he'd got a job, maybe he'd even got a contract for a book of poems, maybe he'd even won one of the competitions he entered and someone had finally spotted his talent and everything was going to be fine, finally. It'd still be a struggle but they'd all be together at last and that was what counted. She could ring Social Services and they could do something about poor Granddad, who was clearly going senile or something, and then maybe when he was sorted again they could all move back to the house; he'd maybe have to stay in a home. Maybe he was even dying.

As she walked, her spirits began to rise. It was going to be all right, everything was going to work out finally. Maybe she'd even get to have another baby, a little girl this time; she'd call her Rose. They'd be able to live in the old house together. Maybe with medication Granddad could come home and be cared for there. It was all going to be lovely.

When she got to the flat, she didn't need a key this time either as the door was open. She stood in the empty room stripped of all possessions and gazed round. A few bits of newspaper crumpled on the floor and a cup with a broken handle on the draining board and an old sock under the edge of the bed were all that was left. The battered old furniture that had come with the flat, supplied from house clearances, still remained, and the three old saucepans and cracked plates and cups still stood in cupboards but everything else, everything personal was gone. Until that moment she had never quite fully understood the phrase "the bottom dropping out of the world," but right now she did. It felt like the ground had caved in under her and she was clinging to the sides of a sheer shaft with her fingernails.

Abruptly she felt her knees give way beneath her and she sat down on the edge of the bed. The lumpy mattress smelled stale and sweaty, the stains made by tea and worse like a map of an unknown world and she held her hands together, twisting them and wringing them as if she might wring some truth out of her own flesh.

"He went this afternoon," said a voice from the door and she glanced up. It was the landlord. "He piled all his boxes and cases into a taxi and went."

He was a big man, heavy and ponderous of middle European appearance, who always tried to excuse his reluctance to maintain his property by pleading lack of money but his expensive suits and his handmade shoes rather gave the lie to this.

"Do you have any idea where he went?" she asked hopelessly. "Did he leave a forwarding address for post?"

The landlord shook his head.

"He was paid up till tomorrow and that's all I know," he said. "He didn't even ask for his deposit back. I think he was heading for the city. I think I may have heard him say something about the city to the taxi driver."

He was watching her.

"You are his wife, yes?" he said and she nodded.

"Then I think maybe you should think about a divorce," he went on.

"Maybe I should," she said and managed to get to her feet. "But it'd be easier if I could find him first. And quicker."

"I know a good private detective," the landlord said. "I had him follow my first wife when I needed to find out if she was having an affair. I can maybe give you his card?"

"Maybe," she said and made her way almost blindly to the door. "Thank you."

Down in the street she racked her brain trying to think where he might have gone. The city was a huge place to just wander in the hopes of seeing him but she knew some of his haunts, bars and coffee shops and wine bars where poets recited their work to a largely indifferent audience, places he'd had gigs and places he had, if not friends then friendly acquaintances. If she caught the train now, she could be there as the night-life made its first blinking appearance in the city centre. She might find him by nine o'clock and maybe discover it was all a misunderstanding, that he'd spent hours trying to find her to bring her with him and Tom. Perhaps he'd meant it as a surprise for her: perhaps he'd found a little flat somewhere in the city for them as a family, a new beginning. She pulled her mobile phone out and checked for any missed calls or messages. Nothing.

She hurried to the station and caught the first train into the city, sitting near the door so she could jump out and be on her way as soon as the train rolled into the station. People were making their way home, or like her were heading out for an evening on the town. The evening air was cold when she left the station and she wished she had a warmer coat; spring wasn't nearly advanced far enough for the light coat she was wearing to be sufficient.

In the city centre, she found one of the big wine bars he'd once taken her to for a gig but it was virtually deserted and the man at the bar had no memory of him having been in recently, so she ordered a glass of wine and sat down to think. She'd have to find a cash point, she only had maybe ten quid or less in her purse and she knew she'd have to find somewhere to sleep tonight. Even if she did manage to get Granddad sorted she'd not manage it tonight, so one of the first things she needed was to find a hotel or something for the night. Everything always looked so much better by daylight, so even if she didn't find them tonight, tomorrow was another day, full of opportunity and hope. She swallowed her wine and a handful of the peanuts on the bar and made her way to the nearest cash point.

At first she thought she must have done something wrong but it soon became apparent that the machine was not going to give her any money. It was saying she had insufficient funds, which was absurd since she'd been paid recently and well, so she rang the number on the back of her card and after the usual robotic pantomime, was told that her account was not only empty but appallingly overdrawn.

"It can't be," she breathed. "I was paid two days ago. There was plenty in it then too. I don't know what can have happened. It must be some sort of computer error."

The distant voice told her that she should speak to someone at any branch in the morning but from the tone it was clear that they certainly didn't think it was computer error that had emptied her account and plunged her so deep into the red that she'd take years to pay it off.

"What if someone has managed to get into my account?"

She was told that was only possible if that person knew her security codes and questions and at that point her whole body went so cold she felt her teeth chatter. She ended the call and stood in the empty street, shaking.

He'd emptied her account of everything; they didn't have a joint account and never had had one but he knew her PIN and her security codes and every damn thing he needed to have done it. It must have been done yesterday; she'd asked him to get some cash out for her and buy them both some lunch, but how could he have just done that and showed no sign of it? He'd been so normal; they'd eaten lunch in a pub near the school she had been working at and he'd been exactly as he always was but he'd been sitting there with thousands of pounds in his pocket and he'd not said a single thing to her that would have made her suspect he'd just robbed her of everything she had. He must have been planning it; he couldn't have just done it on impulse, could he? Perhaps it was him who was going mad, not Granddad at all; his had always been a sensitive temperament and maybe after all the struggles and disappointments and let-downs he was finally succumbing to a nervous breakdown. If she could only find him and ask him; if she could just talk to him; if she could just find where he'd taken Tom. The ifs went on in her head as she stood in the cold street, waiting for her mind to come up with some sort of plan of action that might bring her some solution to the fact that all she had in the world were the contents of her handbag, barely ten pounds in money and the clothes she stood up in, and she had nowhere to go. She'd just lost her home, her son, her husband and all her money in one go and it felt as if she might lose her sanity too as she racked her tired brain to think of some way out of this awful mess.

She spent the next few hours wandering round the bars and clubs she knew he'd done gigs at, and asking if anyone had seen him. It was a miserable business; the music was too loud and after the third bar, her head had begun to pound. No one had seen him for weeks; the only person who had seen him more recently had nothing useful to tell her beyond the fact that he'd seemed very hostile to everyone, not his normal sunny, charming self. He seemed to think everyone was against him, that there was some sort of conspiracy to stop him doing well. This just confirmed her fears but drew her no nearer to finding him and Tom.

After hours of wandering her feet were hurting and she decided that the only thing she could sensibly do was head home; at the very least she had the shelter of the shed to look forward to. There was frost forming on the pavements and her breath hung in white ribbons as she walked back to the station only to discover that the last train had gone ten minutes before, stranding her here. Trying not to cry, she went find the station café, only to find it was closed. She really needed a drink of something hot and nothing was open beyond bars and clubs where she'd pay her last fiver just for a glass of mineral water.

There must be something, somewhere I can go, she thought. Surely there are night shelters with bright lights and stewed tea and doorstep sandwiches and warmth? If there are, I can't see any. You have to know where they are before you need them; I'd never have thought I'd need such places, even in the worst days of the last years I never thought I'd find myself homeless and utterly destitute. What am I going to do?

Away from the city centre, she sat down in a doorway and huddled herself up, hugging her knees to her chest and trying to stop the perpetual shivering. The ground was cold and slightly damp under her and she could feel the cold seeping into her but she couldn't bring herself to get up and keep moving; what was the point? She just wanted everything to stop, to be able to go to sleep and wake and find it had all been a nightmare, but every time she felt herself tipping over the brink of sleep, a gust of wind

116

caught her and made her gasp with the cold of it ripping into her clothes and bringing her to full aching wakefulness again. She didn't want to cry but her body didn't seem to be listening to her any more and a steady procession of fat tears rolled down her face and splashed down her clothes; she watched them without interest as if they belonged to someone else.

"This isn't fair," she whispered aloud to the empty doorway.

David had got home to an empty house, remembering that Rose was staying that night with a school friend, and spending the next day, which was a Saturday, with her. The house felt eerie and he wondered where Verity had got to; usually she was home and had either cooked their meal or was still pottering over the stove when he got in. He ate a piece of toast and then decided he'd best call her to see if that woman she worked for had made her work late; all he got was the voice mail on her mobile. He left it another half hour, hoping she'd say she was on her way, or that she was at the shops and could he come and pick her up, but nothing happened. At this point, he decided to phone Juliet and see if she knew where his wife was; he was quite prepared to give the wretched woman a real rollicking over the phone if she said that Verity was still there. She often made Verity do the cleaning and even a few quid extra didn't really compensate for that humiliation; he suspected she only did it to try and get her own back on Verity for imagined slights in their shared school days. But when he got through to Juliet, she told him quite firmly that Verity had gone home at three o'clock that afternoon.

"I don't know if she had other plans afterwards," she said. "Maybe she was going shopping, or meeting a friend? Shall I ask my colleague? Perhaps Verity said something to her."

He heard her asking someone called Martine if she knew if Verity had any plans for the rest for the afternoon and then her rather grating voice filled the phone again at full volume.

"No, David, Martine says she didn't say anything to her. Mind, she wouldn't necessarily say anything to anyone. You know what they say about still waters running deep," Juliet said and David could help the suspicion that she sounded pleased about something, almost smug. It made him slightly uneasy.

117

He rang off and tried Verity's mobile again; nothing but voice mail. He tried to tell himself there was no reason why she wouldn't have gone off and done some shopping or gone to the cinema or something like that; she was a grown woman, she didn't need to tell him where she was going all the time, but she always had done, and so had he, if something had come up that meant one of them was going to be delayed. It was this deviation from their normal practice that was so worrying. It was far too early to think of calling the police.

He had a sudden thought and hurried out to the shed where her bicycle was stored and wasn't reassured to find it was there. Wherever she was, she had been home first to leave her bicycle. That meant that at least one concern, that she had either fallen off it or been knocked off it by traffic cutting in too close, wasn't going to be the case, but even so, it seemed so odd. Why would she have come home, left the bike and gone out again, and not left a note or something, if she were going to be a while? Her little car was still where it always was on the drive, so wherever she was she'd either gone on foot or by public transport or been picked up by someone.

It was silly to be so worried but he was. She hadn't been at all well and if he were honest, he hadn't thought her well enough to go back to that stupid shop and be bossed around all day by that Mussolini in mascara. Every evening, she'd been wiped out by the time they'd eaten tea and she'd be dozing off over Eastenders if she hadn't already gone to bed; she said she was fine but he had never been convinced she was fully recovered. He made himself something to eat and sat down to wait; surely she would phone soon, or come back complaining about a massive queue at the supermarket when all she wanted was some cheese and a stick of French bread.

An hour or so later, he had a sudden stroke of what he thought was inspiration. It must be somewhere around the anniversary of her Granddad's death, maybe it was today, so she'd have gone to the cemetery. She'd be sitting there right now, in the dark, feeling sad and not wanting to leave the graveside. He got his coat and the car and drove quickly down to the cemetery and found it locked up and deserted. Bang goes that theory, he thought, no sign of Verity, nothing. Damn.

118

He drove home, expecting her to be there but she wasn't. When he tried Rosie on her mobile, he only got her voice mail. He'd even have tried calling the friend where Rosie was staying tonight so he could ask if Rosie knew if her mother had any plans for tonight but he didn't have the number. He gave up and sat down in front of the television and considered his options. He could call all the hospitals in the area, or he could call the police. Both of these options seemed ridiculously premature when she could easily walk in the front door right now and be completely irritated by his panic. Maybe she'd got a call from Carla and they were right now enjoying a meal together somewhere swish; maybe he'd missed her note, or her message on his mobile. He even checked the house answer phone: nothing. He checked all the places she might have left a note: the kitchen notice board, the kettle, the mantelpiece, the dressing table in their room, the table with the house phone. Nothing. He sat back down and put his head in his hands and tried to think where on earth she might be; he thought of the big address book by the phone but when he skimmed through it he was aware for the first time how few names there were in it, and many of them he was fairly sure she hadn't seen since they moved here. He considered calling a few of the women he vaguely recalled his wife having been close to and then rejected the notion; he'd just look silly ringing up after all this time to ask if they'd seen Verity and he knew, with a rather horrible instinct he'd have classified as feminine if he'd had the chance to analyse it, that they would assume she must have left him.

In the end he made himself some coffee and sat and watched the television with blank eyes and mind in neutral, and glanced from time to time at the telephone in the hope that by staring at it he might make it ring with good news.

Chapter 6

David had fallen into an uneasy sleep, stretched out on the sofa, with the television still on but the volume turned low, when the phone did finally ring. He leapt off the sofa in alarm and snatched up the phone; his stomach seemed to do an uncomfortable roll when he heard an unknown voice asking him if he was Mr. David Meadows.

"I am," he said, his mouth dry and his tongue seeming to stick to the roof of his mouth.

It was the city's main police station, ringing to tell him that they had his wife with them. Now he wasn't to worry, she wasn't under arrest and she hadn't been hurt or anything but she'd been found in a distressed state and could he come and fetch her home?

"What sort of distressed state?" David asked.

"She was crying and upset and at first she didn't seem to know who she was but that passed," said the policewoman on the other end of the phone. "She told us at first her surname was Braithwaite, but she then told us it was Meadows. We assume that was her maiden name?"

David muttered something non-committal and said he'd get there as soon as he could and hung up. He stood for a moment, rubbing his eyes and saying to himself, "Braithwaite? Why on earth would she say that?" before he grabbed his keys and hurried out to the car.

The night-life was still spilling onto the streets in swaying crowds, and once or twice he saw someone fall over and stay down as he drove thought the city centre trying to find the main police station. It was after three in the morning when he got there and he was almost twitching with anxiety. Inside, the waiting area was brightly lit, almost garishly so, and when he asked at the desk, he was told Verity was waiting in one of the interview rooms.

"We didn't think it was right she should have to sit out there," said the policewoman. "It was pretty chaotic around the time we brought her in and I think she was rather scared by the group of drunks we were processing. We were hoping to have had a doctor have a look at her but he's been busy with one of our

120

other...clients, but she seems all right. She told us nothing had happened to her, so I guess it's up to you to sort it out now."

He guessed she probably thought it was a domestic matter, a runaway wife who'd got so far and thought better of it.

"We brought her in for her own safety," she went on. "She didn't seem to know where she was or even who she was for a while so we were concerned she'd been hurt, maybe a traffic accident but then she seemed to come round. I'll show you through and then you can take her home. She isn't in any trouble."

Verity was huddled in a chair, clutching an empty plastic cup that seemed to have held tea; her clothes were crumpled and grubby and her face was dirty with tears and grime but she seemed otherwise unharmed. When she saw him, she sprang out of her chair and into his arms; the feel of her arms round him made tears rise to his eyes and when she moved away he saw she was crying again too.

"Let's go home," he said.

The journey home seemed to take far longer than it should have done, partly because he had to be extra careful about the swelling number of inebriated people that seemed to lurch out into the road almost without warning the whole time he tried to negotiate the city centre, but even when he got out and onto the main roads the time it took to drive home seemed too long. The awkward silence, interspersed with sniffs and the occasional sob or the nose blowing seemed to stretch time out like a piece of dough till there seemed to be tears and rips in it. All he wanted was to get home where they would be safe, before he could ask her what on earth had happened, and this long delay before he could start to extract the truth was weighing on him heavily. He had begun to suspect all sorts of horrible things and the sooner he managed to dismiss the worst ones, the better he was going to feel. To make matters worse, she was obviously all-in and in no state to talk but he was adamant that he needed at least a few answers before tonight became truly tomorrow.

He'd left lights on in the house because of his rush to leave but he was glad when he saw the light shining through the gap where the living room curtains didn't quite meet; it made the house seem occupied and therefore less of a void to walk into. He steered her into the living room and sat her down; she seemed to just sit where she was put without modifying her posture or position, rather like a lifelike doll that can be posed but cannot move on its own. There was something limp and unresponsive about her that frightened him and he wondered if he should have taken her to the hospital rather than home. Something was very wrong; perhaps he ought to take her now. He glanced at the clock; it would be better to wait now till morning proper. If he could get her an emergency appointment with their GP, she might be referred to hospital far more swiftly and efficiently than hanging round the local casualty department for hours dodging drunks and watching the clock.

"I'll make us both a hot drink," he said to fill the void and when he came back with a tray of tea she still hadn't moved. He had to put the mug into her hands and hold it to her lips for her to sip.

"Too hot," she said suddenly and her voice seemed rough with disuse.

"Sorry," he said but his heart had lifted with the sound of her voice. She hadn't really spoken to him all the way home and he had begun to worry that she had lapsed back into the catatonic state the police said they had found her in.

"What on earth happened tonight?" he asked.

She shrugged, a gesture very like one he'd expect from their daughter.

"I don't really know," she said. "I don't know I can explain it."

He could feel his relief that she was safe slipping away and anger rising to replace it; the anger a parent feels when the child who has run away is safely home and the need to understand now is overwhelming.

"I've been out of my mind with worry," he snapped. "And all you can say is you don't know. You must know. You were there, you have to know what happened."

He thought she'd cry again but she didn't, just sat there looking blank and broken.

"I'm sorry," she said in a dull voice.

"Sorry isn't good enough," he said. "I need to know why you went to town, what happened to you, why you're sitting there like a basket case. Sorry just won't do."

"But I am sorry," she said, very childlike. "The thing is, if I try to explain what happened, you are going to think I am completely mad."

"Don't tell me you've been abducted by aliens," he said with a rogue flash of humour, and she managed a tired smile.

"Nothing that articulate," she said. "Nothing as easy as that. But please promise me, if you do think I've gone mad, please don't just leave me."

He was appalled, shocked to the core to hear her say this. What could be that bad that she'd think he'd just leave her?

"Is there someone else?" he asked feeling his own insides going icy cold as he asked it.

"No," she said. "Nothing like that, I promise you. But I still don't think you're going to understand or like what I'm going to tell you. I've spent the whole time trying to work it out, work out what has happened and I can only get so far with it. Ever since I found myself at the police station I've been trying to understand it."

He was shaking slightly with the anxiety and when he looked at her he could see she was trembling too. He sat down opposite her and waited.

"I've been having what may best be described as visions," she said quietly. "Not religious visions, nothing like that. And not hallucinations either. I don't think that's the right word. Visions, that's the nearest word."

"Visions?" he repeated. "When did this start?"

"I'm not sure but I think the first one was back in September," she said. "I say I'm not sure because the more it happens the more I worry it's been happening longer than that but I can't quite be sure. When they happen, I can't remember this life at all. It's like I'm in another life altogether."

"Are the visions of the past or the future or something like that?" he said, trying to keep his voice steady.

"No, nothing like that," she said. "It's all very strange. It's like another life I might have had. Some of it is very mundane, nothing dramatic. The first one I remember, that was very disorientating. It's not like a dream or anything like that, or even like watching a film. I'm there, right there, just as much as I am here. The only reason I'm sure that this is my real life is because I can remember the other one when I come back here, whereas when I'm there I have no memory of this life beyond some slight uneasiness about some of the bits of the other life."

"You'll have to explain a bit more. I really don't understand," he said.

"OK. The first one, I had a nine-year-old son called Tom and I didn't have Rosie. Tom had brought home a school friend for tea without asking me first and I was trying to find if we had enough for tea. I still lived in this house but it was pretty much the same as when Granddad was here, you know the décor and stuff. I came back to myself when Rosie came home, and I was still not quite myself and it took me a few minutes to realise that Tom wasn't real, that things had shifted back to the way they really were. I felt weird, really weird. I thought it was just a living daydream but when I thought about it, it hadn't been. I'd been trying on my new jeans when Tom burst in but I hadn't been daydreaming. I'd been thinking about getting on with tea before Rose got home, stuff like that. And then I just had to get on with other things and I forgot about it. I didn't think it'd happen again. I thought it was just stress and such like."

"And it did happen again?" David said.

She nodded.

"One or two tiny ones, and then on Christmas day," she said. "In this one, Granddad was still alive but he'd gone… funny in the head. He was doing a dig at the bottom of the garden and he was so excited about it but when I saw what he'd found I was scared. He'd dug up all this domestic refuse. Oh some of it was old, Victorian or earlier but he was convinced it was something quite other than it was. So the bit of flowerpot was Samian ware, an old fish knife was a Bronze Age dagger: that sort of thing. He got angry with me and hit me with a spade when I walked off holding one of his finds."

"That was when I found you fainted in the garden," he said and she nodded again. "Any others?"

"I had one where I was a supply teacher at your school, but you were just the head of department and I never saw you," she said. "And another when I went somewhere else. Others where I've seen someone who is dead but in the vision isn't. And then today, that was the longest and worst. And I am so scared because until

124

now I wasn't sure if I was actually doing things when they were going on or if I was just standing somewhere in a daze for ages. I went into the city on a train, and spent hours wandering around the bars and clubs. And now I know that tonight at least I have been acting out what I'm seeing in the visions, in this other life, but in this real one. I've never been so scared in my life when I realised that."

David nodded slowly.

"You think I'm mad now, don't you?" she said.

"What is mad anyway?" he said trying to keep his tone light. "We're all a bit crazy at times. I don't understand any of this but I do think you need to see a doctor tomorrow."

"No," she said. "No doctors. I don't want to go to hospital."

"You probably won't need to," he said. "If there's anything wrong, they can usually treat you at home."

"I don't want to see a doctor. I don't want to," she said and he could see she was getting distressed again.

"You don't have to if you don't want to," he said, soothingly. "I just thought maybe they could help you. All right, tell me, in this school vision, if I was just the head of department, who was your husband? Is it one story all the way through or is it like snap shots of different stories?"

"It's like one story," she said. "When I'm in them, I know stuff about it without thinking about it; it's not like I'm out of place or anything. But when I come back, I'm not sure about anything I didn't see or think directly during the vision, a bit like when you watch a film. So I can remember some things but not everything. So I couldn't tell you what colour tie you'd be wearing if I hadn't seen you, but I might know you'd be at that school that day because that was what should be happening. I don't know I'm making any sense. The whole thing is appalling."

You're telling me, David thought but said nothing for a moment.

"OK," he said. "Today, tell me exactly what happened in the vision. You left work at the normal time and then what happened?"

"I went home," she said. "I locked my bike in the shed. Then I went to try and get in but my key wouldn't work. At that point Granddad leaned out of an upstairs window and told me I couldn't get in because he'd had the locks changed. He told me that my husband whom he hates had taken Tom away that morning and since he'd only given me a home because of Tom, I was now out on the street. He spat at me for goodness sake! So I went to my husband's flat."

"You don't live together?" David said sharply.

"No. Granddad wouldn't let him live with us so he has, had this tiny bed-sit flat place in the rough end of town. When I got there, the place was empty, all his stuff gone and the landlord said he'd heard him say to the taxi to take him into the city. So I headed into the city to try and find him. But no one had seen him and when I tried to get some money out of my account I discovered my account had not only been emptied but I was horribly overdrawn. I'd asked him to get some money out the previous day for me and he must have done it then. So I had no money for somewhere to stay overnight. I decided I'd head home and maybe talk Granddad round or at worst sleep in the shed but I'd missed the last train. I must have just wandered for ages then. I couldn't think what to do; my husband and my son were gone, I was broke and homeless and I didn't know what to do. In the end I sat down somewhere and just cried. That was where the police found me. I think at first they thought I was a drunk and then they realised something was wrong so they brought me in and tried to find out what had happened to me. I was very confused for a while. I couldn't work out which life I was in until they went through my handbag and found my details and called you. At that point I remembered who I was properly and I was really, really scared."

"I'm not surprised," he said. "I'm scared at the thought of you wandering round the city bars in such a state. Why would this husband of yours be there anyway? Was he a boozer or something?"

"No, he was a poet," she said, and David made sudden sense of what the police had said to him .It was the first time that night that anything had made any sense whatsoever and it was a poor comfort but welcome nonetheless.

"Nick Braithwaite," he said and she nodded.

"The odd thing is I've never seen him properly in any of the visions," she said. "I've seen him pass but never face to face. And now I think about it, I've seen him from the shop, walking past. I only see him from the back, never face to face. This is really odd."

"What, odder than all the rest?" David said dryly.

"Yes," she said. "Because now I think about it, the only times I've seen him, I'm almost sure I wasn't having a vision!"

David rubbed his eyes; they were feeling gritty and aching with tiredness and very little of this was making any sense but at least she seemed moderately coherent and together.

"I think," he said. "I think you need to tell me about this Nick character and maybe then I'll have some idea of why in this other life of yours he's somehow ousted me as your husband. I don't pretend to have any grasp of what you're been seeing but I'd like to have a more complete story before I try and make sense of it."

She nodded.

"I'd have told you about it before, years ago, if I'd thought it had any relevance to us," she said. "I've always hated the way people make capital about their partner's old flames; I don't think I ever asked you about any girlfriends before me and in the end, the whole thing was so painful I didn't want to even think about it. In honesty, I think I forgot a lot of it."

"Well, all I know is that you went out with Carla's brother when you were seventeen and he died," David said. "I suppose I've assumed it was just a boy and girl type of thing, a bit tragic but nothing to do any lasting grief, but I have this feeling it wasn't like that at all."

"No," she said quietly. "It wasn't like that at all."

She sat up a bit straighter in her chair as if she was feeling a bit better and took a sip of the tea.

"I don't know how to start, really," she said, slowly. "It's all so long ago and really, I stopped thinking about it altogether a long time ago. When I see Rose, I think I was never that young, but I was that young once. I wasn't much older when Nick and Carla came to the school. Carla was in my year but another form and I didn't get to know her at first. We were just going into our O level year, fifteen going on sixteen. Their Dad had just come out of the army and they'd all moved here for his new job and I think now it was a bit of a shock to them after what they'd been used to, living abroad and so on. We'd been back at school for maybe a week when I first noticed Nick. He was in the lower sixth and they had their own common room, a place to hang out away from the rest of the younger ones but they had to come out to move between lessons. I had a friend back then, Diane, and we hung round a lot together. You know how it is with girls of that age: best friends forever, at least until some boy comes along. Anyway, we saw this… vision wafting along the corridor. I seem to recall the whole New Romantic look was around but we'd never seen anything like this: long dark curls and a velvet jacket. Now I think about it I don't know how he got that jacket past his dad! But the funniest thing is neither of us was sure of this vision's gender! I remember Di saying, "It's got to be a girl. No lad looks that good!" and I said I wasn't so sure. It wasn't that he was feminine looking, as such, just I guess a bit androgynous. Some boys are at that age. We argued about it for a few days and then Di got close to him in the queue for lunch and came to me so disappointed and said dolefully, "No girl has sideburns!" It took me years to work out why she was so disappointed, or why she palled up with Carla afterwards and why Carla was so bitchy to her later. I don't think I knew what a lesbian was till I went to university and saw their stand at the Freshers' fair and then so many things just clicked into place. I digress. Sorry."

"That's OK," David said. "So how did you get to meet him if the sixth formers didn't mix so much with the lower school?"

"Carla," she said simply. "I sat with her in English and we got to know each other a bit. She used to find her brother at lunchtime and sit with him; I think she wanted the security of having someone she could really rely on being around. So I ended up joining them too and we were a proper little gang. You have no idea of what their home life could be like; their Dad was horrible, a real martinet, and their mum just used to give way to him and never stand up for the kids. So they spent most of their free time round here. Granddad liked them and Mum and Dad were never here, really. Carla used to flirt with Granddad, would you believe? He knew she was only being silly but he was still flattered. Nick used to talk with him a lot about everything. I think he really liked having an adult he could talk to and not be yelled at all the time. Nick and I… well, we were such close friends everyone thought we were an item but that school year, we weren't. We'd read poetry together and talk about books and art and philosophy and so on, the three of us and had such a good time, but as the year went on, Carla started being difficult. I think she felt I was stealing her brother from her and maybe that's what was happening but as Nick and I got closer, Carla got spiteful and awkward. You know that photo, the one of us in the hammock? That was a great day. Things were as they had been and we were all happy until Nick kissed me. It took the shine off it for Carla, but you can't see that in the photo. She took a minute or two to realise what had happened and then she got the sulks. Granddad got her giggling later and she forgot about being annoyed with me and Nick but by the time we started back at school, with all of us in the sixth form this time, there was no going back. Carla started hanging round with Di, sniping at me when she could and criticizing Nick at every opportunity. But I didn't care. I didn't miss her. Nick was…everything."

She glanced at David but his face seemed neutral.

"It was a strange year," she said. "My parents had managed to persuade Granddad to fund them to buy the bar, so they were going out there frequently after Christmas to arrange stuff. We decided the best thing was for me to stay living with Granddad and finish at school and then go to an English university. I was glad about that as I didn't like Spain. It was too hot for me and I didn't want to move for obvious reasons. And things hadn't been the same since Dad's business went belly up; Mum never quite got over it. She became hard and cold. I've never talked to her about it but I think she went under in a big way. They should have seen it coming and sold the house and put the money somewhere safe, but they didn't and we lost everything. I don't think it affected me as much as it might have done because it was so much nicer living at Granddad's anyway, even though he and Dad never got on. They never did, apparently, even when dad was a child. I think they never quite got their head round why they were so different. Granddad wanted an intellectual son whom he could talk with and Dad wanted an ordinary dad who would come and watch him at the football and maybe go fishing. Granddad got on OK with my Mum most of the time back then, even after the business failed. Dad hated having to go and work as an ordinary builder when he'd previously owned the company and it really bothered him that he was sometimes working alongside guys he'd been boss to before. So really I was glad they were never around. And it was great to have my friends around; I'd never had friends before like that. Granddad never fussed about things like bedtime and meals and he only sent them home when he realised they would be in trouble if they didn't get home by a certain time and when it was just me and Nick, Granddad just said he wasn't interested in what we might do as long as we were sensible."

"And were you? Sensible, I mean?" David asked and Verity giggled, blushing slightly.

"Terribly!" she said. "So sensible we never did anything really."

She glanced at him.

"Are you all right with this?" she asked. "I mean…." She tailed off, uncertainly.

David sighed.

"I've never been a jealous person," he said. "And how could I be jealous of someone who's been dead all these years?"

She shrugged.

"I know," she said. "But even so…This can't be easy for you."

"Look, I'm not some Victorian idiot, about to reject you because I find out I wasn't your first love," he said. "I had girlfriends before I met you. I even loved one or two of them."

"I know," she said. "And I love you, more than anything or anyone else. I just need to explain why it was so terrible when he died like that. Perhaps we'd have drifted apart if he'd lived. I don't know. But it was so utterly intense and powerful; emotionally I mean. Anyway, we spent just about all our time together and we made our plans. Dreams really, I suppose. We were going to go to the same university, we were going to get married when we finished and it was all so right. He was going to wait for me so we could go into the same year at University, but then his Dad said no, you aren't hanging round here for a year doing nothing. He set up this trip for Nick and basically told him that if he didn't go on it, he wouldn't fund him to go to university. You forget now that the idea of a student loan hadn't even been thought of and we were all dependent on grants and parents so it was a horrible threat. Nick's parents' income meant he didn't qualify for a grant and he had to give in to his father. His Dad wanted him to join the army like he had but he'd accepted that if he went in with a degree, any degree, he could go in as an officer and that was what he wanted for Nick more than anything. But Nick had no intention of joining up. Anyone less suitable for an army career you can't imagine! Nick was a sweet, gentle soul and his Dad treated him like the lowest thing that ever crawled. He used to hit him sometimes; I used to see the bruises. I think he sometimes used to hit Carla too but never where it'd show. She was daddy's girl and seldom did anything to really annoy him but Nick used to annoy him just by walking into a room and breathing. So his Dad hatched this plan. He had this pal from the army who'd come out at the same time and had set up this business with his brother-in-law doing these trips for lads. It was quite pricey but basically as long as you were up to a certain standard of fitness they'd take you. It was some sort of sailing boat, old-fashioned thing I think and quite big, and they had so many trained crew and the rest were lads being sent on the adventure of a lifetime. Don't forget, the term "gap-year" hadn't been thought of and there were a fair few people who wanted to go and have some fun before settling down to study or whatever and if they had families with a bit of money, this was seen as a safe but fun sort of option for that year out. It wouldn't have been Nick's idea of fun though, being stuck on a boat full of lads."

"Nor mine," David said, with feeling. "Sounds like a nightmare to me."

"I think it was a nightmare for him," Verity agreed. "I got a couple of letters and he was pretty fed up of it. They were sailing somewhere in the Pacific, I think and it should have been so lovely but it wasn't. The other lads kept picking on him, the crew weren't much better and he was seasick to start with. I don't think I thought anything of it though. I never thought...Well, he'd been gone some time and then one day, just like any other day that summer, I got up like normal. I didn't have any premonition or anything. Then Carla came round. Since Nick had gone she'd been friendly with me again but never as we had been. But as soon as I opened the door, I knew something was wrong. It was her face; like that painting of Lady Of Shalott, just stunned and staring. He'd apparently gone over the side and they thought he must have drowned. There was a search going on but there wasn't a lot of hope. They never even found his body. I held her and held her while she cried and then she went home and then I started crying and I couldn't stop. I couldn't stop, really I couldn't. Granddad was home but it wasn't till teatime that he realised something was wrong; before that I used to disappear for hours either in the garden or in the attic and he'd just see me at mealtimes some days. I cried non-stop for two days I think. I'd go to sleep crying and when I woke I was still crying and the pillow was soaked."

David said nothing but watched her with careful eyes and held out his hand to her. She took it gratefully.

"Granddad tried to get Mum to come home," she said. "He called her and told her what happened. I didn't know about it till later. He told me about it a long time later. He said he called her and explained what had happened and she said, oh well she'll get over it! He wanted to know what he could do to help me and she said, try chocolate; that usually mends broken hearts at that age. I don't think he ever forgave my mum for that, the way she just dismissed what had happened as if it were just some teenage romance breaking up. I'm not sure I can ever forget it either. But Granddad had to do something to try and help me and he just didn't know what to do. He'd been planning to take me on a short trip to France, round the various megalithic sites, but that was clearly hopeless. I wouldn't talk, I hardly stopped crying and I wouldn't eat. I was utterly broken inside. Poor Granddad; he was never very good at emotional stuff but he did try so hard. He decided to try and see if he could at least make me eat and he decided that if he couldn't take me to France then he'd bring France to me. I don't think he'd ever baked in his life but he reckoned that if women could do it, then so could he. So he got a recipe book out of the library and he taught himself to bake. The first I knew of it what when he came and woke me one morning with a tray full of home-made Brioche and chocolate croissants and a mug of that French coffee with chicory. I was so surprised and I was so touched by his face, all hopeful and keen, that I picked up one of the croissant and began to eat because I couldn't bear the idea of hurting his feelings. I think he'd timed it just perfectly. I was starting to take a tiny bit of notice of the world outside my head. The rest of that summer, he spent his time baking and cooking and messing about with sweet stuff to try and tempt me with. You know what he was like; he had to do things

132

just right. And in its own way it tempted me to live again. I piled on the weight but eating did seem to ease some of the pain. It's like a huge emptiness inside, that sort of grief. It feels like you haven't eaten in weeks and eating cake and chocolate does sort of ease it, or at the very least anaesthetise a bit."

She rubbed her eyes.

"By the autumn term, they'd given up hope of even finding his body," she said. "So they held a memorial service and that was that. Carla ditched Di altogether and hitched up with me again but it wasn't the same; I was a poor substitute for Nick and so was she but we sort of huddled together like orphans against the storm. We didn't talk about him much and after a while I taught myself not to think about him either. I worked hard at school and I ate Granddad's cakes and pastries and chocolate and got fatter and fatter and I didn't care. I did my A levels and had the most awful summer waiting for results and then I went off to university all on my own. The first night in halls I cried myself to sleep for the last time and when I woke up the next day, I said, enough! A year and a bit of tears is enough for a lifetime and I didn't consciously choose to think about him again. But sometimes when we were doing tutorials, we'd come across poems and stuff Nick and I had loved and I'd shiver without remembering why and I wouldn't even say his name even in my own head. So I'd avoid that poet if I could, and if I couldn't I made myself go hard and cold so it wouldn't hurt and after a while I stopped even liking poetry much but that didn't matter because it didn't really matter, any of it, any more."

She stopped then and got to her feet and began pacing.

"I'd met you by then and it stopped hurting so much when you were around and I forgot that there was anything to hurt anyway," she said. "It all went so fast and then we were married and it was so good, and then there was Rosie and that was so good too. I forgot about it totally and then all this started happening and I don't understand it at all. I've been so happy, so happy."

"Have you?" he said.

"Yes, I have. Oh we've had some hard times and some sad times but I have been happy," she said. "I couldn't have wished for a better life."

There was a long silence. Then David broke it, saying,

"This other life, the one in your visions, are you happy there?"

She could hear the uncertainty, the insecurity in his voice as he asked it, and she shook her head with feeling.

"No, not at all," she said. "I should have thought that was clear."

"The little boy, Tom, is he the sort of child you might like to have?" he said. "I know we both felt that Rosie was enough for us but if you wanted another child, we're both still young enough…"

"David, no," she said. "This Tom isn't a child I would really like to have. In my visions I love him of course but he's not really loveable or even likeable; he's more than a bit spoilt and he takes me utterly for granted. This isn't about the children we didn't have. I don't know what it is about but it isn't that."

"So you aren't happy in this other life?" he asked again.

"No, anything but," she said. "I get all full of hope and optimism that things are going to be all right or even how I think they should be but they aren't. Nothing has ever worked out like it was meant to; Nick and Granddad hate each other, I do a job I hate, we can't even live as a family, I scarcely make ends meet and nothing Nick does ever prospers, and my son treats me like a doormat. And now Nick's robbed me of all I own, including my son, my Granddad's gone barmy and chucked me out, and I'm on the street trying to make sense of why it all went so wrong. Do you think this is some sort of rosy daydream, all the what-ifs and might-have-beens about my lost love? It isn't. It's anything but. My other life is a shambles and a mess."

She sat back down next to him.

"If I were making up a dream life, I think I'd pick a better one than that one," she said. "I don't know why I've been seeing these things or why after all this time I began thinking of Nick again and it really bugs me."

"It started before you saw Carla again, didn't it?" he asked. "So it can't just be that she's woken things up for you."

"Up until I saw her, I hadn't really let myself think of Nick," she said. "But when I saw her again, I couldn't not. They were so alike; there was only about fourteen months between them and they had always been so close. What made it worse for me was Carla telling me she was sure Nick killed himself."

"She said that? And do you think he did?"

"I don't know," she said. "I would have said once definitely no but after all this time, it got me wondering. I know he hated it and she told me that he'd managed to call home to ask his dad if he'd send him the funds so he could get home but his dad wouldn't and was horrible to him."

"Why didn't he just go anyway?" David asked.

"That's what you'd have done, isn't it? He wasn't like you, David, not at all. He'd not have had the courage to have just got off the boat at the next stop and made his own way back, scrounging lifts and food from whoever would help. His dad had destroyed any courage of that sort from years of undermining their confidence. I guess he just gave in to his dad because he was so scared of him and it took away any initiative he had. I don't think it'd have been easy to have got home from where they were but I can't bring myself to think that he couldn't just have stuck it out and endured it till they got back. I can't bring myself to think of him swimming so far he couldn't get back rather than stay any longer on that boat. Unless something had happened that made it impossible to stay, he'd have just endured it. It was only six months after all. I think he'd coped with worse at home really."

She was biting the edge of her nail, fighting with herself.

"I wish I knew, though," she said. "Whether he did kill himself, that is. And if he did, then why? I don't know there's any way of finding out; apart from me and Carla, I can't think of anyone who knew him that well. His dad's dead now and from what Carla said, I think he thought Nick killed himself; he burned his poems and his old journal. If I'd got his journal I might have understood what was going on but that's gone too. Oh David, I'm so sorry about this. I would have had you worried for the world. But I didn't choose for this to happen and I swear I haven't thought about Nick in so many years."

David was silent for a moment.

"Maybe that's why this has happened," he said slowly. "Look, what happened was a huge part of your life, both being with Nick and losing him like that and you stopped thinking about it, maybe before you should have done, before the grieving was fully completed. Maybe you should have been able to think about him sometimes, shed a few tears, get drunk and all the rest of it. But you didn't. Was it because of me? In case I were jealous or thought you were being melodramatic?"

"The first Christmas after it happened," she said carefully. "My parents came over. They took a week off over Christmas since most of the ex-pats the bar serves had gone home anyway. My mother caught me crying, on Christmas day. She slapped me and told me that the best way of ruining my life was to carry on moaning and groaning over Nick and that no guy would ever want me if I dissolved into tears at the slightest thing even vaguely connected to him. 'People die. Get over it,' she said. 'There's no room in this world for drama queens like you, so stop it now before it becomes a habit,'"

Verity spread out her hands in a gesture of helplessness.

"What else could I do? I thought she was probably right," she said. "So I never talked about it, except with Carla, and only when she mentioned it, and I made myself try and forget everything over the next years and largely I managed it. But when Granddad died, the emotions were familiar and maybe that's what set it going."

"You didn't seem that upset about Granddad," David remarked.

"Just shows then doesn't it," she said. "I was devastated. He'd been the one thing that had been constant in my life since I was a little girl and now he was gone. But I remembered my mother's comments about drama queens and I stopped myself. I saw her look at me at the funeral and I saw her warning me then with her eyes and I kept it all locked down so I wouldn't cave in to it."

David said nothing and put his arms around her shoulders.

"You should have been allowed to grieve at your own pace and in your own way," he said after a while. His own sense of relief was huge; the only other man had been dead for years and even in her strange visions he was far from an ideal husband. What was concerning him now was whether she might actually be mentally ill to be having these experiences.

"Look, maybe I might ask Gavin for some advice?" he said presently.

"Love, your brother is just a GP. A very good GP I'm sure, but he isn't an expert on anything," Verity said. "Were you hoping to ask him about the symptoms of schizophrenia, or psychosis, or brain tumours?"

A little ashamed, he nodded.

"I don't know anything about them myself," she said. "But I can distinguish between reality and fantasy when I am in reality. I told you I am sure this life is the real one because I can remember the other one here. I don't know why this is happening to me. Perhaps there was no... what is the current buzzword? Ah, yes, closure, that's it. There was no real funeral because his body was never found, just a rather awful memorial service. I was only his girlfriend and not his wife or anything else more deserving of sympathy and support, so people thought there was only so much grief that I could claim, and maybe that's what people think: wife gets X percent of grief, mother so much, friend so much, neighbour so much and no more, and taking more than your fair share is being a drama queen and means you need slapping down. His mother and father wouldn't even look at me at the service let alone speak to me, as if it were somehow my fault that he died. Maybe it was in some obscure way."

"Now that really is being silly," David said. "How on earth could it ever be your fault, whether it was accident or suicide?"

She shrugged.

"I got used to everything being my fault and it's hard to let go," she said. "When my Dad's business started to go under, I thought that was my fault. They'd sent me to a private primary school but things had got a lot tighter so that was how I ended up in a state secondary even though it was well before things crashed. Mum said money was a bit tight and once things were sorted they'd send me to a proper school again but it got tighter and tighter and then things crashed and we ended up at Granddad's and I heard them arguing and there was mention of extravagances like private schools and I thought it was because of my school fees that we lost our home and everything. I know it isn't true but that was what I thought because I knew how much the fees had been and that seemed like an enormous amount of money to me. I didn't know that it wasn't really much more than petty cash to a big company. So I ended up thinking they'd spent all their money on my primary school and that it was all my fault. I told Granddad about it and he set me straight but even so, even now I end up feeling as if things that aren't my fault, couldn't ever be my fault, are my fault."

David couldn't speak for a few moments; he was so horrified by what she said he could scarcely breathe. When he did speak, he said very carefully,

"Whatever went on back then, I can tell you that Nick's death could never have been your fault, whether he fell off the boat or whether he drowned himself."

"I know that," she said. "But that isn't what I *feel*. I feel that somehow I might have done more to have stopped the trip going ahead, or somehow written just the right things in my letters or helped him learn to be stronger and tougher. I don't know."

"I should have thought if anyone was to blame for his death, it'd be the people with the boat," David said. "Surely he should have been wearing a life-jacket, even at night. It should have been drummed into all the kids on that boat that out on deck meant wearing a life jacket. Surely there must have been an enquiry of some sort?"

She shrugged.

"I think there was one but no one told me anything about it," she said. "It was months and months after his death and Mr and Mrs Braithwaite didn't have anything to do with me by then."

"If you could find out that it really wasn't anything to do with you, maybe you'd feel a bit better about it," he suggested. "And then maybe you can finish your grieving properly and then this might stop. I can't bear the thought of you wandering around in a daze, at the mercy of anyone who finds you. You've checked your bag, I assume, to make sure there's nothing missing."

"Yes," she said. "Everything is there that should be there. I think I'm only partially acting things out. If I'd really been wandering around your school someone would have stopped me. They insist on things like signing in and out and wearing visitor's badges, and I think someone would have mentioned it if I really had been in. I think on that occasion I was standing outside with my bike for a while and that's all. This time, I obviously did go into town but I don't think I used a cash point, or phoned the bank."

"Even so, I don't like it at all," he said. "Anything might have happened to you."

"But it didn't. Look David, I hope you aren't thinking I should stay at home till this is all over. It's happened here often enough; you can't lock me in and you can't be with me the whole time."

"But we have to find some sort of resolution to this," he said.

"I know," she replied wearily. "Do you think I don't know that? I know you've been worried sick tonight but for me this has been on my mind for months now and I'm still no closer to understanding it or to stopping it than I was in September. I want it to stop. I love you, and I love Rosie and I hate the way this other life is intruding itself and I don't know how to stop it, and if you say I need a doctor I shall probably scream!"

"I don't think you need a doctor," he said hastily and with only partial regard to the truth. "But you do need some peace. I think that if you have a chance to talk about the past with someone who remembers it, maybe that will help give you some peace. Knowing Nick's death wasn't your fault might help."

"But there's only Carla who remembers him," she said miserably. "And she doesn't think much of him and she thinks he killed himself. Their mum almost certainly wouldn't talk to me; she wouldn't then and I doubt she would now. And I certainly don't want to talk to Juliet about Nick!"

Despite himself, David laughed and the sound seemed to relax both of them.

"There must be other people," he said. "Other family, other friends?"

"There was an aunt," she said thoughtfully. "His father's sister I think she was. She and Nick were close. That statuette that Carla gave me, well, that was what she sent Nick that Christmas after he'd died. She was abroad and no one could find her to tell her he was dead. I don't even know if she's still alive but I bet she'd want to talk about Nick."

"You didn't tell me about that," David said, half in reproach.

"I thought it was too complicated," she said. "I didn't want to get into the whole thing of who it had been sent to and so on."

"Fair enough," he said. "I wish you had been able to talk about it, though. Why don't you get in touch with Carla and ask her for this aunt's address. Tell her you want to ask her where she found it, if she knows anything about it; you don't need to tell Carla you want to ask about Nick if you don't want to."

Verity nodded.

"I will," she said. "But the funny thing is that I have a sort of hunch that the reason Carla got back in touch with me properly instead of the nice comfortable card at Christmas is that she wants to talk about Nick too and can't bring herself to say it. Or maybe she thinks I'll get upset about it. I don't know; I never did in front of her even when we did talk so I don't know why... Why do things have to be so complicated?"

David managed a tired smile.

"Life *is* complicated," he said. "You should try looking at things down a microscope! Even the simplest of things like pond water that looks completely empty and yet is full of millions of squiggly things that dart all over the place. The closer you look at anything, the more complex it becomes."

The little triangle of sky visible through the gap where the curtains didn't quite meet had lightened now to a dark blue tinged with the orange of street-lights and David yawned suddenly.

"God," he said. "How many years is it since we last saw the dawn come in?"

"I think Rose was about three or four and she had chicken pox and had kept us up most of the night. Well, me anyway. That's the last time I remember being still up at dawn. Before that, plenty of times when she was a baby. But it's a very long time since we stayed up all night for fun and none of this has been fun," she said, yawning herself.

"Tell you what, we'll have to do a fun all-nighter some time soon, then, before we get too old and staid to manage it," he said.

She tried to get up, and found she was so stiff and aching it was a huge effort.

"I think I am too old already," she said apologetically but David just laughed. Even though he was still concerned, the worst of his worries had vanished and he was feeling strangely light-headed and happy.

"Let's just go to bed then," he said.

Later that day when Rose was dropped off home by her friend's mother, she was at first annoyed and then embarrassed to discover that her parents were still in bed in the middle of the afternoon, and only emerged when Rose had clattered round the kitchen with sufficient noise to wake if not the dead then some very sound sleepers.

Chapter 7

"I'm glad you called, actually," Carla said dipping a muffin into her hot chocolate and taking a big bite out of the dripping cake. "I've got a few other bits for you. I don't have much time for reading myself and when I do, I'm afraid I prefer a nice entertaining bonkbuster novel. Not very intellectual I know but I always left the intellectual stuff to Nick. And I can't see Mum ever wanting to read poetry but it seemed rather a shame to just give them all to Oxfam so I wondered if you'd like them. I expect you might have copies of some of them yourself but…"

She nudged the carrier bag with her foot towards Verity and obediently, Verity peered in.

"I'd have to check but I don't think I have any T.S. Eliot at home," she said. "I used a library copy when we did The Wasteland in my final year. Thank you."

She didn't retrieve any of the books from the bag as Carla had hoped, and flip open the flyleaf and read Nick's handwriting sprawling wildly in gold or silver ink; his own name and the date he acquired it. She didn't need to. She knew what was written on each book; one she knew she'd given him for his eighteenth birthday and it was inscribed in her own rather mundane handwriting.

There was a dusty smell rising from the bag, with a hint of mildew as if the books had been allowed to get very slightly damp over the years, so she folded the handles down and sealed away the smell of years and leaned over her coffee cup and inhaled that instead. It was better than Carla's perfume, which was giving her the start of a headache.

"I wanted to ask you if your aunt is still alive," Verity asked. "You know, the one who sent that statuette. I wondered if she knew anything more about it, since I don't have Granddad any more to ask."

"Barmy Aunt Charlotte? Oh yes, I still get a card every Christmas and usually some Marks and Spencer's vouchers which are always good for buying some new towels or what not," Carla said idly. "I'll have a peep in my little black book."

She rummaged in the handbag that Verity guessed probably cost a lot more than she herself earned in a week and pulled out her address book.

"I'll scribble it down for you," she said and scrawled it on the back of her own business card and passed it across the table to Verity. "She's a bit of a bore so I haven't seen her for years and years, not since Dad died I think. Nick was always her favourite; I never thought she liked me much even. I'm sure she'll have some fascinating tales to tell about how she came by that statue." She gave an elaborate stage yawn and winked but Verity didn't smile and Carla's face fell into a blank expression that was her default expression that rested the muscles of her face and stopped her stretching the skin over much.

"So are you all right then?" she asked, as if uneasy with Verity's refusal to conspire about how boring her aunt was.

"Mostly very tired," Verity said. "I had a really bad bout of the flu and I'm still not quite back to par yet."

"Oh right!" Carla said brightly, relieved that it was obviously down to illness and nothing more sinister that her friend wasn't laughing at her jokes. "So Juliet's let you out early then today?"

"I usually finish at three anyway," Verity said. "She's got another girl working the other hours for her so I slipped out a few minutes early because Martine was there anyway and Juliet wasn't around."

It hadn't been easy to slip away quietly since Martine was hard to escape from at the best of times and in the end it had only been ten minutes early instead of the half hour she'd hoped for. As a result, she arrived at the Starbucks at the same time as Carla rather than before as she had hoped. But she had managed to order her own coffee and avoid any of the sugary offerings by way of muffins and cakes so at least she wouldn't go home feeling sickened both by what she had eaten and by her own lack of confidence in not asserting her own wishes. Carla clearly considered Starbucks to be far too down market for her and was quite happy to hide in a corner with Verity where she was unlikely to be spotted by anyone who might recognise her.

"I wanted to ask you something too," Verity said and felt her stomach lurch with nerves. "I'm not sure you're going to like this though."

Oh God, she wants me to open the school fête or something, Carla thought, and was about to tell her to ring her agent first when Verity continued,

"What I need to know is why on earth you think Nick killed himself when he'd survived a lot worse simply living with your Dad. I know your Dad hit him sometimes and he was forever belittling him and berating him and making life pretty miserable for all of you. So what was so bad about that trip that makes you think he drowned himself?"

Carla stared at her, too shocked to speak for a moment, and tried to think of an easy cheap answer when all she wanted to do was to deny how tough life with their father had actually been.

"That call, that was all. Nick begging to be allowed home, that's why," she said finally. "He was missing you, I think, as well. He just didn't have the guts to keep going; he was a wimp."

"I don't buy that," Verity said. "I just don't buy that at all. He stuck it out with your dad and he only had a few months to get through, and then he'd be home again; he only had to get through university and then he could be free of your Dad altogether. So why, after years of that, with the end in sight, do you think he'd kill himself? It doesn't make any sense at all to me."

Carla was frantic inside but her face was still a slightly smiling blank like a mask. She was furious with Verity but then if she said what she wanted to, things might get very nasty indeed; she wasn't sure she wanted that, not yet anyway.

"No," she said. "It doesn't make any sense at all. It must have been an accident after all."

There was something so bland and calm about her answer that made Verity suspicious and she gave Carla a hard stare.

"I think you're lying," she said quietly and Carla goggled at her in surprise. This was so unlike the usual Verity for whom assertiveness was an almost impossible concept.

"I think you have a theory or something and you don't want to tell me," she went on and Carla was almost speechless with surprise.

"I am not lying!" Carla said, her voice rising in both pitch and volume. "How dare you suggest that? He died by accident and that's all. I was wrong to think otherwise."

"It must be bad if you'd rather admit you were wrong," Verity said and then Carla felt her fury spilling over like badly poured champagne.

"I didn't want to tell you because you'd be hurt," she said. "But since you'd rather think me a liar I shall tell you anyway and have done and if you don't like it you've only yourself to blame for forcing me. I think that on that boat with only guys for company he realised what I'd guessed about him ages back. He was gay. Happy now?"

"Gay?" said Verity. "You've got to be joking. I'd know!"

Carla laughed a rather brash and forced laugh.

"I don't think so," she said. "You never twigged about Di the Dyke after all, did you?"

"Nor did you," Verity countered. "You hung around with her for ages."

"Do you think I didn't know? Christ but you're naïve, Vee," Carla said bitterly. "Sometimes it's good to have an acolyte who'll do anything for you. Di fitted that bill at least until she started getting too pushy and then I had to give her the shove, good and hard. OK, you say he wasn't gay, I say he was. I'm his sister; I should know him better than anyone."

"I was his girlfriend," Verity said quietly. "Doesn't that count for something?"

Carla looked at her with an unconcealed sneer that made Verity recoil inwardly.

"Not a lot, no," she said. "I'd bet good money you never slept with him! Well, did you?"

Verity's pale skin shot through with a mottled blush.

"No," she said. "I didn't. But back then, it wasn't such a foregone conclusion as it seems to be now. We were very young, after all."

"I rest my case," Carla said smugly, folding her arms. "What normal healthy boy of eighteen isn't going to be gagging for it? And your Granddad wasn't exactly a good chaperone, was he? He'd have let Nick stay over if you'd asked."

Verity's mind seemed to be drowning with both the venom and the content of Carla's argument but she rallied and stayed impassive and calm.

144

"He trusted us," she said. "Nick and I agreed we weren't in a hurry. He wanted to let me have time. It isn't that he didn't want to."

"Rubbish," Carla said harshly. "Of all the girls that chased him at that school, he picked the one who was too timid and staid and prudish to want to experiment. You don't think that was an accident, do you? Get real, he picked you as his alibi to get Dad off his back about being queer and keep all those girls at bay. You don't really think he was in love with you, do you? Like I said, you're so naïve, it's ridiculous!"

Verity wanted to hit her but she merely sipped her coffee and said nothing for a moment.

"Then why did he ask me to marry him?" she asked.

"Camouflage," Carla said. "Being married is always the best camouflage. Oh, don't get me wrong: Nick liked you well enough. He'd probably have enjoyed being with you; he could have his own private audience the whole time, adoring him. He liked that. Of course when Dad died he'd have been able to come out; and the rest of the world has changed since we were teenagers anyway. Being gay is virtually obligatory in some professions now. But back then we didn't know that, or even guess how the world would change. He'd have been on this boat unable to get away from all these nice male bodies surrounding him day and night and he'd not have been able to ignore it any longer. He might even have fallen in love; he was a sucker for that after all, a real soft romantic sort, all hearts and flowers. Silly sod!"

Verity could feel her chest tighten and begin to hurt as she tried to get her breath.

"Why are you doing this, Carla?" she said, but her calm voice had developed a tremble.

"Doing what? Setting you straight, pardon the pun, on what my brother was really like?" Carla said. "I think it's called doing you a favour."

"Why? What harm would it have been to let me go on thinking of him as he was? Why do you need to trash the past like this? I haven't done you any harm. I thought we were friends," Verity said.

"I just wanted you to have some of the things Mum and I found, nothing more. It's you that's been dragging stuff up," Carla said.

"No," said Verity. "Do you think I'm stupid? Your Mum moved before Christmas; I've seen the size of those sheltered bungalows. There's no way she's been storing any extra stuff after the move and certainly not a big bag of books. You've had all the things you've given me all this time and you've been eking out passing them on and I'd like to know why."

"I didn't bring it all in case you were upset by it," Carla said, taken aback.

"Why would I be upset? It's a long time ago. The only way I'd get upset is if you went out of your way to upset me, first by telling me you thought he'd killed himself and now by telling me you think he was gay. What did you think would happen? That I'd start pining for my lost love?"

"I just thought maybe you should know about the truth of the past," Carla said uncomfortably.

"Why? What difference does it make to you whether I know the truth or not?" Verity said, her voice rising angrily. "Were you hoping it'd make me cry? I put it behind me, years back, before I got together with David and I haven't thought about it in years."

"Ah yes, nice safe boring David," Carla said. "Trust you to pick someone like that; safe and staid. Never takes a risk, never makes a mistake. God, I'd die of boredom."

"Then it's a good job it's me who's married to him," Verity said fiercely. "Out of interest, what's your longest relationship to date? Three years, isn't it?"

It was a low blow, but Verity was feeling savage with fury and wasn't about to just roll over and die for Carla. No more Mrs. Nice Guy, Verity thought and then saw the look on Carla's face.

"I don't know why you think you're so superior," Carla said. "Staying married is easy when you've got about as much adventure in your soul as a bloody potato. I mean, what have you ever done with your life anyway? You're the wrong side of thirty, and all you've done is marry at twenty-one, have a baby and work in a dead end job. What sort of a life is that? In a hundred years' time, who's going to remember you?"

Verity shuddered inwardly.

"Then tell me how many will remember you?" she said coldly. "An also-ran model, who never managed to be super, a whole host of lovers ready to kiss and tell if there was anything worth telling, and an actress whose career depends on fading looks and who she sleeps with. Is that anything to be proud of?"

The words were out before she had a chance to stop them and her mouth continued speaking regardless of her mind that was shrieking to her to shut up, shut up, shut up.

"And as for me being on the wrong side of thirty, we are the same age," she said. "Even if you do lie about it, it's the truth and the truth will out. At least I did my degree, at least I do what I need to do every day and don't ask others to clean up after me and pander to my insecurities constantly. At least I have a husband and a child and I don't lead a life of consummate shallowness. Fine, I may not have done anything in my life to get in the history books yet but I'm still on the right side of forty and for people like me, things just get better. I've got half my life still ahead of me; the best of yours is already over. If the shelf life of a model-turned actress is limited, then mine isn't. I can still do anything, anything at all; I still have my talents and advantages to turn to."

"What talents, what advantages?" Carla sneered. "You're just a fat suburban housewife with a dull husband and a few pretensions to intellectualism because your grandfather was an archaeologist."

Verity just grinned suddenly, which scared the life out of Carla who was still expecting tears or a tantrum.

"Wrong!" she said with some triumph. "I'm a woman with a first class honours degree and something else so few people have: Time, lots of time. Oh, and as for being fat, I think these jeans are maybe only a size bigger than yours. I might not be a stick insect but I don't think I count as fat these days, but frankly even if I was twenty stone it wouldn't matter. That's only the outside. But then that's all that's ever counted with you, isn't it, with your Prada handbags and Gucci shoes? Take them away and what are you?"

She stopped. There were tears streaking down Carla's face, and she looked as if she were likely to throw something at Verity.

"You were always jealous of me," Carla said.

"Jealous? Why would I be jealous of you?" Verity asked. "I've always felt sorry for you."

147

"Sorry for me? You patronising bitch! I've got everything you haven't: looks, fame, money, excitement, travel, lovers. How dare you feel sorry for me!"

"You assume that I'd want those things? Why? Because you have them? Get real! There's a lot more to life than any of those things, Carla."

Carla was busy gathering up her bag and coat, and she kicked at the bag of books.

"You can keep those," she said. "I would have just binned them as the load of old rubbish they are but I thought, maybe a bit more rubbish would suit Verity. She can con herself that she owns something worth having if she crams that horrible old house with more filthy old books. So there you go, my parting gift. Have a nice life, Vee!"

She marched out of the room with what should have been a dramatic stride except she stumbled at the door and nearly fell.

Verity watched her go and then felt the eyes of the people at the table next to her. She glanced across at the small group of women, ladies who lunch maybe, who were watching her surreptitiously and with barely concealed excitement.

"I think that's me off her Christmas card list, then," she said brightly to them and drank the rest of her coffee and left too.

By the time she got home, Verity was feeling very odd. She would have expected to be tearful, upset and shaking at the very least. Instead she felt as though she'd just won the lottery: ridiculously, absurdly happy, fizzy inside with exuberance and relief. Rose was upstairs, music blasting out of her room and didn't come down or call, so she rummaged to find the card Carla had given her and stared at the name and address that trailed across the surface like the tracks of a drunken spider. The phone number was only just legible. She tapped the card on her teeth as she considered what to do now.

If Charlotte Braithwaite was anything like Carla then calling her was probably pointless, but Carla had said that she reckoned Nick was Charlotte's favourite and she knew from her own memories that they had been close. If there was a chance of clearing this up and stopping these horrible visions by speaking to her then she was going to take it right now. She also knew that if she stopped and thought about all the things Carla had said, she wouldn't be able to do it at all and her burst of happiness would vanish like a soap bubble popping.

Her hands shaking, she dialled the number and waited. After four rings it was answered.

"Hello?" she said, nervously. "May I speak to Charlotte Braithwaite please?"

"Speaking," said a brisk female voice. "If you're trying to sell me something you might as well hang up right now though. I'm immune to sales talk of any kind."

"No, no, not at all," Verity said. "You probably won't remember me, but then I don't think we ever met. I was a friend of your nephew Nick."

There was a silence that seemed to go on for an age though in reality it was probably only a few seconds long.

"Well," said Charlotte after what sounded like a sharp but slow intake of breath. "That's a name I haven't heard in a long time. What can I do for you, oh nameless friend of my nephew Nick?"

Verity had a sense of being gently mocked. "Sorry," she said. "My name is Verity. It was Verity Fairfax but now it's Verity Meadows. I'm sorry if I have disturbed you like this and if it this isn't a convenient time then I shall ring another time-"

"It's perfectly convenient," said Charlotte. "Speak on. What can I do for you?"

Verity swallowed hard to clear the lump she felt rise to her throat, blocking her speech.

"A while ago, Carla passed something on to me that you sent to Nick the Christmas after he died. She said she and her mother had found it when they were clearing the house for her mother to go into a sheltered bungalow," she explained. "Carla didn't know then that my grandfather who was a bit of an expert on these things was dead and wouldn't be around to tell me what it was and where it had come from and how old it was. She didn't know anything about the statue and nor do I and I've been wondering if you know anything more about it."

There was another long silence.

"Remind me what it was," said Charlotte. "It's a long time ago."

"It was a figurine in what I think is bronze, of a woman or maybe a goddess with her arms raised," Verity said. "Not very big but it does seem very old though."

149

"I'd have to see it again," Charlotte said after another pause. "A lot of such artefacts passed through my hands; I can't recall the exact item I'm afraid. It's been a lot of years since then, a lot of figurines and such like."

"Oh," said Verity, horribly disappointed. "If I sent it to you, perhaps you could...."

"I think we can do better than that," said Charlotte. "Why don't you bring it to show me some time? That way you don't have to trust it to the vagaries of the postal system. I think it would be a terrible shame for it to end up lost in the post after all the miles it's probably travelled in its time. Why not come and visit me this Saturday, say?"

This was better than anything she could have hoped for; even a three-hour drive was worth what she might find out.

"That would be wonderful. Thank you, it's very kind of you," she said.

"Kind? Not at all!" said Charlotte. "I gather you have my address and not just my number?"

"Carla gave me it today," Verity explained.

"And how is my niece?" Charlotte asked, after another of the tiny pauses.

"Probably never going to speak to me again," Verity said. "We had a bit of a row. I'm not expecting her to call me again, let's just put it like that."

"Sounds like Carla," Charlotte said. "She was always very good at carrying on a grudge past the point of absurdity. Very well, I shall see you on Saturday some time. I shall be in all day so take your time. If you need directions, just ask."

Verity rang off and stood staring at the phone. Upstairs the music suddenly got louder as Rose opened her door.

"Mum?" she shouted. "Do you know where my trainers for PE are? I can't find them."

"Try the cupboard under the stairs," Verity called back and went to start cooking the evening meal.

"How was Carla?" David asked at dinner.

"Bloody," Verity said and both David and Rose looked at her in surprise.

150

"Mum!" Rose protested. She found it very unsettling if her mother behaved out of character and Verity seldom if ever swore or used coarse expressions at all.

"Sorry," Verity said. "But she was! I don't think I'll be getting a Christmas card this year somehow."

David was watching her with anxious eyes.

"Did you have an argument?" he asked.

"Sort of," Verity said. "Not really, I guess. Not what any sensible person would call an argument. It almost degenerated into name calling, just like in a primary school playground, which about sums the whole relationship up. I just didn't want to play her games any more; that was all. I don't know why I didn't do it sooner. I guess I was scared of losing a friend, but when it came to it, I don't think she was ever a friend at all. More a sort of a habit, actually."

"Not hard to think of Carla as something like nail biting or thumb sucking," David said and Verity grinned.

"What you mean is destructive, unattractive, but strangely hard to give up," she said. "At least I didn't have to paint anything with bitter aloes!"

"I don't understand you, Mum," Rose said, pushing her last potato round the plate with a fork. "You bust up with someone that famous and you aren't upset?"

"Fame isn't everything, love," Verity said. "Now, either eat that potato or stop tormenting it and put it out of its misery!"

Rose spiked the offending vegetable with the prongs of her fork and ate it in one bite.

"Can I go and watch telly now?" she said, sulkily.

"Go on then, I'll help Mum with the washing up," David said and Rose slipped away before he could change his mind.

While they stood at the sink, David said, thoughtfully,

"I didn't think you wanted to talk much with Rosie listening in," he said. "What happened? Have you had any new visions?"

"No, no new ones," Verity said, polishing a plate with a tea towel. "It was a pretty horrible time though. She's so used to me just rolling over and giving her what she wants, she couldn't cope with me saying anything critical."

"You didn't criticise her did you? No wonder she got stroppy!"

"Not at first, no. I did mention how horrid their Dad could be and I think that was a mistake," Verity said. "And calling her a liar was maybe not the best move either."

David started laughing.

"You'll have to tell me the whole story," he said.

Carefully Verity detailed the whole encounter from first coffee sips to Carla's would-be dramatic exit.

"She must really have been upset to trip like that," David said. "After years on the catwalk you don't trip easily. You really rattled her."

"Good," said Verity with some uncomfortable satisfaction. "She wasn't exactly nice to me either."

"No. No, she wasn't, was she? Do you think there was any truth in what she said about Nick?" David asked.

"If we hadn't rowed, I'd have said without hesitation there was no truth in it," Verity said. "But that row made me wonder how many other things I'd got wrong. If I'd got it wrong about my friendship with her, then what else might also be wrong? But I think I've always known she kept me on as a kind of fail-safe friend, someone she thought she could always rely on to massage her ego and remind her how far she's come in the days since we were at school together. A kind of benchmark if you like; at least if she can look at me and my life, it makes hers look better. From her perspective that is, not mine. She can look at my clothes and hair and so on and despise me for them. I don't want to put up with that any more. But about Nick, now I'm not sure and I don't like that."

"If he had been gay," David said and then stopped.

"If he had been gay, it does explain some things, yes," Verity filled in for him. "Anyway, I'm going to see their aunt on Saturday and maybe that'll clear some things up for me. I hate it that Carla has tried to spoil my memories of the past like this."

"Do you want me to come with you?" he asked.

"No, you stay with Rosie," she said. "I'll be fine. I'll have to swap with Martine though. I'm supposed to be working this Saturday. I don't suppose Juliet will care much. She's been very odd lately."

"Odder than usual? Can this be possible?" David said.

152

"Different. Distracted. I don't know," Verity said. "As if she's worried about something. She's been very snappy too. I suppose there's something going on but I doubt I'll ever find out."

"She's probably having man trouble," David said. "Or rather, some guy is having Juliet trouble!"

"Meow!" Verity said. "True but cruel!"

Martine was quite happy to swap with Verity but when Juliet found out, she seemed less than pleased.

"I'd prefer it if you were here this Saturday," she said. "Can't you cancel this outing?"

Verity shook her head.

"Sorry," she said. "Anyway, Martine's has said she'll cover for me. What's the problem?"

Juliet didn't bother answering but just scowled at her and went back up to her therapy rooms. When she spoke to Martine later it appeared that the last Saturday she had covered, a lot of stock had vanished after a group of teenagers came in and, while one of them engaged Martine in a complicated conversation about rose quartz, the others had all but emptied the jewellery case that Martine had failed to lock. Saturday was the busiest day of the week and it seemed that Juliet preferred Verity's eagle eyes watching the shop.

"I was so sure I'd locked that case," Martine said, sadly. "And the girl seemed so genuine too. Juliet was so cross with me since I didn't even notice till we were shutting up later. Anyway, where are you off to on Saturday?"

"Family outing," Verity said, astounded by her own ability to lie so easily.

"Nice," said Martine. "Will's been talking about us starting a family but I'm not so sure. I'm still so young. Maybe I'm too young for such a responsibility."

Verity said nothing; explaining that when she was twenty five she had a child of three was only going to provoke more comments about how women had had babies much younger in the dim and distant past. In her current mood, she might actually say something decidedly cutting and since Martine was doing her favour doing this Saturday it did seem unfair to have a go at her.

It seemed to take ages to get to Saturday and when she packed an overnight bag just in case, it all suddenly seemed far more real than it had done. She wrapped the statue up in a silk scarf and put the letter in next to it and zipped the bag up.

"Are you sure you want to do this?" David said.

He'd been watching her face as she packed. She nodded.

"I think so," she said. "It might just be a waste of petrol and a day I'd otherwise have spent in the shop but I think I need to do it. Other than me and Carla, she's the one who knew Nick best; she knew him all his life but at least she'll have an adult perspective on it that neither Carla nor I can have. I only ever knew him as a teenager myself and Carla's judgement is also coloured. So if I can get any sense of what he was truly like from his aunt, it might help. I don't know. But I feel I need to do this."

"Do you think it'll stop the visions?"

"I don't know," she said. "But I can't not do it now. Now Carla has raised these questions, I need to answer them if I can."

Verity didn't much enjoy driving but it was a lovely day, that Saturday, full of bright skies and sunshine, and she felt her spirits rise slowly the further she drove. Charlotte lived close to the south coast and when she finally found the right house after several wrong turns and dead ends, Verity stood by the car breathing the salt tang of the air and hearing the cry of gulls and felt suddenly sad again as she shifted the figurine to her handbag. She guessed the garden was probably glorious in full summer but today the scent of wallflowers filled the warming air, and the opening buds of shrubs and the fading daffodils showed both future beauty and past glories. There had been rain in the night spoiling the tulips, bending the pliant stems so that the flowers now leaned drunkenly, spilling rainwater and petals onto the path. Over the front door there were small wind chimes, made by wiring together pieces of sea glass and shells and hanging them from bits of weathered driftwood. As she paused at the door, a sighing breeze shook the chimes, making a strange sound almost like bones knocking together, an oddly dull sound without resonance but pleasantly soft after the chimes at the shop with their metallic brash clanging and tinkling. She knocked hesitantly.

It was strange but when the door opened, Verity not only recognised Charlotte immediately, though she was pretty sure

154

they had never met, but also had the sense of her being so very familiar. She had the same long slender bones as her niece and nephew, the same eyes, though a little faded from the rich chocolate colour, and her hair had once been the same shade of dark brown but now was mostly grey, twirling in corkscrew curls much as Nick's had done whenever it was allowed to grow longer. She wore an old denim shirt and jeans so disreputable that Verity immediately felt comfortable in her own.

"I'd shake hands but mine are covered in potting compost," Charlotte said. "I was pricking out seedlings at the back. Come in and I shall get clean and then we can shake hands if you like!"

Verity followed her into a hallway filled with pots of flowering bulbs; the air was heavy and sweet with the fragrance of hyacinths.

"You don't mind kitchens, do you?" Charlotte said and led her through to a neat bare kitchen with a scarred old deal table in the middle of the room, and began scrubbing her hands at the sink.

"I've travelled most of the world but these days it's so good to live all year in one spot and see it change every day," Charlotte said, vigorously attacking her nails with a nail-brush. "You never think when you're young that being still could be so satisfying, nor that waiting and watching for seeds and bulbs to come up or for fruit to ripen or leaves to fall could be so fulfilling."

She half turned and gave Verity a smile of such sweetness that it brought tears to her eyes. She seemed so like and yet unlike Nick all at once that it made Verity's head whirl uncomfortably with a whole range of thoughts that she thought she'd never think about again.

"There," said Charlotte shaking her hands to dry them. "Now some tea or some coffee I think. Did you find me easily enough?"

"A few wrong turns but nothing much," Verity said, watching her move around the room about her task.

"It's a nice day at least," Charlotte said. "A bit too cool to sit out in the garden which is what I'd hoped to do, but that breeze still has teeth. What can I get for you? Tea, coffee? It's a bit early for a proper drink and as you're driving…"

"Coffee," said Verity hastily. "That'd be lovely."

Charlotte made a pot of coffee and brought Verity through into the living room. It seemed strangely bare, devoid of the kind of artefact Verity had half expected to litter the place after a lifetime of buying and dealing with such things, but even the furniture seemed new and scarcely used. There were few pictures on the walls and none of the usual row of family photos. The view from the patio doors at the end of the room led the eye down the richly planted garden; Verity imagined it in summer, vivid with flowering shrubs and lush with greenery.

"I originally had a flat in London," Charlotte explained. "But when I retired, I bought this. I wanted to be away from traffic and the frantic pace of life, and have a bit of earth to call my own and to cherish. Funny after all the years on the move how good it felt to be still."

"You must have travelled all over the world," Verity said.

"Most of the interesting places, yes," Charlotte agreed. "Most of which aren't on any tourist map I hasten to add! Do you have the statue?"

Verity drew the figurine out of her handbag and stood it gently on the coffee table next to the tray. Charlotte gazed at it for a moment, her eyes seeming to mist over a little, before taking it in her hands and running them over it slowly, like a woman reacquainting herself with her lover's skin after a long absence.

"Yes," she said after a long silence. "I thought I remembered it. I didn't know much about it when I found it, and that hasn't changed. I bought it from the private collection of a gentleman in Cairo but it almost certainly isn't Egyptian; I am almost sure it's far older. He was in the process of selling as much as he could to realise some money so he could slip out of the country, so he wasn't haggling. He was in a real hurry if you know what I mean, so this cost me virtually nothing. I hung onto it till I got a chance to post it to Nick. I think I might have been the other side of the world by then though. As for my Egyptian gentleman, I don't think he even knew what it was or where it came from. If you really need to know, I'd suggest you write to the British museum and ask them. But be aware my gentleman in Cairo probably didn't come by it in any legal or even ethical way and it may open a can of worms about ownership."

"Oh," said Verity, disappointed. She'd just have to drink her coffee politely and then leave. She felt her spirits sag.

"I bought it for Nick because he'd written to me not long before he set off on that trip," Charlotte said. "He told me about you, you see. He described you as his muse, his goddess, so when I saw this, I thought, how perfect! It was a shame he never saw it; he'd have loved it. But how did it come to you so late? I would have thought that Joyce would have passed it to you straight away, all those years ago. She must have read the letter."

"I think she must have done," Verity said. "But after Nick died, his parents didn't really speak to me again. I'm not sure I'd have found out about his death so quickly if Carla hadn't come over and told me."

Charlotte's eyes widened in surprise.

"Why? I cannot understand that at all! I was under the impression my brother and his wife approved of you being with Nick," she said.

Verity shook her head.

"I don't know why," she said. "But at the memorial service they hardly spoke to me and after it, I don't think they ever spoke to me again. I kept in touch with Carla simply because we had another year at school together after Nick's death and we sort of clung together. She gave this to me after she'd helped her mother move to a sheltered bungalow. She said they'd found it when they were going through all the stuff her mother had kept hoarded away. I know Carla read the letter so I assume your sister-in-law had done too."

"Then I would have assumed that since you had been likely to become their daughter-in-law that they would have at least been friendly to you and supportive," Charlotte said thoughtfully. "I know Jack wasn't an approachable sort of father at all; I know he and Nick were always arguing. But even with that I would have thought Jack would have behaved better than that to you."

"I did see them afterwards," Verity said. "You know, in the street or the supermarket. But they ignored me. I guess it's still too painful, remembering Nick I mean."

"You're very forgiving," Charlotte said dryly. "I had a huge row with my brother when I finally got back to England and found out what had happened; we barely spoke after that. We were still not reconciled at Jack's death five years ago. I always felt that they could have made greater efforts to find me; the company I worked for knew where I was and it wouldn't have been hard to find me like that. I can assure you it wasn't easy coming back to England after almost six months abroad to find my nephew dead and no one had thought to tell me. The inquiry was done and dusted by then; even the memorial service was long past."

"You didn't miss much," Verity said. "It was a horrible service. I kept thinking they were talking about someone else entirely, not Nick at all. I kept thinking he'd have found it very funny. It was so very unreal, like something on the television, you know, staged. But then, I couldn't take in the idea that he was dead."

"Not could I," Charlotte said. "I wanted to collect all his poems, his writings together and maybe publish them, privately obviously. These days you virtually have to sell your soul to the devil to get poetry into print professionally so there was no thought of that. And I found that my brother had burned Nick's poetry book and his journal in a fit of ...well, I don't know what. Guilt perhaps, rage, I don't know, but not true grief I am sure of that. Grief can be destructive, but not like that. It devastated me all over again when I discovered what he'd done; all I had was the newest journal."

"You have that?" Verity said so shocked she almost spilled her coffee. "But he took that on the boat with him."

"And he posted it to me the first chance he got," Charlotte said. "He said in his letter that the lads he was sharing his cabin with kept trying to read it; they were always going through his stuff and he was getting very upset about the thought of them reading what he was writing. He wanted to be sure it was safe so he sent it to me asking me not to read it but just keep it safe till he got home. Of course, it was among the post I found when I got back, including a rather horrible little note from my brother telling me to get in touch as soon as I got home. When I did just that, of course that was when I got the news about Nick. I could hardly take it in."

"I see him," Verity said, unable to stop herself. "Now, I mean. I keep seeing him. Not as he was then but as he would be now."

Charlotte nodded slowly.

"For some years after he died, I kept thinking I'd seen him in the street somewhere or other often somewhere utterly improbable like Marrakesh," she said.

158

"No, I mean recently," Verity said. "Not when he died. Just the last eight or nine months I think. Since September at least."

"That's very odd," Charlotte said.

Verity could feel the blood rushing to her face, making it turn a deep pinkish red.

"I know," she said. "It's made me wonder if whether, maybe, perhaps he didn't die at all?"

Charlotte didn't seem surprised.

"One would wonder that," she said. "But the boat was anchored nearly a mile off shore when he drowned. I don't think Nick was a strong enough swimmer to have covered that distance, even without the various hazards like sharks and undertows and strong currents. Leaving aside what he would have done then, why would he do that? And why would he return to where he lived as a boy, so many years later? Not to mention why would he want us all to think he was dead?"

The questions were all phrased quite gently but Verity could feel her eyes filling up with tears.

"I don't know," she said. "Maybe he lost his memory. Maybe it wasn't deliberate at all, maybe it was an accident."

"It was an accident," Charlotte said. "Falling overboard, I mean. Look, what you are talking about is something from the realms of fiction. People rarely fake their own deaths and never without good reasons. Don't cry, darling, please don't cry."

The tears were dripping slowly down Verity's face and Charlotte passed her a box of tissues.

"Nick's death was a horrible accident," Charlotte said. "I came back too late to ask any useful questions but I am certain he is dead. How could he not be? How could he not have come back for you, at the very least? He did love you so much, you know. I can understand him wanting to punish his father. Jack was vile to him and to Carla when they were growing up, but there was no reason for him to have done that to you."

"Carla thinks he killed himself," Verity said thickly, her voice muffled by the wad of tissues she was pressing to her eyes and nose.

"Why on earth would he do that?" Charlotte said quietly. "Nick loved life. I cannot imagine a single reason why he would do something as terrible as that."

"Carla thinks he was secretly gay," Verity said and blew her nose loudly.

Charlotte sighed wearily.

"Bloody Carla!" she said ruefully. "Always the drama queen. Is that what you and she argued about?"

"That and other things," Verity said. "It was like opening Pandora's box. You don't think he was?"

Charlotte laughed.

"No, I don't," she said. "Jack was always going on about it; it was the ultimate nightmare for a macho man like him, to have a gay son. He was terrified Nick would turn out gay. That was one of the reasons he and I fell out after Nick's death. He blamed me, you see."

"Why on earth would he blame you?" Verity asked.

"It's complicated," Charlotte said. "This coffee has gone cold. Shall I make some more?"

Verity went to use the bathroom while Charlotte made fresh coffee; when she saw her puffy red eyes and swollen nose, she was glad she hadn't bothered with any make-up today. If she had put on her usual work make-up she'd look like a rabid panda by now. She splashed her face with cold water and returned to the living room.

"To understand why Jack blamed me, you have to go back to our childhood," Charlotte said. "If you think Jack was a horrible father, you should have seen ours! I know Jack hit the children, Nick in particular, but as far as I know he didn't use a stick. My father did. That's maybe why Jack got so anxious about what he perceived as masculine in a person. He saw gentleness and softness in a man as a sign of both weakness and effeminacy. He wanted Nick to be tough, a real man. And Nick didn't want to do any of the things his father wanted him to do. From about the age of eleven it got tricky. And I was seldom welcome in the house. When the children were little, I spent a lot of time with them. I read to them a lot: lots of Arthurian tales and epic poetry you know, The Idylls of the King that sort of thing, knights in shining armour, maidens in distress and dragons and treasure and so on. They both loved it but Nick took it in very deep. I didn't realise how deep it went for a long time. He seemed to breathe the whole chivalry thing. By the time Nick was about ten or eleven it was a part of him and Jack began to hate it. It was all fantasy to him without a shred of relevance to him or to what he saw as the real world. He began to blame me for making his son a softy; so I came at Christmas and seldom at any other times. But Nick and I wrote to each other from time to time and that was how we kept in touch. Very occasionally, I would phone at a time when I knew my brother was going to be away. Joyce might not have stepped in to stop the worst of Jack's bullying but she never made things worse by telling him I'd called or I'd written. I'd be careful of what I wrote too, in case Jack decided to start opening letters. I don't know why they decided to ignore you when they should have cherished you but maybe it was down to my last letter that I sent with the statue."

"No," said Verity. "That didn't come till months later. I just don't think they wanted to think about me."

"Maybe not," Charlotte said. "Maybe Jack decided to blame you for some of his own failures, the way he tried to blame me. I remember he said to me, "You made my son gay with all your namby-pamby poems and stories." I told him not to be so silly, that Nick wasn't gay at all. He wanted to know then if he wasn't gay why had he killed himself?"

"So none of this is news to you?" Verity asked.

"No," Charlotte said. "You see: Carla was around when these rows were going on and even though she wasn't in the same room, she'd have listened at the door. Any teenager would. That's why she thinks what she does. But I am certain she and Jack are both wrong. You see: I knew Nick. I know what he was really like. Most teenage boys go through a stage where they question their sexual orientation. Even back then, while it wasn't something that was talked about, it happened. We've all come such a long way since then. Nick was a late developer in many ways; he didn't like the way girls seemed to chase him, but not because he was gay. Oh no! He saw the whole thing as somehow cheapening, demeaning even. Not because he didn't have urges, as I'm sure you're aware, but rather because he saw them as something to be controlled rather than given in to. He'd absorbed so much of the ideals of chivalry and so on that he didn't want to get sucked into the messy life most of his peers were thrashing around in. You know, who's sleeping with who, who's just

161

dumped who and why. He saw it as pointless and cheap. He was an odd lad, I'll grant you that, but he wasn't gay."

"Carla seemed adamant about it," Verity said.

"She would," Charlotte remarked. "Carla's a difficult girl in many ways. She idolised her brother and there's nothing like turning out to be just an ordinary human by doing something as ordinary and dull and human as dying for souring worship. I often used to think that there was something very unfair about the way certain qualities had been shared out between the two of them. Nick got all the talent and the soul but Carla got all the restless ambition and drive. That's why she's gone as far now as she ever will. She craves more but there's something lacking in her. I don't quite know how to explain it but one of the reasons she only got so far as a model is nothing to do with looks at all. The models who go to the absolute top have something else, something indefinable and elusive, beyond extraordinary good looks, and that something was what Nick had and Carla didn't. It'll be the same with her acting; oh, she'll have the technical ability as well as the looks but there'll always be something missing. And the worst of it is I think she knows it, deep down."

Charlotte sighed deeply.

"If Nick had lived, I have often wondered what might have become of him," she said. "In some ways, Jack was right about him being soft. He never seemed to have the drive Carla did; if something didn't come to him, he didn't chase it. He didn't fight back when people had a go at him. By eighteen most lads would have thumped their father back if he'd hit them, but not Nick. It infuriated Jack no end that he wouldn't even try to stand up to him; every time they had a row, it would end as it did when Nick was little: with Nick in tears and Jack shouting and yelling and Joyce trying to smooth it all over. I think Jack knew he'd been in the wrong sending Nick on that trip; he'd effectively blackmailed him into it. When Nick died, I think Jack was thrashing around with the guilt and he'd blame anyone rather than take his own fair share of the blame. If Nick had been another lad, he'd have defied his father, refused to go, fought back. That's what Jack could never cope with; he'd made Nick what he was with the constant bullying and abuse, so that Nick couldn't fight back. So Jack believed that Nick must have killed himself rather than face his father with unpalatable facts; I think that if he'd been right about Nick being gay, I am almost sure that's what Nick would have done. But he wasn't. You should know that."

"We never-" Verity said and blushed again.

Charlotte chuckled.

"I wouldn't have expected Nick to have done, not that early on," she said. "Like I said, he was a late developer in many ways. And since you and he had been friends for some time, it would have taken time anyway. Otherwise it feels too much like incest. You were his sister's best friend; that's pretty close. He would have taken it very, very slowly. But you haven't told me anything about your life since then. Have you ever married? I know you said your surname has changed but these days one is never sure..."

Verity nodded.

"Yes," she said. "I married very soon after I graduated. We have a teenage daughter. I've never done terribly much though, with my life. It's been very quiet. That was the other thing Carla and I rowed about, I suppose. She seems to despise me for what I've done with my life."

"Tell me about your husband," Charlotte said encouragingly and after some hesitation, Verity told her about David and about how they had met and fallen in love and their life since. She lost track of the time as she talked and Charlotte asked a few questions and then sighed.

"You've been a very lucky woman," she said. "Your David sounds like a wonderful man."

"He is," Verity said. "But Carla said he's boring and staid. But then she thinks that of me too. She was horrible about it. I wasn't exactly nice to her in return though."

"Carla is simply jealous," Charlotte said. "She's got a problem; a big problem in fact. There's never going to be a man in her life who is ever going to measure up her brother. If you like, he was her first love."

"But the way she talks about him you'd think she hates him," Verity protested.

Charlotte shook her head.

"She does," she said. "And she always has done. That's the problem. You see, when you're young you think that love and

163

hate are opposites, that they can never exist together, that one will cancel out the other. It isn't true. The opposite of both love and hate is indifference. Love and hate are almost the same thing; they are the same thing but seen from different places. You can love and hate someone in almost equal measure. Why do you think that the vast majority of murders are committed by people who are closest to the victim? It's because love and hate are mixed in almost equal proportions in most relationships. Carla loved Nick. Carla hated Nick. Simple."

"I can understand her loving him but why should she hate him too?"

"Because he was everything she was not," Charlotte said simply. "Because he was better at the things she wanted to be good at."

"But she always said she wasn't really interested in the things that he was interested in," Verity said. "When we were all together, the year before Nick and I got together, Carla used to go so far with the things we talked about, poetry and philosophy and life and then she'd just start laughing and poking fun at us."

"That's just what I mean," Charlotte said. "Was that when the topic was becoming very difficult or intellectually demanding? Yes, I thought so. She'd gone as far as she could. She wouldn't want either of you to know that she'd reached her limit so the best way of changing the subject was to ridicule it rather than let on she was struggling to keep up. You also need to remember that Carla adored her father. Undeserved, I admit but she did. She would see that Nick simply provoked their father into his rages."

"But she used to complain about him all the time, especially after he'd hit Nick," Verity said.

"That means nothing," Charlotte said. "If any outsider had said anything, she'd have defended her father to the hilt. Oh, nothing is ever simple and clear-cut with family. I think you'd have found things would have got very sticky between you and Carla if Nick had lived. She'd have resented you utterly for taking away her brother."

"She already did," Verity said. "She could be very nasty to me back then; bitchy, you know."

Charlotte nodded.

"It would have got worse," she said. "Though I would hope that it would have settled down in time. In some ways, Nick dying damaged Carla irretrievably. I see her sometimes. I've even met some of her boyfriends. The disturbing thing is that all the ones I have met had more than a passing resemblance to Nick. She's got unfinished business with him. So it's easier for her now to say he killed himself because he was afraid of coming out to his family than to say to herself my brother was more talented than I am and the world is a poorer place for his passing. It's easier to despise his memory than to look at her own emotions towards him and admit they were far from healthy."

It took Verity a few moments to fully register what Charlotte meant and when she did she found she couldn't speak. It must have shown on her face because Charlotte nodded sympathetically.

"I know, it's shocking to think of," she said. "And I'm not suggesting anything ever happened, because I think Nick would have been revolted and appalled. But Carla had a deep attachment to him that goes some way beyond the boundaries of filial affection. You must have thought it odd how close they were."

"I didn't think about it," Verity said. "I just thought they were close because they were the only constant thing in each other's life. I thought that it was because of the way their father was, how difficult it was at home."

"There is some of that, I admit. And when they were small children, I think that was the case. But they were in their mid-teens when they came to your school; did you not think it odd that they hung round together, after the initial adjustment to a new school was over?"

"No," said Verity. "I just thought it was rather sweet. I'm an only child, you see. I'd have liked a brother or a sister to have been looking out for me."

"When you started going out with Nick, how did Carla take it?" Charlotte asked.

Verity stared at her feet for a second.

"Not well," she said. "She didn't want us to have any time together alone. We'd have to try and give her the slip. She got the hint eventually but she was so nasty to us at times."

Charlotte nodded sadly.

"I thought so," she said. "I think it would have passed eventually, if Nick had lived. But Carla was left with stuff she hadn't a clue how to handle and she's still where she was all those years ago: confused."

That's me, too, Verity thought but didn't say it. It had been hard enough telling David about the visions; telling Charlotte would be far worse.

"When people die, they leave questions behind," Charlotte said. "It's often bad enough that they are dead but the unanswered questions, the unresolved issue, the things we all left unsaid can be a torment. Once I got back and discovered Nick was dead, I read that journal for clues. I wanted to be sure that there could be no truth in what Jack said. I found nothing there to suggest that either Nick was gay or that he was feeling suicidal. You can have it, if you like. I've made my peace with his shade, if you like. I wonder if you have."

It was such a strange thing to say; Verity heard the words like some distant bell, tolling far away.

"I don't know that I have," she said slowly. "Life stopped, you know, back then. Just stopped."

"Did it?" Charlotte asked thoughtfully. "But it started again. You met David. Have you ever asked yourself what would have happened if Nick hadn't died?"

What a question!

"What do you mean?" Verity asked.

"Well, if you and Nick had gone to university together, would you still have met David? Would you have fallen for him if Nick had been there too? Would you have been faced with a choice between them?"

Verity gazed at the floor.

"I don't know," she said. "Maybe I'd never have met David at all. I don't know. But Nick is dead and that's that."

"Is it?" Charlotte said. "You see, when you get to my age, sometimes you sit down and wonder what if life had gone other ways. I told you a little of my history. My father didn't believe in educating girls beyond the essentials; I stayed on at school far longer than I ever thought I'd be allowed but when it came to university, my father wouldn't even consider it. He thought it was a waste of time and money, that I would just marry and have children and never use it."

Verity swallowed hard.

"So I ran away," Charlotte continued. "I ran away and somehow managed to fund my own way through, much like the Americans do now. I got a degree, I got a brilliant job and I proved my father wrong. Or so I thought. I never married, never had children, never had a proper home. I rolled from continent to continent, buying objects d'art and minor antiquities and curios to be sold to American tourists and Brits with too much money and too little taste. I came home to a tiny, empty little flat with no one to welcome me home, no one to miss me when I went away again. When I retired, I thought about all the things I'd seen and they meant nothing. You can travel the world and still never see what's under your nose. I bought treasures for others and nothing for myself. And here I am, finally still, and what I find gives me most comfort is the pleasure of growing things, of creating beauty that is temporary and yet eternal. And what I wish now is that I'd not been so hell-bent on proving my father wrong; I had the chance to marry many times and I wouldn't take it and my lovers grew tired of waiting for me to make up my mind. All because I believed my father's lies."

"Lies?"

"Yes, lies. I doubt he knew it but what he said was totally untrue," Charlotte said. "What he said was based on a fundamental misunderstanding. Learning is something for its own sake; it enhances life the way beauty does. It doesn't have to be used, like a blade or a machine or a tool. It just is; it simply enriches the people we are. I could have done my degree, done my job and still had a husband and a family but because he insisted that the two were incompatible, I believed it blindly. I only discovered this when it was too late for children, if not a husband."

She gave a short, rueful laugh.

"Would you have liked children?" Verity asked shyly.

"I've no idea really. Perhaps I'd have been a terrible mother. I don't know," Charlotte said. "Maybe I'd have hated it; maybe the life I had was better. But I wish I'd been able to choose with all the facts before me."

Verity felt sad but Charlotte was smiling as if she was reconciled with her life as it had been and did not pine for a past that had never been.

"I'll get that journal for you," Charlotte said. "I'd rather you had it. It may help you be at peace with the past."

She opened a drawer in a nearby sideboard and passed the faded book over to Verity.

"Please keep it safe," she said. "I don't think I shall ever forgive my brother for burning Nick's writings. This is the only thing left of him, I think."

"Carla gave me a few poems she found when she and her mother were sorting the house," Verity said.

"That's something," Charlotte said. "What about you? Nick told me you wrote poems and stories. Do you still write?"

Verity shook her head.

"Other than essays at university, nothing since the week he died," she said.

"That's a shame," Charlotte said. "Nick said you were better than him."

Verity shook her head.

"I don't think so," she said. "He was brilliant."

"He said you were better," Charlotte said and Verity blushed at this praise from a lost past.

"He was just being kind," she said.

"If he'd said it only to you, maybe," Charlotte said. "But he said it to me, and he never bothered with things like false modesty. He meant it."

Verity said nothing, too shaken to reply.

"Anyway," said Charlotte. "Would you keep in touch with me? I'd like that. A rolling stone like me gathers a lot of temporary friends, but few really close ones that last. I've not got much by way of family; I see Carla once in a blue moon. I think the last time was probably at Jack's funeral. We were never as close as Nick and I were and Carla has always resented that, resented me. If you had married Nick, you'd have been my niece. I know it never happened, but perhaps we could be friends?"

"I'd like that," Verity said. "I seem to be rather short of friends too."

Charlotte smiled.

"Then that's settled," she said. "Can I offer you some lunch? You must be famished."

"I'd like that," Verity said.

Chapter 8

Verity lay down on the bed, limp with exhaustion and finally let her mind run through the thoughts she'd been holding back for hours. She'd had a late lunch with Charlotte, and then made her excuses but ten minutes after setting off home, she knew she was too tired, too confused to drive safely all the way home, and pulled over at a service station. She rang David while her coffee cooled enough to drink.

"Find a B and B for the night and come home tomorrow," he'd said.

So here she was, in the safety of a bed and breakfast bedroom, lying sprawled across the bed and trying not to go mad. It wasn't so much the volume of the thoughts as their conflicting nature. Nick was gay; Nick was straight. He'd killed himself; his death had been an accident. Nick was dead; Nick had somehow survived. Carla loved Nick; Carla hated Nick. She'd have chosen Nick; she'd have chosen David.

"Just stop it," she said aloud but her rebel mind ignored her and rattled on like a caged squirrel rampaging around the bars of its prison. Her head was beginning to hurt.

You used to have a good brain, she told herself severely, so why don't you bloody well use it? All right, I will, she replied to herself severely. Take things one at a time. First, was Nick gay?

She sent her memory back in time, something she had never done since she had met David, to the time when she and Nick had been together, to the breathless time of kisses that threatened to burn them with their power, of cautious exploration of skin, of tenderness and timidity. Carla believed him to be gay because that was what their father had feared beyond all other things but it didn't make it true and her long hidden memories were beginning to confirm it, to the point of feeling very slightly disloyal to David. These days she knew beyond doubt what passion felt like, what it looked like and how it made her feel; this simply confirmed her memories. The hours spent alone had not been spent simply talking and reading poems; a vivid picture of Nick's eyes, smoky with arousal, swam across her mind and made her shudder.

Fine, that answered that one. Great; now what about the next one?

He'd killed himself, had swum away from the boat one still clear night and had drowned himself; that was Carla's belief. But that belief had come directly from her father, who saw it as a consequence of his son being too afraid of his father to come out as gay. So if he had no reason strong enough for suicide, then his death must have been an accident. Did he have any reason for suicide, any reason at all? Carla said he was a wimp and would rather have taken the easy way out of any hard situation but had it been that hard on the boat that he might prefer to die rather than put up with it for months? It was laughable really; however tricky things had been aboard the boat they could never compare with life at home, with a father who regularly punched him, humiliated and abused him. Even with seasickness and the lack of privacy, even with homesickness and missing Verity, nothing could be as bad as what he lived with at home.

Brilliant, another one sorted. Nick died in a tragic accident, sad but not as appalling as suicide. Next please!

Carla loved Nick; Carla hated Nick.

She let her mind run over what Charlotte had said about love and hate and felt as if the conflict melted away in the heat of that wise argument. It was perfectly possible to love and hate at the same time; people are not machines that require logic alone to function but are complex beings that can hold feelings that seem diametrically opposed to each other. Love and hate are aspects of the same thing. Carla had loved Nick beyond what was acceptable for a sister to love her brother; it was shocking but not as much as Verity would have once felt. Over the years, if Nick had lived, the feelings would have faded as Carla matured and developed but she had never matured, not really, and was still caught in both the power and the shame of those feelings. So she had continued to resent Verity as the girl who took her brother away from her and had never moved past those feelings. And because these were thoughts and emotions that she would never allow to reach the light of day and be cleansed, they had festered, twisting both the love she'd had for Nick and the friendship she'd shared with Verity until they became vicious hatred she had let loose last time she and Verity met. Perhaps the unearthing of those bits and pieces in her mother's house had stirred up the mud in her soul; perhaps then with time it might settle again and some semblance of a friendship might be restored.

No. Verity knew she didn't want that, now she thought it. The wounds in Carla were too deep, too dangerous to be ignored now; there must be either healing or death for that relationship. Patching things up would be just that and no more, a plaster over a festering sore, hiding the decay but never healing it.

OK, another insoluble question solved. I am doing well, she thought, rather pleased with herself, and then she thought about that last question and she sat up abruptly and felt a tidal wave of panic rise within her. This is silly, she told herself fiercely. I never had to choose so what does it matter what I might have done?

She got up from the now crumpled bed and began to pace the small room, six steps forward, swing round, six steps back again. Just think, simply think, she thought angrily. Try to remember how it was and mix that up with how it would have been.

She sank back onto the bed, the burst of nervous energy exhausted, and let herself remember her first meeting with David. She'd been doing her laundry in the Student Union basement and the door of the washing machine had jammed. David had come in with his laundry and had helped her sort the door out. It had been a chance meeting; they had gone for some coffee while her washing was in the drier and that had been that. Ten minutes either way, they'd have missed each other; they were in different faculties, had no common societies, went to different bars, lived in different halls of residence, led utterly separate lives, in fact. But for them both choosing that morning to take their laundry to the Union, they would perhaps never have met. In another life, the chances were she'd have been with Nick, they'd have done their laundry together and she'd never have met David at all. So there might well have never been the dilemma of who to choose; and had they met, in all probability she would have not fallen for David at all. It had taken some time before she'd been able to think of him as a boyfriend and not just the good friend of myth, simply because even with Nick dead she had continued to feel a loyalty to him. If Nick had been alive, she would not have been able to let her feelings for David develop into something deeper.

She'd have avoided him, not allowed proximity to undermine her first love. That was how she was, how she'd always been, and nothing would have changed that. Even in those visions, she had continued to be loyal to Nick even though her life was far from roses with him. She could remember from the teaching vision that she had admiration for the Mr. Meadows who was only the head of department in that life, liking him and even feeling something very like awe at how he managed his classes but anything more had been so strongly repressed she had no awareness of it.

Great, another one answered; she'd never have had to choose between them because it just wouldn't, couldn't have happened like that. Only one more and you can hang up the funny coat with the arms that fasten at the back!

She knew she'd been putting this one off because it was the hardest of all, in some ways. Was Nick dead? Charlotte said yes, he was dead. She couldn't imagine how Nick could be alive and not have come back for Verity or why he might have faked his own death. And yet, she had seen him too, or thought she had seen him in exotic, improbable places years gone by. Was that simply the wistful thinking of grief or was it something more. Were her own sightings of him part of the visions or were they something else? The more she thought about it, the less like the visions those sightings seemed. Nothing else in them changed; she was always in places her real life would have her in, and those were not places that other life would have had her be in. And to add strength to that argument, she never saw him face to face.

Think!

She clutched her temples and rolled onto her stomach. Fine, let's go over this logically. There are three possibilities here. First, that it really is Nick and he somehow survived but maybe with no memory of who he was and has by some bizarre twist come back to where he lived as a teenager, or maybe simply that he didn't dare come back after all this time and confront those who thought him dead. Second, maybe this is a ghost. Third that it is another of the visions, just a little different. Oh God, this is insane! He can't have survived, and even if he did it's just too unlikely he'd ever come back, knowingly or not. It can't be a ghost because he'd be eighteen as a ghost and he's not. And if it isn't a vision, I don't know what it can be.

She groaned and sat up again. The only way of getting to the bottom of this, the hardest question, was to somehow manage to confront him next time she saw him, even if it did mean hurtling down the street yelling his name. At this rate she'd end up being locked up for something even if it wasn't insanity but breach of the peace! Even all this still didn't answer her biggest concern, about what the visions were about and how she could stop them. The thought that she might be subject to these aberrations for the rest of her life made her shudder with horror.

The journal was still tucked into her handbag, with the statuette, but she hadn't managed to open it yet and most of her was dreading doing so in case what was in it was somehow going to undermine everything she'd just carefully thought out. She'd go out for a walk, maybe find a pub for some dinner, and then and only then was she going to open that journal. Charlotte had said she'd found nothing in it to suggest suicide was an option but even so, she was in no hurry to see for herself and not just for that reason. Nick had been fiercely protective of both his journal and his poetry book, she remembered that, and it felt still like an invasion of his privacy that anyone but he should look in it. He used to hide both books so that no one in his home might sneak a look. He'd said on occasions that Carla used to try and read them but his real fear had been his father. He had locked those books in the drawer in his desk; his father must have forced the lock open to get at the contents once it became clear that Nick wasn't coming back. She wished now that she had thought to offer to look after them for him but it had never once occurred to her all those years ago to suggest it. If she had, then all his work would not have been lost.

Verity got up and ran her brush through her hair before tying it up again in the tidy knot she wore it in when she wasn't at work. She could feel her headache pounding and decided that some fresh air and a bit of a walk would clear it; failing that a proper cup of coffee might do the trick. She picked up her handbag and headed off into the late afternoon sunshine. She felt the brisk breeze pull at the strands of hair that had escaped her attention and whip them into her eyes as she walked; maybe that was what was making them water at any rate.

She walked for some time, trying to calm down, before finding a nice quiet little pub and settling in a corner with a coffee and the menu. As she put her purse back into her bag, she touched the journal and her skin began to tingle. Feeling oddly guilty, she pulled out the faded notebook and stared at it, the worn green cardboard cover showing how many times over the years Charlotte's hands had held it. It took a lot of effort to open the book and turn the first page. The flamboyant handwriting was subdued by the ballpoint pen he'd used, the ink paled by years to a shade nearer brown than black on the yellowing paper. The first entry was an untitled, unfinished poem, marred by crossings out.

My pale ghostly Viking-
No edged iron runs in your veins!
A twist of silver gilt lies across your throat,
A living torc, shining truer than the metal
Till a careless hand brushes it away,
An axe to my aching heart

She shivered; it was about her. She had often worn her hair in a single plait, and if she lay down, it would fall across her throat like a necklace. He'd joked that she looked like a Viking with her pale hair and sea coloured eyes but he'd been struck by the incongruity of it. She deplored all conflict and would capitulate with Carla rather than continue a row beyond a certain point; anyone less like a warrior she couldn't imagine.

Turning the page, she saw different ink and sensed that this was the point he'd gone on board the boat; the handwriting was erratic as if the boat were shifting enough to make writing tricky but not impossible. It wasn't dated. She began to read.

If she'd expected great literature, she would have been very disappointed. It was really just a stream of consciousness, a rambling litany of the events of days long gone. He'd tried to faithfully record his experience of life on the boat but it was a disjointed narrative, leaping from subject to subject with occasional comments about his own inability to keep track of things properly, and how much harder it was to do anything worthwhile when he felt so sick all the time. Apart from the first unfinished poem, there were no more poems, but right at the end,

174

there was a line she half recognised but could not place or identify. He'd been writing about how inadequate his own command of language was for what he wanted to be able to do, in fact how inadequate language itself could be for conveying the kind of thing he sought to communicate. The next line he had enclosed in speech marks as though he were surrounding it with a bodyguard, to keep it separate from his own words, and his writing seemed to change, becoming stronger, more upright and less inclined to wander:

"My words strain, they crack and sometimes break, because of my burden, because of my tension. They slip, slide, perish, decay and they won't stay in place, will not stay still."[1]

The words had a sense of familiarity but she couldn't place them and she found she had become chilled much as if she had been sitting in a draught for hours. She cupped her icy hands round her coffee cup and shivered. Charlotte had been right; there was nothing in this book to suggest anything untoward was going on. Nick certainly hadn't been loving his "adventure of a lifetime" but he hadn't been falling apart either. Apart from seasickness and a cold, he had been well enough for what duties he couldn't evade. He hadn't been happy but he hadn't been desperately unhappy either. He'd even commented that it made a nice change to only get yelled at for making mistakes, but how much of that was sarcasm and how much truth she was unsure.

She went to tuck the book back in her bag, and held it for a moment to her chest, feeling a surge of gratitude that it had revealed nothing that would send her into another spiral of confusion. Then she slipped it into the bag, zipped it shut and concentrated on choosing her meal.

The following week felt like the time after Twelfth Night, when all the decorations have come down, all that remains of the tree are a few dried-out needles of appalling sharpness and persistence, and the bills are due. To say it was an anticlimax was a simple understatement. She'd spent most of Sunday discussing her visit with David while trying to avoid letting Rose overhear anything but when Monday came round with its usual crush for the bathroom, the odour of toast and coffee, and the grey skies full of spring rain, she felt flat and dismal. She watched as usual as first her daughter and then her husband left the house and as the final echoes of the slamming front door vanished, she felt her heart sink. She glanced round uneasily as if she expected her grandfather to appear and her whole world shift to another life altogether.

"Bugger that," she said aloud and then giggled because she knew it wasn't something she'd have ever said in front of her daughter, and picked up her little bag of make-up that waited by the hall mirror, and took out her eye-liner and slid off the lid.

She stopped, seeing the hard black pencil and recoiling from it.

"This isn't me," she said, to her pale reflection, and dropped the eye pencil back into the bag.

When she got to work she expected to get scolded by Juliet for not putting on her make-up but Juliet largely ignored her, beyond demanding her coffee at eleven. Juliet could be moody at the best of times so she didn't take any notice of this and when Martine came in at half past two, Martine looked a little frazzled herself.

"How was Saturday?" Verity asked.

"Oh fine, fine. No shop-lifters at any rate," Martine said.

"Juliet seems a bit withdrawn, just to warn you," Verity said.

"She's been like that a lot lately," Martine said. "Poor soul. She's so sensitive to the sorrows of this world; it does affect her so much at times."

Verity shrugged without commenting; after all if Martine chose to believe Juliet's moods were down to her being affected by the events of the wider world, then it made her better able to bear the harsh words and bad moods that bit better and even feel virtuous about it. For herself, she suspected man trouble and had no illusions about Juliet being a soul of such tenderness that a famine in Africa and a war in the Middle East could darken her mood.

"I'm off in a minute," she said. "I've put the list for the wholesalers on the side of the till so Juliet can either order or she can maybe pop over there some time. We're getting very low on those big packs of joss sticks. I was pretty sure I told her about the stock levels last week but maybe she's been too busy."

"It's been pretty quiet actually," said Martine artlessly. "Quite often she hasn't had any clients after three so she shuts up shop and gives me my treatments."

Verity raised her eyebrows but said nothing and went to get her jacket.

"Right," she said as the minute hand on her watch passed three. "I'm off to Starbucks for my fix. See you tomorrow."

At the counter of the coffee shop, she deliberated over whether to have an espresso or a cappuccino, and when the assistant turned to her, she recognised him as the lad who'd wanted her number.

"Hello," he said. "You've not been in lately. The guy you thought you knew has been in a few times, by the way. I told him he keeps on missing you but he's upstairs right now if you want him. Tell you what, I'll bring you your coffee up so you can catch him."

A good loser then! How refreshing.

"Thanks," Verity said. "I'll have a nice big cappuccino, please."

She put the correct money on the counter and almost sprinted for the stairs, and though she didn't run up the stairs she found she was taking them two at a time in her determination to catch Nick before he vanished again. The upstairs coffee lounge was quite busy with shoppers refuelling before heading home and she glanced around frantically before spotting a curly head over by the window, a newspaper stretched out on the table in front of him. He was facing away from her and she felt her knees begin to tremble with such emotions she could scarcely name them as she walked quite slowly around tables before coming to stand right next to him. She could see the strands of silver shining through the curly brown hair that scraped his collar and smell the coffee he was drinking, hear his breathing even; the room seemed to have become so still, so very still.

"Nick?" she said, her voice quavering.

The head turned in some surprise; hazel eyes gazed at her quizzically.

"Sorry," said the stranger. "Wrong man."

She staggered against his chair, the floor seeming to tilt unbearably, and she dropped her bag. In some distant part of her mind, she was glad she hadn't carried her coffee up herself or she'd have dropped that too.

"Are you all right?" the man was saying, and he had got up from his chair, scattering sheets of newspaper all over both table and floor.

"This is the lady I was telling you about," said the lad from downstairs, appearing bearing Verity's coffee and blithely putting it down on the table.

The man she'd thought was Nick had steered her to the chair opposite him.

"You look like you might faint," he said.

The assistant stood as if waiting for some sort of explanation but when none was forthcoming he shrugged and headed back down the stairs.

"I'm sorry," said Verity. "I am so sorry. I really thought you were someone else."

"I gathered," said the Nick-clone. "I'm sorry too. I was intrigued when Bruce said someone thought they knew me. I thought it was maybe someone I knew years ago and lost touch with but we've never met, have we?"

"No," said Verity. "I am so sorry to have disturbed you. I'll take this somewhere else and stop being a nuisance."

"Don't do that," he said. "And stop apologising."

"I'm sorry," she said again automatically and then giggled. "Force of habit."

He grinned at her. He didn't look that much like Nick now she'd seen him properly but in height, build and colouring and especially that hair he was like enough to have passed for him in the street. His eyes were a hazel colour and his face was a different shape really but his smile was rather like Nick's and she found herself grinning back at him.

"This is very embarrassing," she said. "I kept catching glimpses of you and I was so sure you were someone else."

"Sorry I wasn't," he said. "Maybe you'll bump into him some other time."

"I don't think so," she said. "You see, I was so shocked to see you and think it was him because he's been dead for years."

"Dead? I don't think I'm quite so flattered now," he said, laughing.

"Sorry," she said. "I didn't mean-"

He waved his hand in a negating manner.

178

"I know you didn't," he said. "I understand. Anyhow, how come you should suddenly imagine you'd seen someone who should be six feet under?"

"Because his body was never found," she said. "I guess my imagination ran away with me."

"At least you've got an imagination," he said, smiling. "My wife can't think of anything beyond what she sees and usually it's shoes that she sees beckoning her from shop windows!"

"A good imagination is sometimes a bit of a burden," she said. "Especially when you start concocting bizarre theories about faked deaths and so on when what I should have been thinking was the very obvious solution, that someone just closely resembled him! I do feel so silly!"

"Don't worry about it," he said. "It's given me a bit of a thrill anyway! It was very briefly like being in some sort of novel or thriller. And even with the obvious explanation, there's clearly quite a story. How come the body was never found then?"

"He was lost at sea," she said.

"Oh," he said, looking slightly disappointed. "So did you never think of the other way of finding out if he really is dead?"

She was surprised by this question.

"I didn't think there was another way," she said in some confusion.

"Oh, it's all very melodramatic," he said airily. "Why don't you ask a medium?"

"A medium what?" she asked, perplexed.

"No, just a medium. A spirit medium," he said. "Voices from beyond the veil, that sort of thing."

"I'm not sure I believe in any of that sort of thing," she said,

"Then it can't hurt, can it?" he said. "Anyway, I must get off back to the office. I try to schedule myself a meeting with Mr. Starbuck once a week or so. The doctor told me I needed to reduce stress a bit so I diary an hour out now and again, go to the park or something but if it isn't nice weather I usually end up here. Nice meeting you anyway."

He got up and sauntered out of the lounge, even his walk very like Nick's had been. No wonder she'd been so convinced it was Nick! And all along it had just been a look-alike and she'd never even once considered that as a possibility. David was going to laugh himself silly over this when she told him.

"Doh!" he said, hitting his forehead dramatically. "Why didn't I think of that? Now all we have to do is find a sensible explanation for the visions and we're home and dry!"

"Other than that I am going mad, I don't think there is a sensible logical explanation," Verity said, thoughtfully. "If you think I'm going dotty, you'd better not have me sectioned. I don't think I'd find that easy to forgive."

David glanced at her curiously.

"Don't worry," he said. "Besides, you have to be a danger to yourself or others to get sectioned and I don't think you're either."

Not yet, anyway, Verity said in the silence of her own thoughts but said aloud,

"This guy did suggest something interesting, though."

"Oh yes?"

"He suggested I see a medium. That way I find out for sure if Nick really is dead, and if there's anything I should know, I might get told it," she said.

"That's if you believe in that sort of thing. Most of it's just a rip off, you know. Frauds taking advantage of the vulnerable and grieving, telling them what they know they want to hear," David said.

"Yeah well, I deal with that every day at work as it is," Verity said bitterly and David shot her a look that plainly said it wasn't a comment he would have expected from her. "Anyway, I note you said most of it is a rip off. Do you think some of it is genuine, then?"

David took a moment or two before answering and when he did speak, he spoke quite slowly as if he were thinking as he spoke, thinking very deeply.

"Yes," he said finally. "Some of it has to be genuine. There'll never be proof, of course. But if all mediums and the like were fakes, sooner or later the whole thing would have died out utterly. People don't like being conned and tend to be vicious when they wake up to it. There's that guy in Scotland, the psychic barber they call him. The evidence is pretty compelling for his work. Either he's got the most amazing powers of mind reading, which is astounding in itself, or he really is in contact with the spirits of the dead. And since so many cultures have a tradition of communing with the spirits of the ancestors, it seems to be endemic to the human condition to have a belief in the survival of the soul beyond death. If you think it'll help, go ahead, but the chances are it'll be a waste of money, unless you strike it lucky."

"How on earth do I go about finding a medium let alone a reputable one?" Verity said. "I don't suppose I'd find them under M for medium in the Yellow Pages?"

David chuckled.

"Try under P for Places of Worship," he said. "Look for a spiritualist church and ask them. I'm sure they'd pass you on to someone who at least isn't going to rob you blind."

Verity made a phone call and left a message at the spiritualist church she found in the phone book and waited several days for a reply. She had just got to the point of phoning again when her call was returned. She was told a number of mediums who attended the church were happy to do individual sittings but that it was necessary to ask for remuneration for these sittings since the mediums (or should that be media?) needed some recompense for their time, whereas if she were to attend a regular meeting it would be free, though putting something in the collection plate was considered good practise. Verity noted down the names and numbers of the mediums and rang off without further conversation. She felt decidedly odd doing this, almost as if she were doing something out of bounds, something forbidden and taboo.

The first name she dismissed with a wry smile: Madame Sosostris 2. Someone either knew their Eliot very well or not at all. She chortled slightly over that before remembering the drowned Phoenician Sailor. If she were looking at omens, this was either a very good one or a very bad one but she had no experience of knowing which it might be, so she decided that someone who called themselves Madame anything had to have a streak of the theatricals a mile wide and from knowing Carla, was less likely to be what Verity needed. She opted for Catherine Perry, which sounded a sensible enough sort of name and left a message for her.

The next day at work, Verity had to virtually bite her tongue to stop herself from snapping back at Juliet, whose bad mood seemed to have deepened and hardened. There seemed to be something of a lull for the therapies, which meant that Juliet spent half the day picking fault with the quality of Verity's dusting or with her hair, which she'd taken to plaiting neatly in a single braid which fitted under her cycle helmet easily and kept her hair tidy all day, or with how much coffee powder she put in Juliet's mug.

"For goodness sake!" Verity said finally, exasperated. "I can't make instant taste like real coffee however many granules of Nescrap I put in! If you want decent coffee, buy a filter machine or something, or go to Starbucks."

Juliet looked as though she were about to slap her but instead she turned sharply on her heel and stormed upstairs, leaving her rejected mug steaming on the counter. The door chimes tinkled and Verity turned to greet the customer with a smile she didn't feel.

"Please, please, please tell me you aren't Juliet Flannagan?" said the man from Starbucks, her Nick-clone.

"I'm not," she said. "Why would it be a bad thing if I were, though?"

He grinned at her wolfishly.

"Because I am about to give her what is known in business as a right rollicking," he said.

"That must be a technical term," she said, and he grinned again, but she could sense both anger and tension beneath the smile.

"Is she here?" he asked.

"Just went upstairs a minute ago," Verity said. "I'm just the minion. Do you want me to tell her you're here to see her?"

"Better than that, I'll come up with you," he said, and Verity turned over the closed sign on the door and bolted it firmly.

"This way," she said and led him up the stairs to the therapy room flat.

The door to the Reiki room was ajar and music was playing softly in the background. Verity tapped politely on the door, her arm stretched across so he couldn't just barge straight in. She hadn't asked him what he wanted to see Juliet about but she had the feeling it wasn't to book an appointment.

182

"Go away," came Juliet's voice. "I'm meditating. Go away. I shall talk to you later."

He looked at Verity.

"Does she always talk to you like that?" he asked and when she nodded, he said, "You shouldn't let her. You're better than that, better than this place."

"You don't know me," she said.

"I know enough," he said. "You must be Verity? Right?"

"You have the advantage of me," she said and he grinned again.

"I'm Will," he said. "Martine's husband."

Light of sorts began to dawn in Verity's mind and she tapped again on the door, calling,

"Juliet, there's someone here to see you."

"Do they have an appointment?" called Juliet in return but Will had clearly had enough and gently moved Verity's arm so he could push the door open and step in.

Juliet was seated on the sofa in an approximation of the Lotus position and she glanced across as Will entered. She scowled at Verity as she stood just inside the door.

"That will do, Verity. You can get back to the shop now," she said and Will frowned.

"I don't think so," he said. "I'd like Verity to stay, actually."

Juliet got out of her pose rather awkwardly for someone who was supposedly proficient at yoga and stood up, her eyes raking over Will in a manner he clearly found disturbing.

"You'd better sit down," he said to her and Verity expected Juliet to argue but she sank back onto the sofa as gracefully as she could manage.

"What can I do for you? I don't have many men visiting me for my help but it would always be refreshing to see a man taking care of both his body and his spirit," Juliet said, her voice low as she darted angry glances at Verity.

"That won't be necessary," he said. "I've come to inform you that my wife Martine will no longer be working for you."

This wiped the rather sickly look off Juliet's face.

"I don't take resignations second hand," she said sharply. "I think Martine can speak for herself if she no longer wants to work for me."

"I don't want her working for you, actually," he said. "Though how you can call it work when you've never paid her a penny, I don't know."

"That's an arrangement between myself and Martine; she does the hours she does in exchange for my services. It's all perfectly legal," Juliet said.

"Perhaps it would be if there had ever been an employment contract between you," Will said. "It's bad enough that you take advantage of my wife's naivety without the fact that as part of one of these so-called therapies you've encouraged her to be unfaithful to me!"

"I'd hardly expect you to understand the deep spiritual complexities of my work," Juliet said loftily. "You after all are the very man who has enslaved poor Martine for hundreds of years. I have simply encouraged her to find her way to true spiritual freedom and rebirth."

"Bollocks," said Will flatly. "That club she started going to, for those who've been to this Mayan heart thing, that's just an excuse for screwing around! You told her that she'd got her heart back but she wouldn't keep it long, that I'd take it back from her if she didn't sever her vows to me. At least I found out before she went ahead with it. She was like a kid on her first date, that's how I knew she was up to something, and she couldn't keep up the lying for long."

"You monster!" Juliet snarled. "Stopping the poor child expressing her freedom. You deserve a lifetime of slavery to understand what it means. You're evil."

"Not me!" he said cheerfully. "If the cap fits wear it, love. So consider this Martine's resignation and if I ever catch you near her again I shall take out a restraining order and believe me I will know if you come near her again so don't think you can sneak round."

He glanced at Verity, which reminded Juliet that she was still there, listening to everything.

"You can get out," Juliet snapped at her. "Get back to the shop. There's plenty of cleaning to be done. Go on stop gawping like a goldfish and go and do something useful."

"Don't speak to me like that!" Verity said. "I'm not your slave."

184

Something had burst inside Verity, something long dammed up and repressed.

"You'll damned well do as I say!" shrieked Juliet. "It's me that pays your wages so I can tell you what to do."

"So she actually pays you?" Will said curiously.

"Oh yes," said Verity. "I don't think I'd exchange hard cash for one of those stupid therapies."

Juliet was on her feet and had slapped Verity across the face before either Verity or Will could stop her.

"How dare you speak of my work like that!" she said furiously.

Verity put her hand up to her stinging face and winced. There'd be a bruise for sure.

"Work?" she said. "Don't make me laugh! Juliet, I've known you since we were eleven and I've never for one minute thought that deep down you truly believed in all this-" she waved her hand vaguely round to indicate the room and its contents, "beyond it being a good business opportunity, so don't try and pretend you really think any of what you do is real. Apart from the Reiki, all the therapies are so clearly get rich quick schemes designed to con the unwary. What's it going to be next then? Colonic soul exploration- the way the twists and turns of the lower bowel mirror the soul's journey through life?"

Verity heard Will snort with laughter at that one but she took no notice.

"It's all of it moonshine," she said. "And since I can see you're itching to sack me, don't bother. I resign."

"Rats leaving the sinking ship?" Juliet said bitterly.

"I wasn't aware it was sinking. I thought I'd sailed about as far as I want to," Verity said. "I did this job because it came up when I needed it and I've never had the energy to find something better, but you've treated me like a slave the whole time, never as a friend and quite frankly I'd rather go and work filling supermarket shelves than work here a day longer, so if you don't mind, I'd like my wages now and then I shall be off."

Juliet glared at her.

"I'll write you a cheque," she said coldly.

"If you don't mind, I'd far rather have cash," Verity said.

"I'm not sure I have that much cash on me," Juliet said, getting her handbag and rummaging for her chequebook.

"I said cash," Verity said firmly. "From the till, or from the safe if need be."

There was an awkward procession down the stairs and Verity stood with her arms folded across her chest as Juliet fumbled in the till to find the right money; she had to go to the safe to make up the right amount. Will was standing nearby, grinning maniacally, and watching it all with evident glee.

Juliet counted out notes into Verity's hand, her face set like week-old custard and when Verity had stuffed the notes into her own handbag, she peeled off her work tunic, a horrible item in green and yellow tie-dye and held it at arm's length before dropping it on the floor with such relief that Will started laughing again.

"You're lucky I don't go to the police and have you charged with assault," Verity said when she'd grabbed her jacket and helmet from the back room. Juliet merely raised her eyes heavenwards and ignored her.

"I might still do that if there's a bruise in the morning," Verity said. "Just start praying there isn't."

With that, she unbolted the door and swept out into the street, followed closely by Will, who was nearly hysterical by now. In the alley behind the shop, Verity unlocked the chain and freed her bicycle from the down-pipe she chained it to every day, and glanced up to see Will was still with her.

"You all right?" she asked, tucking stray wisps of hair under the helmet before fastening the chinstrap.

"Yeah," he said. "That was amazing! It was like watching ice catch fire."

She shrugged, modestly.

"I think I enjoyed it," she said. "It's something I ought to have done years ago. But I never had the motivation to look for a better job so I never bothered. I just went on day to day, putting up with crap from her. I'm sorry about Martine, by the way, I had no idea Juliet would tell her to be unfaithful too."

"You mean she told you to, as well?" he said.

She nodded.

"I was appalled but I thought it was just down to her being jealous of my marriage. I never thought she'd be telling other people that too," she said.

"It was quite a little industry," he said. "They had this club. You had to pay extra to join and then more to have a therapist assess whether someone was compatible with someone else, and then more for the venue and so on and so forth. Luckily I smelled a rat before Martine had gone too deep but rest assured, I shall be making complaints. The trouble is I don't think they have done anything illegal; all of the participants are over eighteen, of sound mind and all that. It's no worse than some dating agencies, really. I'd like that woman to get a taste of the kind of pain she's caused us, and others for that matter. God knows what might have gone on: orgies or anything. Martine's a child in many ways: very naïve. That woman played on her insecurities about her looks. She's terrified of getting old or losing her looks and that woman just used that to snare her. I say, though, I wouldn't have had you down as being interested in that sort of therapy."

She grinned at him.

"I'm not," she said. "It was Juliet's idea of a Christmas present and she caught me at a bad moment when it was easier to give in than it was to fight her. Look, I'm so glad you came today. It gave me the push I needed to get out of that place. Good luck with everything and give my best wishes to Martine."

She swung herself onto the bike and waved goodbye before steering the machine out of the alley and onto the main road. The wind in her ears made her feel as though she were flying, which in some ways, she was.

Chapter 9

Initially, Verity felt exhilarated by her resignation, and indeed David had been utterly delighted that she had at last told Juliet what she thought of her.

"I hated the way she pushed you around," he said. "She spoke to you as if you were either an idiot or somehow subhuman. And it wasn't as if she were paying you well. And she didn't give you any sick pay either when you were off."

"I won't miss it," Verity said, but after the first euphoria of her escape wore off, there was a gap in her life that no amount of housework could fill.

"You don't have to go and get a job if you don't want to," David said. "You don't need to work now. The money comes in handy, I admit that but it isn't essential. We'll manage just fine."

"I know," she said, for the last year's worth of her wages had simply been squirrelled away in a savings account. Sooner or later, they'd need major work on one of the cars or a new car even, or they'd need new windows or roof work or something but at the moment, the money was just sitting there, slowly multiplying itself.

"Give yourself a while to look around and decide what you might like to do," he said. "I don't want you to end up in another job like that one. You're looking so much better for leaving it."

She knew it was true, but some of that was simply the relief of not having to rush to and from work, as well as preparing meals and keeping the home running smoothly. She didn't miss the job at all; it had been tedious at best. But she did miss having some sort of focus to the day, however irritating it had been.

About a week after leaving, she caught the train to the city to do some shopping she'd been putting off for ages. Her alternate Saturdays had been too precious to waste on shopping but she needed new sandals, and having scoured the local shops for something that fitted, looked nice and wasn't too extortionate in price, she knew she'd need to go further afield to find what she wanted. As is the usual way of things, she found the sandals within the first hour or so rather than taking half the day as she had expected. The day was unusually warm and sunny and all the coffee bars and pubs had dusted off their outdoor tables and chairs and set them out in front of their premises as if to welcome in the uncertain British summer, and the crowded pavements seemed to hum with life and a very Continental atmosphere of conviviality seemed to fill the city. A busker with a penny whistle was playing a tune that made Verity's feet suddenly want to dance with the feeling of lightness and freedom, so impulsively she chose a table outside a coffee shop and ordered the biggest cappuccino they did and a Danish pastry, and settled down to enjoy the sunshine, her foot under the table tapping surreptitiously to the rhythm of the jig from the penny whistle.

The sunlight was like white gold on her face as she leaned back in her chair, closing her eyes but seeing the red of her own blood glowing through the lids as the sun lit up her face. The steam from her coffee swirled around her hands and the smell rose invitingly from both the drink and the pastry, and sighing with pleasure she opened her eyes again and gazed round the square without any real focus. The square was filled with buildings that were either Georgian or built in that style, often four stories high, the first and ground floors occupied by shops but the higher floors often either flats or premises for various small businesses. She thought how rarely one looked up at the rooftops, the skyline from the ground often a kind of lace-work made of ornate chimney pots and ledges, many with figures and carvings that could barely be seen from ground level. She also noticed that in many cases the upper floors of some of the buildings seemed desperately run down, in sharp contrast with the exclusive and smart shops and businesses that occupied the lower levels. Some of the upper windows were mean and poky, the glass sometimes cracked or even absent altogether. Some had the shreds of old curtains fluttering at them; in some she occasionally glimpsed movement behind the blind glass but she rarely saw an actual person at those high windows. It was another world away from the expensive shops below, and a somewhat sad and dilapidated one at that.

She took a sip of coffee, wiping the froth from her upper lip while she squinted against the sun.

I'll maybe get some new sunglasses too, she thought idly. The old ones are too scratched to be a lot of use.

She tilted her chair back slightly, leaning onto the two back legs just like you are always told not to do at school, and the sun slipped behind a cloud so she could suddenly see properly without half closing her eyes against it. There was movement at a window high up in the building to the other side of the square; someone was struggling to raise a sash window. She watched idly, without curiosity, as the distant hands wrestled with the recalcitrant window before finally wrenching it open and shoving a stick or something in the gap to prop it open. As her eyes recovered from the brightness of the sun and finally found their focus, she found she could see the figure at the window clearly. It was Nick, that curly hair and the stance and grace of movement were unmistakeable.

She jumped inwardly but didn't move. She was sure he'd seen her; sure that was why he'd opened the window. It had been weeks now since he'd vanished with Tom, and despite informing the police, there had been no sightings, nothing. She'd come into the city centre as frequently as she could, usually at this time on an afternoon, often stopping at this café to watch for any of his old acquaintances who might know where he was; still hoping against hope he would wander by. It had been too much for Granddad, and he'd finally passed over in a towering rage when she'd come to the house from the bedsit where she'd been living. The thought that he'd lost both his granddaughter and his great grandson to Nick had driven him to the brink and then finally over it. It had only been a matter of time before she'd have been forced to have him sectioned so at least he'd been spared that. He'd died of a massive heart attack in the hall of the house while she'd tried to save him, and the memory of that would haunt her for years. But at least she had her own home back, even if it had taken a week to clean it properly after the months of neglect and confusion. She'd buried him yesterday and today she was simply trying to take time to get herself back to normal, if such a thing existed. David at the school had been so nice about it all; what a lovely man he was. Why hadn't she managed to meet someone like him instead of...

She stopped that train of thought before it had even left the station. Once she found Nick and sorted things out, it would all settle down. If they could all live together again it would all be

190

wonderful, just like she'd always wanted it to be. After all these false starts and problems, they'd be fine.

What was he doing? He'd propped the window open and then gone back into the room, and she couldn't see anything more as the sun had come out again, dazzling her. Perhaps he hadn't seen her at all; or perhaps he'd started off down the stairs and any second now, he'd appear across the square, running and waving at her. It'd take a few minutes; there would surely be a lot of stairs.

The indistinct figure had reappeared at the window, but low, as if he were sitting at a chair by the window. Then she saw something poke out of the window, resting on the sill as if to steady it. It must be some sort of telescope, she thought, but it did seem ever so thin for a telescope, long and very thin, and very distantly she could see his face, a round pale blank at the end of it. Even at this distance the impression was of intense concentration.

There was a sudden sharp crack that rang out in the square, alarmingly loud and she felt herself thrown back and as she glanced down, she saw the great red flower blooming before her eyes on her shirt, spreading wildly and then she felt pain, cold and hard in her shoulder, blossoming too like an evil bloom inside her.

Dear God, he's shot me, she thought, and fell off the chair.

She lay on the concrete for less than a second before the woman at the next table reached her.

"Are you all right?"

What a stupid question! Couldn't she see the blood?

Verity looked down at her shirt; it was still pale blue, unmarked and clean. She gave her head a little shake, trying to remember where she was.

"I think so," she said, letting the woman help her back into her chair. "I was leaning back on only two legs and I think I must have slipped."

"But you're not hurt?" said the woman.

"I don't think so," she said. "Do you know, I never used to believe teachers when they said not to do that. Now I do." She managed a rueful smile and the woman returned it, kindly.

"My teachers used to say you'd break your back," she said. "I didn't quite believe it either. Mind you, I thought you'd maybe been stung by something since you sort of did a bit of a jump as if you had a wasp sting you just when you fell off the chair."

Verity felt around her shoulder, where the bullet had struck, and pretended to find a sore spot.

"I think it was something like that," she agreed. "But hitting the concrete rather took my mind off it!"

"Try Boots," said the woman. "They do one of those creams or sprays for stings."

"I will," she said and left without finishing her coffee, so very shaken inwardly that all she wanted was to get home as fast as possible.

That evening she told David about it and he looked very worried.

"Why on earth would he have shot you?" he said. "And where would he have got the gun from?"

She sighed.

"I think it might be because Granddad had died and left me the house," she said. "I think he was desperate for money, I mean really desperate. I also think he was in debt to some very dangerous people. If they thought the only way of him paying back what he owed was to get rid of me, they'd have given him the means to do it. He couldn't have done it close up; this way, he could just pretend it was target practise. I have a memory that I was going into the city centre quite frequently in the hopes that I'd find him; I guess that was how he knew I'd be there. Or maybe he had been following me. I don't know. But somehow or other he knew I was likely to be at that café some time; what with the weather being so nice, I'd been sitting outside quite often. It makes me shudder to think of it; the thought that he'd been watching and waiting for his chance to kill me."

"Would he have known how to shoot?"

"His was an army family; he'd done a year or two of cadets before he finally started to stand up to his father. They do air rifle shooting. I know it's not the same as using a real rifle but I think he was a good shot; I do recall his father saying something of the sort, deploring the waste of his skills once he'd stopped with the cadets," she said. "I can hardly believe he'd really do it but he didn't kill me. It was a nasty wound but it probably wouldn't kill me."

192

"I wonder," David said and stopped.

"What?"

"Just that thing with dreams, the folklore that if in one of those dreams where you're falling that if you don't wake before you hit the ground, you really die? Would you really die in this life if you died in that other one?"

That was a thought!

"I don't know," she said. "It was really scary. And it still feels horrible to think that someone I loved would be driven to try and kill me. If he'd asked me, I'd have done anything to help, sell the house, anything. But he didn't even ask. Which makes me wonder quite how bad things were that he was that desperate. I had thought it was over, that there might not be any more visions. Clearing up the other sightings made me wonder if the other stuff was over too."

"Obviously not," he said.

She could see he was worried. "This one only lasted a minute at the most," she said as if to reassure him. "And all I did was fall off my chair. So it is maybe slowly dying away."

She wasn't really convinced of this and plainly neither was he but they left it at that; there didn't seem much point in discussing it further. Strange really how the extraordinary became everyday and how easily you accepted weirdness when you had no choice.

It was more than a week after this incident that Catherine Perry phoned back.

"I was away on holiday," she said by way of apology for not getting back to Verity sooner. "You said in your message you wanted to arrange a sitting? Have you ever been to one before?"

"No, never," said Verity. "Is that all right?"

There was a rich chuckle at the other end.

"From my point of view, it's great," said Catherine. "That way there's none of the stuff I sometimes get where people tell me that when they went to Madame So-and-so, they got told this or that. If you're coming to it for the first time, you won't have any preconceptions that might get in your way. Some people like a more theatrical sort of sitting than I give. I think they feel it's better value for money somehow. I don't dress up and I don't mess about."

"How much will it be?" Verity asked nervously.

There was a pause.

"I don't actually charge," said Catherine. "I suggest that if a client is happy with what I do, they make a donation to a charity of their choice. I don't do this for a living. I have a job and somehow charging money for something I do naturally seems wrong. So the donation is up to you, both how much and who to. Of course, if I don't manage to make contact with anyone for you, then you may feel the need to go elsewhere and that's fine. It's no skin off my nose. Sometimes they queue up waiting for the chance to speak to their loved ones. Other times there's no one much there waiting on the other side. I hope you won't be too disappointed if that happens."

Verity made an appointment for a Saturday a week or so away and put down the phone feeling surprisingly happy about it. Catherine had sounded both nice and normal; she didn't use jargon and she sounded so matter of fact about it that it didn't feel weird at all. Verity had become used to Juliet using as much New Age jargon as she could possibly lace her speech with and conversations with her (monologues really!) had been peppered with chakras, auras, psychic thises and spiritual thats and countless other terms that seemed to mean virtually nothing but were an insider's way of excluding the outsider, like herself. Catherine had used normal everyday words and hadn't seemed remotely spooky or weird.

She sighed. It was like when you were a child; even a week seemed an aeon to get through before the desired treat could be reached. She made a note of the appointment and went back out to the garden which was looking somehow rather surprised at the amount of attention it had suddenly begun to receive lately; even the ancient apple trees at the end of the garden seemed to be watching her in anticipation of her next move.

"You can relax," she said, patting the oldest one on the trunk as she went by to retrieve the wheelbarrow. "The worst thing you're getting is a bucket or two of manure forked in round your roots. You've been neglected for too long."

Talking to plants now, she thought laughing inwardly. Well, no one can say that's mad when even royalty does it; I shall count myself mad when the plants start talking back and not until then!

Breathe. Just breathe. That's all you have to do: breathe, Verity told herself sternly. The echoes of Nick's poem came back to her in her own thoughts as she stood on the path outside Catherine Perry's home and panicked helplessly. It was as though her lungs were working flat out, but were still failing to deliver the oxygen to her fogging brain.

Fine bloody start this'll be, me having the vapours on her doorstep, she thought irritably and managed to even out her breathing before pressing the doorbell. She had the feeling Catherine had been there, just waiting for her to ring the bell, as she opened the door only a second after she rang, but her first impression of the woman at the door was a thoroughly positive one. Catherine was around her own age, maybe four or five years older but it was hard to tell; she was pleasant looking without being pretty. The word handsome perhaps fitted best, taller than Verity but not lanky and dressed in very ordinary clothes. The hallway she ushered Verity into was spotlessly clean, and smelled of lavender; she spotted a bowl of it on the table near the door, and saw Catherine stir it automatically with her hand as she passed it.

"Through here," Catherine said and indicated a door to the side of the hallway.

Verity found herself in a small room, with a two-seater sofa and an upright wooden chair, a low coffee table and a small desk with a computer on it, thought the computer screen was covered with a scarf. It made her think of covering budgie cages to keep the occupant quiet. Catherine seemed to notice her glance.

"I keep it covered mainly to keep the dust off it," she explained. "I don't use it very much but having a blank screen is rather off-putting to some people, a bit like having an extra eye in the room. It can make them uneasy."

The walls were painted a soft pale blue and were mostly empty but for a wooden cross and a few icons. One she thought might be Christ raising Lazarus, but she wasn't sure. It fitted anyway.

"Can I make you some tea? Or maybe you'd like to use the bathroom?" Catherine asked.

"Yes, to both," Verity said, and she was shown to the impeccably clean bathroom. When she got back the little room was empty but she could hear Catherine in the kitchen making tea, singing softly to herself. She seemed like a happy sort of person; maybe an inalienable belief in the survival of the soul would give such apparent serenity. The tea was brought in and she drank it with a growing nervousness as they chatted about how the roads had been, what the weather was likely to do and all the other inconsequential chit-chat that fills in the growing silence between people.

"Right," said Catherine with the air of someone getting down to the real business of the day. "If you've never been to a sitting before, I need to explain how I work. I like to sit in quietness for a short while. This is to help me get into a receptive state. Some people talk of going into a trance but I find the term is misleading. Technically speaking I shall be in a trance of sorts but a very light one, not dissimilar to the kind of trance we all go into when we watch TV or similar. People expect something weird or dramatic or even a bit scary. All you'll see is me sitting quietly with my eyes closed to begin with. I won't thrash around or anything alarming; I won't speak in a strange voice and there won't be any goo coming from my mouth. Hollywood has a lot to answer for! All I shall be doing is becoming receptive to those who have passed over and relaying to you anything they tell me. Is there any one person you are hoping to contact? Don't tell me a name; I find it helps to ease the nervous sceptic if I can get things like names without being told."

"Yes," said Verity slowly. "There is one special person I want to contact."

"Good," said Catherine. "That's usually better than a generalised wish to meet someone from beyond the veil. I do get people coming who just want to see if there really is anything there; it's fair enough I suppose but it does make it a little tricky. OK, I'm going to get comfortable and then I shall say a very quiet prayer. Please don't talk to me until I speak again but when, or maybe if, I get through, you may ask me questions to ask your loved one."

Catherine seated herself on the wooden chair, very upright and alert but seeming still quite relaxed, placed her hands in her lap and closed her eyes. She took a deep slow breath in and then let it out again even more slowly. Verity saw her lips move but she couldn't hear what she said, but saw her make the sign of the cross and then fall very still and very silent.

The silence became like a living thing, like a great tree growing in the room, filling it with tiny flutterings and breezes. Far off, Verity could hear a dog barking, a car door slamming and the sounds of children playing; she could even hear her own heartbeat as she tried to stay quiet.

Then quite abruptly the atmosphere changed. It was like that moment when the new chill to the air tells of the passing of summer even though the sun is still shining and the flowers look the same to a casual glance, or the way a familiar aroma heralds the arrival of a dearly loved person before they quite reach the door and the eyes of those within. The stillness of waiting had been replaced by the stillness of arrival. Verity wouldn't have been at all surprised to hear a polite little cough from somewhere unseen. Catherine's eyes opened and she smiled at Verity.

"I have a young man here to speak to you," she said, almost as if she were an old-fashioned telephone operator connecting a call. "He's wanted to speak to you for a long time. I'm getting a name, yes, thank you, Nicholas. Sorry, you prefer Nick. He says you've worn better than his jumper!"

Verity jumped; she'd worn the old Guernsey sweater almost without thinking about it. It had been hers so long she had almost forgotten it had once been his. He'd left it at her house the last time he'd been there before he left and she had cherished it all that long summer and after, holding and cuddling it, inhaling the residue of his body scent every time the pain became too much for her. It had been a year before she'd washed it, laundering it by hand, tenderly, like a sick baby.

She found she could still breathe; she had stopped for a second as if winded by the words Catherine spoke.

"He says there's so much he wanted to say to you but now you're here, he's sort of tongue-tied," Catherine went on. "He says his own words seem so inadequate now. My words strain, they crack and sometimes break, because of my burden, because of my tension, that's what he's saying. They slip, slide, perish, decay and they won't stay in place, will not stay still."3 Catherine frowned, as if puzzled. "He says there's so much he wants to say but he knows he can't. He says he doesn't have the words to explain it all, and there isn't time. If you had a lifetime, there still wouldn't be time. And he has to say goodbye and let you move on. He's glad you've been happy but there's things you need to sort out before you can move on properly."

"I don't know how," Verity whispered. "I don't know where I went wrong. I don't know how to move on or where to go."

She wasn't crying but there was a prickling in her eyes and that ominous burning at the back of her nose and throat.

Catherine closed her eyes again for a second, her face intense with concentration.

"He says, if I came at night like a broken king…"4 she said and tailed off as if listening to an unheard voice. "All shall be well and all manner of things shall be well, he says, that's surely Julian of Norwich, then something about tongues of flame and crowned knots of fire, then he says the fire and rose are one."5

She rubbed her eyes and the atmosphere in the room changed again, became oddly empty.

"I'm sorry," she said. "He's gone now. He got very emotional and he had to go. I don't think he was upset, just rather overwhelmed. Do you have any idea of what he was talking about at the end?"

Verity shook her head.

"It was sort of half familiar, almost like something I heard as a child but I couldn't place it," she said. "I'm sorry."

Catherine made a negating gesture, waving her hand as if shooing away flies.

"Don't be," she said. "I'm sure it will come to you. I'm sure he wouldn't have said it if it wasn't going to mean something to you. How long ago did he die? Was he your son?"

What a question!

"No," said Verity. "He was someone I was going to marry a long time ago. Almost nineteen years ago in fact."

"I had a feeling it was quite a while ago but time is different over there," Catherine said. "He's wanted to speak with you for a long time."

198

"You said," Verity said, slowly, her mind running over the words.

If I came at night like a broken king.[6]

She came back to herself with a jerk of awareness that she had been sitting ignoring her host.

"I'm so sorry," she said. "I'm just so mystified about what it could all possibly mean. Thank you so very much. I can't believe it happened. Did he say anything else or did you have any other impressions of him?"

Catherine smiled.

"He seemed such a nice young man," she said. "I have the impression his death was peaceful but he regretted not being able to say goodbye to you especially. There was something else he said. It didn't make sense to me. Something about a door you never opened into a rose garden.[7] It was all a bit muddled. He was trying to say everything at once and it got jumbled. I did my best to decipher it but I maybe didn't get his words quite right. I hope I did."

"Thank you," Verity said and got slowly to her feet. "You've been very helpful. I've been dreading it in case it was all a fraud or maybe worse and be utterly banal with messages of light and love from beyond the veil and nothing useful. But I can, well, connect with what you said. He'd always introduce himself as Nicholas, and then reduce it to just Nick virtually in the same breath. His father used to call him by his full name when he was angry so he didn't like his full name much since his father seemed to be angry with him all the time near the end. It's all so strange though. What broken king? Come where? And what rose garden? There never was a rose garden either at my house or at his, never mind opening doors into it. And that bit about the fire and the rose? I'm baffled."

"You'll figure it out," Catherine said. "It's something he thought you'd recognise. Go back in your mind and you'll find it."

Impulsively, Verity hugged her and broke away, embarrassed.

"Sorry," she said. "That was-"

"That was very kind and very sweet," Catherine said firmly. "You need to stop apologising, you know. You seem to be saying sorry far too much, you know, and I doubt you have very much ever to be sorry about."

"I'm not so sure," Verity said, darkly.

"I am," Catherine said. "I'm a good judge of character. I think you need to be gentler with yourself. I don't encourage repeat visits but if you ever want to come again, I wouldn't refuse. I don't like people to get addicted to speaking to people beyond this world. Sometimes we need to, simply to clear up things we maybe should have done before they died but really, they need to move on and so do we. But if you do need to speak to him again, ask me. But I think you have the strength to see this through without it."

"Thank you," Verity said and as she left the house her mind began turning things over and over, like an oyster-catcher or other wading bird on a pebble beach, searching for the truth like some tasty morsel of shellfish, hidden in the damp recesses between salt encrusted rocks.

When she got home, David was in the study, marking books. A full but cold mug of coffee was at his side and he glanced up at her with unfocussed eyes as she walked in.

"How was it?" he asked, putting down his red pen.

"Odd," she said. "But amazing. I don't think I expected to hit the jackpot first time. I think I was expecting to have to try a few before I managed to find one that was genuine."

"Did she get through to... to Nick?" he asked hesitantly.

"Yes," Verity replied. "Where's Rosie?"

"Gone round to a friend's house," David said. "So you're safe from curious ears bar mine! So she did get through to him. Are you sure she wasn't faking? You didn't tell her anything about yourself beforehand did you?"

"Do you think I'm stupid? No don't answer that; I was only joking!" she said. "She told me something that no one else knows about; all I told her was my name and telephone number. I didn't tell her anything about who I wanted to contact or why. But she knew that this jumper was Nick's and said so. She said he said I'd worn better than his jumper."

David stared at her in surprise.

"I didn't know that!" he said, almost sounding hurt.

"I'd virtually forgotten myself," she said. "I've had it so long it's just become my comfy old jumper for wearing when I'm feeling cold or fragile. It was virtually new when Nick left it here. It's lasted well really, but I'd almost forgotten where it came from. Anyway, she even knew his name, and other things too. The thing is that the rest of what she told me he was telling her doesn't make any connections for me. There were some words he'd written in his journal as well, well she repeated those which was odd and then there were a few other things he said that I don't recognise at all; it sounds sort of half familiar but I can't quite place it. You know, like a tune you sort of know but you can't quite remember where from or what it is or what comes next. It's maddening in the extreme because I am so sure it's important."

"It'll come," he said, with such certainty she had to smile. "What's so funny?" he asked in response to her smile.

"Just you," she said. "Being so sure I'll crack the puzzle. No wonder your pupils do so well at GCSE! They hate to disappoint you when you have such confidence in them. Shall I make some fresh coffee that you can forget about?"

He grinned at her and held out his mug with its congealing contents.

"Please," he said. "And then you can tell me all the rest."

Chapter 10

If I came at night like a broken king.8

Verity let the words run through her head as she washed the dishes, stroking the cloth over plates slowly as the words played round senselessly like bored children.

If I came at night like a broken king.9

She pushed the trolley round the supermarket and placed items in it to the rhythm of the words, letting them become a mantra.

If I came at night like a broken king. 10

She sorted laundry into piles and stuffed the first load into the washing machine, measuring the laundry liquid into the dispenser as the mantra droned on and on in her head, making her want to scream by the end of the day when every task, every moment was accompanied by the backing track of those words repeated endlessly, maddeningly, frustratingly in her mind.

This is going to make me crazy even if I am already crazy, she thought, helplessly. What king and why is he broken? Are we talking about a real historical king, or a biblical king, or a chess piece king or even a flaming Burger King? And why should I come at night anyway? Come where exactly? Oh come on Nick, this isn't like you. You didn't go in for mysteries and puzzles and all that stuff. You didn't get a kick out of how far parsley sank into the butter or the curious affair of the dog in the night-time. You didn't even much like Scooby Doo so why the puzzles now? This just doesn't make sense. Was it really you speaking to Catherine or was it all a fake and a fraud?

If I came at night like a broken king.11

What the hell does it mean? Is that what I have to do to clear this whole thing away? Arrive at an unspecified location at an unspecified time of night like an unspecified monarch broken by unspecified ways and means? What the hell does it mean?

David had been as baffled as she was, playing with anagrams and other word games but getting nowhere. She'd written it down and the other things, about the rose garden and about the fire and the rose becoming one, and words slipping but none of it was going anywhere. She was starting to feel very resentful that if the dead truly spoke then why couldn't they speak plainly and not in riddles? It was all starting to sound like a matter of smoke and mirrors but she couldn't deny that Catherine had known Nick's name and about the jumper, something no one, not even Carla nor David had known about.

I just have to hang onto that and let myself figure it out in my own time. I have to step away, do something else until it just clicks.

She sent off for brochures of all the further education and community colleges in the area, and browsed through endless lists of courses, covering everything from further maths (no way!) to flower arranging and yoga, not to mention all the beauty therapy courses. She wandered round the local job centre, peering at all the jobs available. She read the situations vacant columns in both the local and the national newspaper; she seemed to be either vastly over-qualified for most of the jobs or hopelessly lacking in experience even if any of them had even remotely interested her.

I just have to face it, she thought despondently in the end, I'm fit for just about nothing but what I'm already doing. But a trained chimp could stuff a washing machine; there must be something right for me. I'm just not looking in the right place. But where the hell is the right place? Maybe the job at the shop was about as good as it gets. God, that's a horrible thought. Hell might not really be other people but Juliet was certainly Purgatory! I'd like to know exactly what I must have been atoning for if that was what I was doing there.

She rinsed out the cloth she was using to wipe down skirting boards; since she'd stopped working, the house had never looked cleaner. She'd even been considering clearing out and decorating the attic bedrooms, though since she had no reason to do so beyond the fact that she was getting bored and restless staying at home the whole time she had not made a start yet. She could hear a car stopping outside the house but since really there was no one likely to call, she was astounded when footsteps sounded on the path and the doorbell rang.

"Please God don't let this be Juliet or Carla," she whispered as she dropped her cloth into its bucket and ran to answer the door.

She almost didn't recognise the person waiting on the step, so much had Martine apparently changed in the intervening weeks. She looked absurdly younger and it took Verity a moment to figure out why; she had left off the layers of make-up that Verity had never seen her without and her face looked childlike and far sweeter.

"Hello," said Martine, rather shyly. "I hope you don't mind me calling on you like this."

"Not at all," Verity said, and stepped back and said, "Come in, please."

Martine did so, and Verity saw that she was wearing trainers and not the usual foot-crippling high heels she'd always worn before. Martine looked round the hall much like many people gaze round the Sistine Chapel.

"This is so lovely," she said. "It's like something from a film."

Verity wanted to ask what sort of film but wasn't sure she would really appreciate the answer.

"I was just going to stop and have a coffee," she said. "Can I offer you one?"

"Ooh yes please," said Martine as if she'd been offered something rather exciting rather than a humdrum cup of coffee.

In the kitchen, Martine peered through the window at the garden. The trees were in full leaf, and there was a lot of colour from various shrubs.

"You've got a lovely garden," she said.

It was such an un-Martine-like comment that Verity couldn't help wondering what was going on; no make-up, no heels and now an interest in gardening.

"Will and I are thinking of moving house," Martine said as Verity made coffee. "Somewhere in the countryside. Not too far from town but not so close either. I'm going to have a baby, you see and we want the very best for it."

Verity glanced at Martine's flat stomach.

"Congratulations," she said. "When is it due?"

Martine gave a little tinkling laugh.

"Oh, I'm not pregnant yet," she said. "We've only just decided, you see. But we need to make plans now, after all. That business with the shop just brought it all home to me; I was just drifting along. No wonder Juliet decided to con me."

Verity took her through to the living room and Martine gazed round with wonder.

"All those books," she breathed, in some awe. "Have you really read them all?"

Verity nodded.

"Just about all of them," she said.

"Have you heard from Juliet?" Martine asked and when Verity shook her head went on, "I have. I know she wasn't supposed to but she rang me a week or so back. I was very upset by it. She screamed and screamed at me. Kept telling me it was my fault. Oh and your fault too."

"What was?" Verity asked mystified.

It took some time to patch together a complete story. Martine was never going to win Brain of Britain, even with her apparent change of character, so she didn't seem to be able to tell a story straight or get her facts clear. It appeared that while Verity had been off with the flu, a client of Juliet's had had a severe allergic reaction to whatever gunk Juliet had been using on her; Martine was unclear which therapy had been in operation at the time. This had resulted in an appalling skin rash that would probably scar, maybe permanently. Now this was bad enough but it turned out that Juliet had never bothered to take out any professional insurance that might cover such an eventuality and the client had decided to sue for compensation, feeling that scarring had not been an agreed part of the therapy. Since Juliet had no insurance to cover claims for malpractice or anything else for that matter (which explained why she had been so furious about the shoplifters who had emptied the case of jewellery when Martine had been in charge of the shop) she was going to have to find the money from somewhere else, and rather than simply sell her house (and that was news in itself to Verity that Juliet had a house rather than the small flat she'd said she had) and move into the flat over the shop until things improved, Juliet had opted to sell the shop.

"Will says she must be stupid to do that," Martine said. "After all, the shop is her livelihood."

But word had got round about the allergic reaction and clients had been dropping away as fast as they'd once flocked and clearly confidence had been lost completely in her and her therapies.

"Maybe the house is worth less than the shop," Verity suggested but Martine shook her head.

"No," she said. "Will reckons that the house is worth maybe double what the shop is worth."

"Double? That's absurd," Verity said.

"Oh yes!" said Martine. "I saw the house once. She invited me over once after my first heart therapy session to meet a lot of other people who'd had it too. It was ever so big, very nice too; lots of white carpets and white furniture. No good for children but ever so nice to look at."

Verity tried to imagine how Juliet could have afforded a house like that and then thought of the hours she had worked herself for very little over the years, and how tight-fisted Juliet always was and how prices always seemed on the high side, and still couldn't figure it.

"Will says he reckons she's probably been lying about her income to the tax-man too," Martine said and Verity nodded. That might explain it but there were probably a few other sidelines she didn't know about that brought in a lot more money than flogging joss sticks and crystals. So jettisoning the shop was probably the best move; perhaps Juliet planned to set up therapy rooms at her own home, if she hadn't already done so. It also explained why Juliet had been so very irritable in the last weeks Verity had worked for her; things were going badly and she was taking it out on anyone who was there.

"Rotten cow," Verity said suddenly. "She didn't say a word to me about any of this. I'd have liked some warning that I was about to lose my job. OK, I know I resigned anyway but it was only because your Will gave me the courage to do it. I could have just turned up for work and found it all closed down and she'd never have bothered telling me. Did you know anything about the compensation claim?"

It appeared that Martine had to some extent been in Juliet's confidence, having accidentally opened a letter from the client's solicitor mistaking it for her own post. It sounded an unlikely story from anyone but Martine; she had brought her own post in to open one Saturday and had picked up the post on the mat when she came into the shop and had somehow confused the two. She'd had to tell Juliet why her letter had been opened and had also to confess that she'd read it and was there anything she could do to help? Juliet had told her the story, emphasizing that it really wasn't her fault the wretched woman had such sensitive skin and how she had chosen not to have any insurance.

"Because, she said, all insurance companies are such crooks," Martine explained. "They take your money year after year quite happily but when you come to make a claim they always wriggle out of paying it. That's what she said. It never occurred to me that anything could go wrong with her therapies. It's not as if she was doing anything with bones or joints or anything."

"Why didn't you tell me what was going on?" Verity asked.

"Juliet told me not to," Martine said. "She said you'd been so ill, it wasn't fair to worry you. She also said she didn't think you'd understand. She said you weren't terribly enlightened and bringing in more negativity would just make the situation worse. Like attracts like, she said. She said we just had to bring lots of light into the situation and it'd all be great, the woman would drop her claim. She'd see she was harming a true light-worker and drop it given time. We just had to pour lots of positive vibes into the universe and it'd all work out for the best."

Martine rubbed her eyes in a strangely childlike gesture, a little girl trying to wipe the sleep from her eyes along with the residue of the nightmares.

"It was all rubbish, wasn't it?" she asked very sadly.

"Most of it, yes," Verity said gently. "I never had a lot of faith in her, you know. That's why she said I wasn't enlightened. I can't help remembering the spiteful girl she was at school; I couldn't see much real change since then and certainly nothing to suggest that she was a real healer."

"Then why did you stay?" Martine asked, artlessly, and Verity laughed.

"Money," she said. "Filthy lucre. I needed the money and I just didn't have the confidence to even look for something better. It was convenient and local and I didn't have to worry about childcare or long hours or anything else like that. Nothing more than that."

"What are you going to do now?" Martine asked.

Verity shrugged.

"I really don't know," she said. "Even if I do sound like Mr. Micawber, something will turn up."

"Is he a friend of yours, Mr.Micawber?" Martine asked and Verity had to stop the laugh she felt rising inside her.

"In a manner of speaking, yes," she said. "I'm giving myself the time to look around and really find out what I want to do with myself. I'm not in any hurry, not really. What about you? Are you hoping to move soon or when the baby's on its way?"

"Oh, soon," Martine said. "I can't wait to have a new home. It's so exciting. Will says I can do most of the choosing for the décor. I've never done that before. But I'll tell you one thing; I'm not getting any white stuff at all. Juliet's place had loads of white and the slightest thing shows up. It might look nice but you can't live in it!"

Verity smiled; Martine might be really rather stupid but she did have some common sense at least, more than she'd have given her credit for.

"I hope it goes really well," she said. "Keep in touch. Let me know how it goes."

When Martine had gone, Verity felt oddly bereft; it wasn't as if they were really friends at all. While she liked Martine, it was largely because it was hard not to like her in the way it's hard not to like a child. There was nothing in common between them and their association had simply been by proximity and now that was gone, the likelihood was that they might never meet again. There might be a card at Christmas for a year or two and then nothing. It was the way most things went unless you held onto them for dear life, even past their natural lifespan. That was what she had done with both Juliet and with Carla and probably with all the other people she had thought of as friends and yet never now saw unless chance brought them together. She felt herself shiver at the very thought of it; she could be passing David in the street and not know him beyond that vague sense of recognition, of wondering where she knew him from before walking on and forgetting it. It was so easy to lose people; it didn't take a boat in the wide blue ocean to do it. Time did it; time and indifference and the simple pressure of living did it.

The contents of the bucket were like dirty ice water and the scum had begun to form on the top, so she tipped it all out and stowed it away in the cupboard under the sink. She had had enough of cleaning for one day and she went out into the garden to think where the sun shone and shadows hid from it.

"Mum?" said Rose one Saturday a week or so later.

"What?"

Verity was curled up on the sofa, doing nothing much, and her daughter had a purposeful air that was a trifle alarming.

"The swimming coach asked me if I wanted to go on the summer camp this year," Rose went on. "They've had someone drop out and there's a place spare. Only… it's the first week of the school holidays and that's when we usually go away."

"And you want to know if you can go to that instead of going away with your Dad and me?" Verity said. "I don't really see why you should have to drag around with us every year, now you're older. If you prefer to go to swimming camp then I don't see why not."

"Cool!" Rose shouted, evidently relieved that her mother had not had the fit she was clearly expecting her to have. "I'll let Coach know tomorrow. I'll need a cheque for the deposit…."

"Ask your Dad when he takes you to the pool," Verity said.

"Mum?" Rose said, halfway out the door.

"Yes, lovie?"

"You keep muttering something under your breath," Rose said. "You've been doing it for ages now. Are you all right?"

"Well, yes, I'm all right," Verity said, touched. "It's just something someone said to me a while back, a few phrases. It's been driving me mad, trying to work out where I heard these phrases. You know what it's like, with a song or something. I can't quite remember if it's something I should remember or if it was just something that was said years ago in passing and has somehow stuck."

Rose thought for a moment.

"Why don't you Google it?" she said.

"Google it? What on earth do you mean?" Verity said.

"The internet? Computers? You know!" Rose said. "I mean, Google! It's a search engine. Don't you know what that is?" She was staring at her mother with kind contempt.

"Of course I know what a search engine is. It just never occurred to me to use one," Verity said. "Surely it won't help!"

"You never know till you try," Rose said. "Go and ask Dad. He'll show you what to do."

She was gone then, back to her lair upstairs. Verity sighed. She couldn't see how a search engine could possibly help her understand words spoken through a medium from a boy dead so many years. She lay there for a minute and then decided that if nothing else it couldn't hurt and went through to the study where David was staring despondently at a pile of exercise books. He glanced up.

"I was hoping that you might have made coffee," he said. "Though I think I need something stronger to face this lot."

"No, but I can make some if you want it," she said. "Rosie just gave me a thought. Why not Google the words Nick said?"

David looked rather stunned and then began laughing.

"Out of the mouths of babes," he said. "I don't see why I never thought of that myself. I guess I just got too caught up in it. I'll start the computer. If you make some coffee, we can have a look together. Anything has to be better than year nine homework!"

When she came back with the coffee, the computer was humming contentedly and David had got Google on screen.

"Go on, then," he said. "Just type the words in that box and then click on search."

Verity took a deep breath. It was silly; how could a search engine contain those enigmatic words. But she typed in "If I came at night like a broken king"12 and with another deep breath clicked on search.

"Oh my God," she said a moment or two later, letting out her breath noisily. "How could I have been so thick? Of course! It's not I but you, look, at it!"

David took a look at the screen.

"It's from a poem?" he said.

"What other way would a poet pass on a message?" she said. "It's from T.S. Eliot's 'Four Quartets', from 'Little Gidding'. I gave Nick the book for his eighteenth birthday. We read it once together. I never understood most of it and I never read it again. No wonder it felt familiar. But even so, I can't think what on earth it means."

"But at least you know where the words come from, now," David said.

She nodded, but her mind was absent and her eyes had become unfocussed and hazy.

"I don't know why I never thought of Google," David said after a moment. "It seems so obvious now."

She gave a very distracted smile.

"I know," she said. "But I thought the words must have been from one of his own poems, one of the ones that his father destroyed, so it never occurred to me that it was from someone else's work."

"Isn't Eliot the one who wrote Old Possum's Book of Practical Cats?" David asked. "I do recall reading those to Rosie when she was tiny till I was sick of them. Are the Four Quarters like that then?"

"Four Quartets," Verity corrected. "No. No, they're not at all like Old Possum. I never understood them then. I did The Wasteland at university but never Four Quartets; I somehow managed to avoid it. I didn't understand The Wasteland either but I gather no one does. You just have to glean your own meaning from it. I think most of Eliot is like that. Actually, most poetry is like that. Short of asking the poet what they meant, you just have to figure it out. Or not, as the case may be."

"Do you want me to print out a copy of it?" he asked.

"I don't think so," she said. "I have a feeling that the book I gave Nick is one of the ones Carla passed onto me. I'll go and have a look."

David followed her upstairs to the attic where she had left the bag of books; she had been too upset to sort them out and had simply left them in a corner. As carefully as her grandfather might have unearthed some pottery from a dig, she took each book out of the bag and set it aside until she came to the last one.

"It's here," she said, holding up the thin volume.

Chapter 11

Verity didn't notice David slip quietly from the attic as she opened the book and began to read. The odour of years rose from the book, somehow yeasty like rising bread, and the powdery dust that coated the edges transferred itself to her fingers like dirty flour as she flicked through the pages. Her own writing on the frontispiece, more hesitant than it was today, less sure of itself but still recognisable as hers, made her shiver as she remembered biting the end of her pen trying to think what to write and ending by writing something simple and plain because all the other things sounded so overblown and absurd. These days, she pitied the girls who in a similar fit of devotion had the name of the object of their affections tattooed on some body part, to be grieved over long after the emotions were dissipated and gone. All she had been obliged to worry about was a few lines on the inside of a cheap paperback book; she'd at least managed not to blot or make any errors in those few lines, but then she could also remember practising them on scraps of paper till she was sure she would get them right.

It was at first like starting a new exercise regime, making muscles that had been unused for years work harder than they were used to. When she had begun cycling to work, it had been agony the first week or so, with aching legs and lungs puffed out; this felt similar, using mental skills she had not touched since the day she walked out into the June sunshine with her last exam behind her. To tease out of individual words their many meanings was at first unfamiliar and then much like bicycle riding, she found she had not forgotten it at all. She found that she would read some lines over and over again and fail to take in their meaning while others leaped from the page as if highlighted by some strange light.

There were some lines that made her shiver and others made tears prickle in her eyes, and yet others made her gasp aloud at their implications. To explore the very nature of time in a poem seemed to be so far beyond the scope of the art and yet, and yet, somehow it seemed to touch on it in ways that made her want to talk to the poet, to wring the meaning out of him from the hints and clues and tentative exploring, and yet he too was gone beyond, gone where she could not go.

She read aloud from the first of the poems, Burnt Norton, where the rose garden and the door that was never opened was mentioned, and almost heard those echoing footsteps from a past that had never happened. 13

So that was what Nick had been talking about. Had he meant their planned life, that had never come to pass, was the rose garden never visited? But rose gardens are only pretty for a very short time; in winter they are simply a wasteland of dead, thorny twigs with no hint of what might come. And even though she had never grown roses, she knew they were in many ways the least rewarding of flowers, taking mountains of manure, hours of weeding and pruning and picking thorns out of bleeding thumbs, to produce that brief lavish display of blooms all too easily despoiled by a summer storm. If, as Eliot suggested, all time is eternally present, then somewhere in time, she had truly lived that other life. 14

Her mind was aching with the effort to understand; this was beyond mere poetry. This went into the realms of the philosopher, the mystic, the saint and the astrophysicist. She'd once read about the theory of alternate universes, in a sci-fi novel; it had hardly registered at the time, as she'd been more interested in the story than the pseudo-science. But now it made her wonder if it were true, that at each branching point of a life, one reality went on one way and the other went another way altogether. In another universe Nick had not gone on deck in the night, had not tripped, fallen or dived from the ship. He had come home and everything had been different.

She read from Burnt Norton, and pondered on how much reality a human could bear 15 and then laughed aloud. "You're telling me birdie!" She thought of her phantom son, playing in the apple trees with his school friend, hiding and giggling among the leaves and shivered so much she dropped the book.

I can only bear so much reality, she thought and picked the book up and stared at it. Where has all this come from? From within me, or from beyond, from somewhere I can never quite grasp?

She opened the book again and found words that seemed to speak to her and only her, as clear as a voice in her mind.

She read about dust on rose leaves in a bowl and shivered. Was that what her life had become, a bowl of petals gathering dust and fading in the light of increasing years? 16 Better not to just blow away the dust, better to return the petals to the earth and fetch new ones full of colour and scent and meaning. If somehow this made her turn her life into something fresh, then that was purpose enough for disturbing the dust. Sometimes you just never noticed how faded and worn things had become; sometimes it took the irritating finger of the troublesome guest dragged through the layer of dust that furred up the mantelpiece to make you realise it was there at all. After her grandfather had died, she'd had a window cleaner round to clean all the windows; it had been years since it had been done and the difference it had seemed to make to the light levels had been astounding. Sometimes such simple acts were all it took for a new perspective to come in.

She went back downstairs, the book tucked under her arm, and carried on with her chores, letting some words flow through her till they seemed to merge with her own thoughts; till she was unsure what were her thoughts and what were the poem.

She muttered to herself as she rummaged in the freezer for something for their dinner that evening about how only things that are living can actually die.17 Well, that was true enough. How many lives, countless lives, went into the dark and were gone and lost utterly, compared with the very few whose names and stories remained alive, becoming legend, becoming myth, becoming more than they had ever really been in life? "Love is unmoving," 18 she whispered as she chopped onions and if tears fell, well, it was only the onions after all.

David came through later and saw her in the garden from the kitchen window, wandering amid the ancient trees, and came out to join her in the sunlight.

"Are you all right?" he asked and she nodded, silent for a while.

"Yes," she said finally, her hand resting on a gnarled old trunk. "Yes, I am all right. This has done something inside me. I can't explain really. It's like feeling something unlock and become free again."

He watched her, curiously. There was something different, something lighter, less artificial and more natural about her face; she had so long worn a guarded look that held back from expressing any real feelings. He hadn't realised it till now that her face had been almost unnaturally still, like that of a living statue.

"Good," he said. "Do you think you might be getting at whatever Nick wanted to say? Is the poem making sense to you?"

"Good God, no!" she said with a laugh. "Some of it makes some sense but then I move a few lines and I hardly understand a word of it. And then some lines I might almost have written myself."

"Such as?"

"I told my soul to be still and let the dark come upon you," she said. 19 "I wrote something very like that when Nick died. Of course, I destroyed all my poems and his letters too so I can't remember what I wrote exactly, but it was about letting the darkness come upon me like a dark tide. Oh, I can't explain to you how much these words hold, what worlds and gods they hold, and what hope too."

He saw she had tucked the book into her waistband, like a sword.

"I'm glad," he said, and realised he was. "When you're ready to try and tell me, I'll be ready to hear."

He put his arms round her and felt her lean into him, warm and relaxed.

"Come on in," he said. "I reckon dinner will go better with a glass or two of wine each, don't you?"

She nodded slowly and turned with him and went inside.

To live with words inside that glow like live coals in the pit of the soul is to live in an almost pregnant state; the startling jerk of unconscious recognition of a truth beyond one's own ability to express is very like the kick of the babe unborn. It comes when it chooses and sleeps when it wants and the sense of watching over that tender sleeping form curled up on itself like a nautilus in ancient seas gives a huge and almost overwhelming feeling of responsibility: this thing is mine to care for, nurture and protect as it grows within me though what I shall give birth to I do not know, but guard it I will whatever may come.

To explore ideas that are old to the world and yet new to the individual is like children exploring a wood that generations of children have wandered through as Eden or as fierce jungle: to each new explorer, the next corner turned may reveal treasure or dragons or possibly just an escaped shopping trolley or next door's cat. It is the exploring not the territory that changes. Perhaps old men ought to be explorers but few children grow to be explorers; we believe there are no more uncharted lands to discover and do not see the vast areas that are only ever incompletely investigated and those are the places both close to home and in the very soul of each of us and they blow like lost maps, dropped and discarded once the words Here Be Dragons have been written at the edges.

Using the poem as her map, Verity explored, taking words and phrases as road signs and tracks. On the Monday, when the door shut as first David and then Rose left for the day, she did not hear the slamming of the door as the sound of prison door shutting her in but rather as the heavy castle door shutting the world out so she could be free to wander where she needed to. In the attic rooms, she moved quietly as she paced up and down. Sometimes the rain beat heavily on the roof, other times the dust rose and danced in the beams of sunlight that filled the rooms through panes of glass now in need of a good clean. And whatever the weather, she sat or walked or worked on household chores, letting herself wander through thoughts and feelings she had not touched since she was truly young and had believed that she might somehow change the world in some small way. Funny to think that once she had believed she had mattered, that her abilities might one day count for something beyond the tarnished glow of exam success and school prizes; it seemed more than a lifetime ago.

Sometimes she held the book close, like a pious nun with a treasured missal, and other times she would leave the book carelessly wherever she felt like it, coming to retrieve it when she needed to check the order of words. At a certain time in the afternoon she would come back to herself and begin cooking the evening meal for the family and returning to the quiet and orderly world she lived in, her head still glowing with the day's experience.

She took walks in the area around her home, a space she had known most of her life and had known well in her teens, and found it changed from her memories of it. The old house a few streets away on her old route to school that had been virtually derelict for years had been bought up by a keen young family and was being steadily transformed and restored to its original beauty; the tidy garden she had admired as a girl, bending sometimes to smell the roses that leaned onto the pavement courting the passer by to admire them, had been paved over to make hard-standing for a small fleet of cars. The small shop where her grandfather had bought his papers had been bought up by a chain of newsagents and was filled with the exact same range as anywhere in the country; all the sweets and magazines in bright, homogeneous displays and the fridge filled with chilled drinks and cartons of milk. The elderly cat a street away that had greeted her some days and scratched her hand on others was long gone, replaced by a kitten now itself growing old but a living replica of the ancient ginger tom of such varying moods. This cat had rubbed against her legs like an old friend when she paused to pet it. She walked the streets and parks like a tourist, mentally pausing to notice, admire or be repulsed by a vase of flowers in a window, or a china doll or a sleeping cat or a row of plants. Ordinary things seemed somehow extraordinary, taking on a kind of luminous glow that lit them up from within.

She spoke aloud to herself as she came out of the house one morning. "Fare forward. There's no going back. I'm not the person I was yesterday and I am not the person I shall be tomorrow. So I shall fare forward and let that be all."[20]

She walked into town and saw Juliet's shop boarded up, the sign up announcing it was for sale, and saw that already the vultures of the urban jungle had been there, pasting posters on the newly dead corpse, annunciations of forthcoming gigs by DJs with bizarre names.

I must be getting old, she thought, to be so contemptuous of the new culture where a man who spins and chooses records is king. At least I'm unlikely to ever sound like my own mother; I hardly know what she sounds like to start with. The day I start saying "in my day" is the day I shave my head, pierce my navel and nose and start smoking something illegal.

She spoke aloud to the crowded street of how the past has a pattern not a sequence [21], and those passing assumed she was speaking to someone on a mobile phone with a particularly neat and inconspicuous headset. Oh, the blessings of technology! She could talk to herself as a mad person might and no one thought her mad at all. Indeed no one gave her a second glance as she wandered from shop to shop collecting the groceries she had chosen to buy and walked home.

The words in her head would often shift from the words on the page as her own mind and soul assimilated them and brought up new thoughts; well, new to her anyway. It felt like one of those dreams where you are searching for something and each time you turn away the landscape changes, sometimes dramatically and sometimes subtly but always confusingly. What you thought you had found is gone and something irrelevant but oddly endued with meaning is in its place; or the object that wasn't there a second before is there, shining in front of you, and you had to grasp it then and there or else lose it utterly. It was the oddest way to live and had she had any close friends, any friend at all, they might have worried she was losing her mind or her grasp on reality. To David, she had the look of a pregnant woman, carrying secrets within her and guarding the profoundest mystery, while wearing an expression that reminded him of the Mona Lisa. It had never occurred to him before how sexy that expression had truly been and he looked at her as if with new eyes.

"I do wonder about Da Vinci sometimes," he said one Sunday morning. "He painted that damn woman and created endless speculation about her and yet did he see what others saw or did he merely record it without ever experiencing it?"

"That's a good question," she said sleepily. "Don't know."

"Don't care either?"

"I didn't say that!" she said, stung. "A man who paints like that sees. Sees whatever is there. He doesn't have to feel what others feel but he does see; and for someone to be able to transmit that in any form so that any other person has the chance even hundreds of years later to see and understand and maybe even feel what he did, is astounding. It's what poets and artists and writers and so on and even scientists have tried to do in their own way for... well, forever really. Even cave art done tens of thousands of years ago has the power to move us even now with our twenty first century brains and preoccupations. It all comes down to the same thing really: do you see what I see, do you hear what I hear, do you feel what I feel? We seek not to be alone, even in our own heads. To know that another person thinks and feels what I think and feel means I am not alone in the dark forever."

"And what do you think and feel right now?"

"You know!" she said.

"Right!" he said, getting out of bed. "Is it tea or coffee you want, though?"

"Neither," she said and he got back into bed.

"You know something," he said a little later. "When we were first together, or when things were so tough when Rosie was tiny and we hadn't any cash to have fun and we were both so shattered, I might have been jealous if all this had happened back then. I might have been resentful of Nick then. But now, now you seem to have changed so much, like you've been sleepwalking all this time and you've just woken up, I'd shake his hand if he had a hand to shake and thank him, poor sod!"

"Am I really so different?" she asked, leaning into him.

"Different and the same," he said. "I can't explain it. It was as though you've been a pale copy of yourself all this time."

"I've always been pale," she said, with a half laugh.

"You had a kind of translucency," he said. "As if you were only half here, a ghost or something."

She nodded, though he couldn't see.

"I know," she said. "Sometimes it felt like that, or like I was behind glass and everything was muted, both sound and colour and everything. And I'm not translucent now?"

"No," he said but he didn't know how to explain how she seemed to be filled with a kind of light now, that pregnant glow he'd only ever seen in expectant mothers who were satisfied with the prospect of motherhood.

There was a polite rap at their door, making them both jump and then giggle.

"Mum?" came Rose's voice, tentative and a bit irritated. "I can't find my swimming costume. Do you know where it is?"

Verity yawned and stretched.

"I think it's in the clean washing from yesterday," she called back. "Give me a minute and I'll go and have a look."

"I've got swimming practice today though and I need it now," Rose called back.

219

"Patience is a virtue. I'll be five minutes," Verity called back. "You don't need it till later but you want it now. Learn the difference."

She rolled out of bed as she heard her daughter's over-loud sigh and then footsteps leading downstairs. She pulled on her dressing gown and then glanced at David who was laughing soundlessly.

"What's so funny?" she asked, doing up the belt.

"You, being assertive," he said. "I can't remember the last time I ever saw that."

She snatched up a pillow and threw it at him.

"Ask Juliet," she said. "She knows how assertive I can be."

"She's probably still in shock," he said. "Look, if Rose is going on this swimming camp, what shall we do? Do you want to go away or do you want to just stay home?"

She paused at the door, thinking.

"I'd like to go to the seaside somewhere," she said and he sat bolt upright in surprise.

"The seaside? But you hate the seaside," he protested.

"No, I've never hated it, love," she said quietly. "I was always afraid of it."

He followed her downstairs and filled the kettle while she rummaged amid the clean laundry for Rose's costume.

"I don't understand," he said.

"What don't you understand?"

"I really thought you hated the seaside," he explained. "Every time we went you wouldn't even paddle, wouldn't walk near the shoreline or anything. You can't even bear to watch Rosie at a swimming gala, never mind swimming in the sea."

She shrugged helplessly.

"I was scared," she said. "Now I'm not. At least I don't think I am. That place we went to in south Wales, when Rose was about five, that sticky out peninsula bit along from Swansea, can we go there? Take the tent and have a few days or so there. I wouldn't promise a week since you know what the weather can be like in Wales, but a few days would be nice even in the rain."

He shook his head, in puzzlement.

"If you want to," he said. "This is so weird. Everything has changed and yet everything is really still the same. I'll have a look at the tent later today, put it up in the garden just to check it's still all right."

"And that you remember how to," she said, grinning. "You know how every time we get it out you have to learn how to put it up all over again."

He laughed and bowed.

"Sherpa Tensing at your service," he said. "Everest an option, the Gower peninsula a certainty. Right, now do you want tea or coffee?"

Rose came into the kitchen as they were kissing and made a disgusted face.

"Oh for goodness sake," she said crossly. "Get a room!"

One Monday, David came home from school with the local paper, a thing he never did.

"Someone at school gave it to me," he said. "Just have a look at the headline."

He passed it to Verity who read it aloud.

"'Local businesswoman arrested on vice charge?'" she said and pulled a face.

"Just have a look at the name of said local businesswoman," David said and she peered closer at the slightly smudged type.

"Good God, it's Juliet," Verity exclaimed nearly dropping the paper in surprise. "I don't believe it!"

"Just read it," he said.

"Is this the woman you used to work for Mum?" Rose asked, fork half way to her mouth.

"Mmm," Verity said. "OK, here it is. 'Local businesswoman Juliet Flannagan, 32', well, either the paper's got it wrong or she's taken to lying about her age."

"I'd give it fifty-fifty either way," David said. "Go on, read the rest."

"OK, OK," Verity said. "Give me a chance. Right, 'Juliet Flannagan, whose well-known shop The Enchanted Kingdom recently closed due to financial difficulties, was arrested at her home last week and charged later with running a brothel. A variety of illegal substances were also found but Ms. Flannagan has not yet been charged in connection with these and it is believed that the substances were the property of the "guests" attending her exclusive "parties". The accused has been running invited guests only swinging parties for some time but following an anonymous tip-off, police raided the premises and arrested a number of people, all of whom but Ms. Flannagan were released without charge later. She will appear at court, blah, blah, blah.' Crikey, what's the betting it was Martine's husband who tipped the police off?"

David shrugged and grinned.

"Looks like you got out just before the ship sank without trace," he said. "I bet the police might have a few questions to ask you. Just pray she doesn't ask you to be a character witness in court."

"She'd be very stupid if she did," she said. "And while it does look like she's been pretty stupid, she can't think I'd ever stand up for her after the years of rubbish I got from her. No wonder she's been able to just sell off the shop if she's been running that sort of party."

Rose wisely said nothing at this point, aiming to make sure she wasn't sent off so she wouldn't hear any more of the very interesting gossip.

"We do live in interesting times," David said. "There must have been a lot of money changing hands for the police to get involved. Technically swinging is illegal but I think a blind eye gets turned, so she must have been charging a hell of a lot for them to bother. And then the drugs too, that's bound to be a bit of a black mark. Do you reckon she'll get sent down?"

"I have no idea," Verity said. "I hope not."

"Mum, you are too damn nice," Rose said, unable to keep silent any longer.

"I wouldn't wish that on anyone," Verity said. "However nasty she was to me, she never did anything that really harmed me. However, before you accuse me of being too nice again, Rosie, I will say I am horribly pleased she's turned out to be a total fraud. I couldn't stand her holier than thou attitude; sometimes that was worse than the rudeness and the low pay. Anyway, I don't think you need to hear about such sordid things at dinner, dear."

"Mum, I am fourteen," Rose protested.

"You can wait till you've washed up then and you can get your dose of sordidness from Eastenders instead," Verity said.

Chapter 12

"It doesn't feel right without Rosie in the back, asking 'are we there yet?' every ten minutes," Verity said about half an hour into the drive.

"She stopped saying that when she was eight," David remarked. "Once she could read road signs and her watch, she didn't need to ask. But I take your point. I don't think we've ever been away together, just the two of us."

She cast her mind back carefully over the years.

"We had that weekend straight after we got married," she said.

"That hardly counts!" he said. "That was only because the flat wasn't ready for us. The old tenants should have been out but weren't. A weekend in a B and B down the road hardly counts. And certainly not as a honeymoon!"

"Shall we tell people we're on our honeymoon?" she asked, grinning at him.

"Better not!" he said. "A week in Wales is hardly exotic by today's standards. Fifty years ago it might have been but these days people go to Bali or somewhere for the honeymoon. If people really think this is our honeymoon, they're going to start edging away, because either we are very boring or very strange."

"Or worse: both," she said and leaned her head back into the headrest. "It still feels weird without Rose, though. Do you think she'll be all right on this camp thing? She does have enough credit on her mobile to ring us if she needs to, doesn't she?"

"Quit worrying!" he said. "I bet she hasn't given us a thought. She couldn't wait to go. She'll love it: loads for her to do, friends to hang round with when the activities are over for the day, no chores, no washing up. Paradise, in short. What's she missing? A week or maybe less on a camp-site on what you so elegantly described at the sticky out peninsula bit down from Swansea. She's too old for buckets and spades, too young for the night-life. She'd have been bored senseless after a day or two."

"There's night-life on the Gower?" Verity asked, her voice full of suspicion. "It's changed then!"

"I lied about the night-life," David said. "There were some nice pubs though. And there was a bus into Swansea, and they do have nightclubs there. You'd just have to get a taxi back or sleep in a doorway and get the first bus in the morning. Bit of a dead give-away for the dirty stop-outs, coming home with the milk-float, still in your glad-rags and sporting a hangover."

"I don't think I've ever done that," she said.

"You haven't missed much," he said. "I think I was about seventeen the last time I did that. It made me certain to plot my route home with more care in future. Sleeping rough is not to be recommended. It's bad enough waking at home with a mouth like the inside of an old sock, when you can get to the bathroom and maybe have some kind person feed you tea till you feel human again, but waking in a shop doorway with no prospect of tea or sympathy till you've remembered who you are and where you live....Well, I leave that to your imagination!"

"Yuck!" she said. "I think I agree, I haven't missed much. It's going to be strange having the whole tent to ourselves too."

"Yep, no shoes to fall over but our own. No soggy swimsuit left with the tea towels. No sulks on rainy days. No one saying "I'm bored" three times an hour when we're having a quiet morning," he said. "Not to mention other things. Why is sex so much better when camping?"

"I hadn't noticed but I'll oblige seeing as you want me to ask the question. I don't know: why is sex better when camping?"

"Because the excitement's in tents!" he said and she looked blank. "In tents. Intense. Get it?"

She groaned at his awful joke.

"You should be shot for that," she said. "That was so juvenile!"

"It would be," he said. "One of my nicer year tens came up with that one when I admitted I was going camping. I promised him I'd tell my wife that one, so promise fulfilled."

"Good," she said. "You didn't tell them where you were camping though, did you?"

"Nope, I couldn't face all the sheep jokes," he said. "Anyway, I like Wales. I hated that time we went to Spain."

"I thought that was just my parents," she said.

"I didn't much like the place either," he said. "I wouldn't have minded getting out beyond the beaten track a bit and wandering around and exploring, but your father kept saying there wasn't anything worth seeing. Hiring a car at that point was tantamount to saying I thought he was a liar."

224

She laughed softly.

"Sorry," she said. "Inflicting not only myself on you but my awful family too!"

"I liked your Granddad," he said. "As Rosie would say, he was cool."

"He was," she agreed. "I do still miss him, but at least he was spared the indignity of losing his marbles one by one. Maybe one day we can go further afield and explore other countries. At least in Wales they do speak English. It was painful when you tried to order a beer in phrasebook Spanish."

"I know, I know," he said. "And when I'd finally managed to get the words out in the right order, the bastard behind the bar asked in a cockney accent whether I wanted Stella or Carlsberg. How humiliating! He even looked Spanish. He could have at least worn a badge that said, actually I'm English!"

The conversation went on as the miles went by sometimes with agonising slowness as the inevitable jams were joined.

"Considering I though everyone went abroad for their holidays these days, there's a hell of lot of traffic on the way to Wales and not all of it can be the Welsh coming home," David remarked. "Next set of services we come to, I'm going to get off this bloody car park and go and get some lunch. Maybe later the road will have cleared. There can only be so many people going to Wales otherwise the weight will tip the whole damn land into the sea. And I for one don't want to be there when that happens!"

Despite David's cunning plan, the roads were still congested after lunch and they had to sit and edge along inch by inch. The journey extended horrendously and by the time they made it to the camp-site any thought of an afternoon at the beach had long gone, along with the best part of the day. Setting up the tent took longer than they'd planned and by the time they'd got it standing, the sky had begun to turn a beautiful shade of pale azure blue that deepened steadily as they got everything else sorted and the first stars were twinkling faintly as they cleared away the remains of their supper.

"We're out of practice with this camping lark," David said. "And let's face it, Rosie was very good at pumping up air-beds and running errands like finding milk and bread. I always thought we just invented tasks to keep her out of mischief but now I can see she had her uses!"

"Mercenary git!" Verity said and threw her tea towel at him. "I miss her. Maybe we can have a second week away once she's back, all of us together. Even if it is a disaster, I'd like to have one seaside break where I'm not miles from the beach quaking at the edge of the sand. I can't make up for all those years when I couldn't do it but at least we can have one proper old fashioned seaside holiday."

"See how this one goes first," David said wisely. "You never know how you might feel tomorrow when you get to the beach. You might freeze utterly. Now, I recall putting at least one bottle of bière blonde in that cool box."

"One? You put six in there!" she said. "And before you ask, I'd love one too."

They sat outside the tent, as the evening cooled and the sky turned navy blue, spangled with white stars and smeared here and there with a wisp or two of cloud.

"I reckon it's going to be a nice day tomorrow," he said.

"I think you're right but you can't be sure this close to the coast," she agreed.

In a tent not too far from theirs, a small child was protesting bedtime and they both smiled at their memories.

"It doesn't seem five minutes since Rosie was that age," David said. "Come on, let's go to bed. I'm bushed from that dreadful drive."

"I did say I'd take over if you wanted," she said, starting to fold her chair and bring it under the tent awning.

"I was into it by then," he said. "I'd not have anything to moan about if you'd done half. As it is, I can complain about my poor aching shoulders and give you enough of a guilt trip to give them a good massage."

"As I said before, you're a mercenary git, David Meadows," she said severely. "I brought some of that massage balm though. I know you too well by now."

He grinned and folded his chair up with a crocodilian snap.

"Time for bed then, Zebedee!" he said. "Or should that be Florence?"

226

"Just as long as it isn't Dougal, I'm not complaining," she said. "I hated The Magic Roundabout because the kids at school all reckoned I looked more like that damned dog. That's when I stopped wearing my hair loose."

"That's another nice thing about Rosie being elsewhere. I don't have to translate every one of our childhood reminiscences for her to say, "I really wanted to know that, Dad. Not!" each time," David said as they pottered about the tent. "It loses so much in translation!"

"It does," she agreed. "But I still miss her."

"Just think, though," he said. "Tomorrow morning we can be up and on that beach without the usual hassles and delays and having to go back at least twice for some essential that she's left in the tent."

"I suppose," Verity said and indeed the next morning, when she stepped onto the huge wide beach, she felt some relief that her daughter wasn't there. Not because there had been none of the usual messing about and false starts, but rather because when she peeled off to her swimsuit, her legs in particular were white from years of hiding in the shade, and the addition of heavy duty sunscreen made her looked even more pale. Rosie's amusement at that would have been hard to bear and might have sent her scuttling for her clothes.

"I look like something that crawled out from under a rock," she said, gesturing at her lower half. "I don't think these legs have seen the sun in years."

He gazed at them.

"No," he said. "You don't look like something that lives under a rock. You look more like something carved out of the finest white marble."

She snorted.

"About as buoyant as the average rock, then," she said. "Did you know that most classical statues were usually painted to make them look life-like? It's only modern ones they leave maggoty-white. I knew I should have got some of that fake tan. I really look like one of those witchety grubs!"

"OK, you're very pale," he said. "But why is that a problem? It's only idiots like Carla who buy into the tanned-is-best philosophy. If you're so bothered, I'll race you to the sea and you can hide."

He'd started running before she realised what he was up to, so she dropped her bag and sprinted after him and was ankle deep in the sea before she registered that finally, after so many years of avoiding it, she had broken that unrecognised taboo. Her first thought was that it was bloody cold and her second was that it felt marvellous.

"Well done," he said, and scooped up water in both hands and splashed her with it. "Welcome to the world of the surf dude. Have you seen how many surfboards and body boards there are? We'll have to get some later. Are you all right?"

Verity didn't answer but simply splashed him in return.

Long days in the sun had turned Verity not brown but a pale shade of gold, rather like the sand that covered the enormous beach. Even the highest factor cream couldn't keep it out altogether but she didn't mind. It was rare enough to get sunny days in succession in Wales, famed for its rain, and living mostly in her swimsuit mean that most of her clothes didn't get worn and therefore didn't require washing. That made it even more of a holiday for her and the evenings they spent either in the nearest pub or outside their tent, reading until the light faded too much. They took long walks along the beaches and up on the downs, lying amid the heather and listening to the skylarks and grasshoppers, and spent hours in the sea and as the last day approached, they were both reluctant to go home. On their last evening, they ate early and headed off down to a tiny cove about a mile or so from the camp-site intending to watch the sun go down there. The evening was still warm and the air was aromatic with the scents of both shore and sea. Sheep bleated in the fields above the cove, and gulls wheeled in the sky, calling each other.

"Fishermen used to believe that gulls held the souls of those who drowned at sea," Verity said as they picked their way down the steep and rocky path. "On a stormy night you might almost believe it but on an evening like this, they're just birds."

She licked her lips and tasted the salt from the air on them.

"I have so enjoyed this holiday," she said as they walked, her sandals quiet on the sandy path. "I never thought I'd ever go near the sea again."

"Why were you afraid of it?" he asked. "I might have understood it if you were a fisherman's wife. But you've only been a tourist, a visitor. Were you so scared that it might take me or Rosie too?"

"No," she said. "Well, yes, that too but not as much as something else and I don't know that I can explain so it makes any sense, never mind good sense."

"Try," he urged.

"Let me get past this bit and I will," she said. They had come to the start of the cove and the path had vanished amid massive rocks and boulders and she need to concentrate to pick her way down.

It took some time before they got to the wet sand, held between two arms of rock that seemed to guard the little cove. Verity slipped her sandals off and wriggled her toes in the damp sand and began to walk along at the shoreline her feet covered with the foam of the tiny wavelets. The sea sucked at her feet with some force and she could sense the change in the direction of the tide.

"Tide's turned," she said. "It's coming in now."

The sun was slowly sinking and the air from the sea was cooler and she moved further back, away from the little waves that touched her feet and at the rocks she sat and dusted off the sand that stuck to the soles of her feet and put her sandals back on.

"Even though Nick died the other side of the world," she said. "I've always been somehow afraid that he might wash up somewhere for me to find. Doesn't that sound mad? His bones lie at the bottom of a very different sea and yet I was scared that I would find them on the shoreline of this country. You know how you find all sorts of flotsam and jetsam at the high tide mark. Most of it is the usual rubbish, plastic bottles and flip-flops, the odd bit of rope and tin cans. But every time I've been near the seaside since then, when we went when Rosie was little, the first thing I always saw when we got to the sand was a bone. Weird. They're probably bird bones from gulls or even chicken bones from picnics but every time I'd see a bone and it froze me to the core."

"You never said," he said gently.

"How could I? It sounds mad now, doesn't it? How could I explain the whole story? I didn't know where to start even if I had

229

thought I could bring myself to think about it," she said. "This has been the best holiday ever. It's healed something in me I'd never known was wounded. I've had time to think and time to simply be."

She drew her knees up to her chest, and held them to her. David thought she looked a little like a mermaid with her hair blowing loose around her.

"Are you cold?" he asked.

The wind from the ocean was cool and after the heat of the long day it was a bit of a shock to the system.

"A bit," she admitted. "I should have brought a jacket with me but I didn't think."

"Tell you what, why don't we have a fire?" he said.

"I'm not sure we're allowed to," she said.

"Bugger that; who's going to stop us? The tide's coming in, it's going to get dark soon and I hardly think anyone would really mind if we made sure it was cleared up afterwards," he said. "I've got matches."

"What can we burn anyway?" she asked, but he simply reached down and picked up a damp bit of driftwood.

"That'll never burn," she said.

"The stuff above the high tide mark will be bone dry," he said, not registering quite what he had said. "It doesn't have to be a big fire; just a bit of a one to keep warm by for an hour or so."

"You're just a big boy scout," she said and got off her rock and padded over the pebbles to where a tangle of driftwood and rubbish marked the highest tide of the year. Blue tufts of nylon rope, frayed and tattered by weeks or more at sea poked out from the mess of seaweed, wood bleached white from exposure to sea and sun and the inevitable rotting trainer. The wood was indeed dry and brittle, and once David had built a makeshift hearth of rocks it took only a few matches to get the mass of wood and desiccated seaweed alight. As the light leached from the sky, Verity cast along the high tide mark for more wood and found armfuls to carry back and stack near the crackling, spitting bonfire. The flames were many-hued and didn't give off a lot of heat; perhaps the wind caught it and whisked the warmth away before she could feel it.

She sat and wrapped her arms around herself, hugging her own body to keep warm. The smell from the fire was of salt and that unique smell of the sea, slightly fishy but somehow mysterious. David sat opposite her, watching her in the colours of the fire that flashed and changed with the crackling flames like the Northern Lights caught on earth.

"Have you had any more visions?" he asked quietly and she shook her head.

"Not since I saw Catherine," she said. "I don't think I will have any more, not like that anyway. I've done a hell of a lot of thinking lately, trying to figure it all out. I did worry that I was somehow being haunted by Nick, being punished for moving on, marrying someone else and all sorts of other silly fears that might make a good scary movie but they're nothing to do with life, real life. Him giving me clues through Catherine meant I had something to work from, even if it nearly drove me mad trying to remember where those lines were from. I have wondered why he couldn't just tell me directly what I need to know but as I spent time with the ideas and concepts I realised that there was no way of directly expressing them in a few simple words and not run the risk of me getting hung up on those words alone. In many ways, it goes beyond words. That's what he was trying to explain when he quoted the bit about words slipping and decaying into imprecision."

"But why did he use a poem to get his message across?" David asked. "Why could he not have explained it in his own words?"

"Because I needed to understand it in my own words," she said. "Not his, not Eliot's, not yours, not Rosie's nor Charlotte's nor Carla's. Mine. Oh, it's complicated but in the end what better way for a poet to communicate but by using poetry? His own had never reached the kind of sophistication that he needed to get the right effect; don't forget that however good a poet he might have been, he was still only a kid when he died. So he turned to the only poetry he knew that even came close to addressing the kind of issues he knew I needed to face."

David nodded, though he wasn't sure he really understood. She looked very distant, sitting there only a few feet away while their little bonfire crackled and spat and the light from the flames danced in her eyes. She looked so different from the carefree

231

holidaymaker of only hours ago, but he knew she was still the same person he'd always loved and he wasn't afraid.

"There were words in that poem that hold volumes, libraries even," she said. "They express what I don't have the words to express. At least not in any way that resembles sense and meaning. The poem talked of how we die when our loved ones pass, and then they come back and bring us with them. 22 That's what grief is. A little bit of us dies when our loved ones do. We go down into death with them while the grief endures. When the grief pales, we return with what gifts our loved ones gave us in life. I didn't come back. I grieved for Nick, yes, but I never quite came back. A part of me lived on as if he'd never died. Maybe in an alternate universe, maybe just in some dark corner of my head, that life I never lived, was lived. I didn't come back fully from the world of the dead to be reborn with my changed life. Some of it never changed."

"Is that why you had the visions?" he asked.

"I think so," she replied but her voice was dreamy. "There's more to it than that though. I didn't allow myself to think about Nick much and maybe I should have done. That way I might have reasoned that the life we planned for ourselves was not likely to work well. As the years went by and experience taught me things you can't guess at seventeen, I never said to myself, well thank God I didn't marry Nick. I didn't think about it and therefore the life unlived gained power. When Granddad died, he was the last real link with that time, the last person who might have talked with me about it and the pain I felt at losing him is what I think triggered the visions, though I think something was bound to give sooner or later. We had the busy time of sorting the house out, moving in and all that and then when things became quiet, that was when it started. I wonder now if I saw Will around town for months before the vision began and was reminded unconsciously of Nick. He looks enough like him to have fooled me for a second or two at a distance. However it occurred, I started having the visions and now everything has changed."

David threw on another branch, shattering the pictures he had been seeing in the flames.

"What has changed then?" he asked. "Maybe you'll be able to put this behind you now and get on with life?"

"I can't do that," she said quietly. "It's changed too much for that."

Oh God, David thought, suddenly afraid. No wonder she was so keen to have this holiday. It's the last one. Oh God.

He put his arms round himself, to keep himself from shaking with the dread of it.

"It's OK," she said, gently, as if sensing his alarm. "Nothing terrible is going to happen. Relax. You know I love you. I'm not going anywhere. But putting all this behind me is not something I should do even if I thought I could. Putting things behind me is what's nearly destroyed me. I put behind me something I should have worked with and transformed. You never knew I wrote poetry when I was young or why I stopped writing or why I was so scared of the seaside. It wouldn't have worried or upset you to know any of these things but I never told you. Part of me stopped when Nick died and that part of me has come back to life now. I think that same part of me would have remained dormant if Nick had lived so don't get the idea I think my life might have been better. What I have seen of that life tells me I was still sleepwalking in that life too. I convinced myself that Nick was the one with the talent, the gifts to share with the world, and that my gifts were secondary to his. So I worked in a job I hated and was no good at and gave me nothing in return so I could support him. I negated myself. And I hate to admit it but I've done the same here by default. I took a job I never much liked rather than ask myself what I really wanted to do with my life and time just slid by and I never made any moves toward finding out what I could really do. There's a line that is so poignant where Eliot talks about being in mid life, wasting twenty years of his life. 23 I haven't wasted twenty years but I haven't exactly made use of them either. I'd hate to get to the end of my life and think, is that it, is that all there is?"

"You won't," he said.

"I will, though, if I don't make some choices now," she said. "When I was seventeen I invested a whole load of my own personal ambition and hopes and dreams in someone who then died. But had he lived, there's every chance our lives would have been a miserable mess. I thought his dreams and my dreams were the same thing and really they weren't, even if they resembled them. When I saw Catherine, Nick gave me back my dreams through the words of Eliot's Four Quartets; he gave me back my own dreams. I've spent weeks mulling over them all, squeezing meaning out of each word, each line and every time I think I've exhausted it something else comes up. The thing is, we're meant to be explorers, all of us. Each experience is a vital, living thing, each place new and exciting, and we don't see it. I'd lost that, perhaps through grief at first, then through the pressure of time and life and family. Life has no savour lived like that; I didn't have a life as such. I wrote a poem a week or two back that about sums it up. It's the first poem I've written since I was seventeen and it's not very good but it says what I feel and that's what counts."

"Can I see it?" David asked, very quietly, and she rummaged in the belt bag she wore to hold keys and money. She fished out a piece of folded paper and straightened it out.

"It's just called V," she said and began to read.

"I don't have a life," she read.

"I exist in the corners
Of the lives of others
Kind enough to lend me space.
No, don't shake your head,
Protest and frown,
Condemning me for self-pity.
It's true: the words say it all.
Wife, daughter, friend, mother.
They define me by my
Relationships with others.
My name: a jumble of sounds
Meaning nothing in themselves,
A label by which to identify,
Quantify, stratify and forget:
Put me in my box
And hope I stay there.
Me, I reduce my name
To a single initial.
It takes up less space, less attention.
And maybe, just maybe,
Beyond all names,

234

I may shine alone."

The words hung like smoke between them, before the stiff breeze from the sea blew it away. Verity twisted the paper softly between her hands, pleating and rolling it, turning it into a boat, a flower, a hat.

"Since I've been thinking about all of this, so much has come back to me, things I loved and enjoyed doing," she said. "I never wanted to teach, certainly not kids anyway. I don't even much like children if I'm entirely honest. But I did want to work with words and I've never done it. I stopped writing back then and I found out from Charlotte that Nick thought me a better poet than him. That gave me a jolt. To get back my dreams and find that they still have some meaning for me, well, I don't know how to express how much that means to me."

"We all need our dreams," he said. "Even if we never achieve them, we need to have them. I've always wanted you to be able to be more than you seem to be. I've always known you are more than you appear. But I never knew how you could ever reach it."

"There's a line at the end of the final poem, 'Little Gidding'," she said. "He talks of never stopping our exploration but that the end of the exploring will be to return to where we began and know it properly for the first time.24. I've come back to where I started, in so many ways. I've come back to a point before I met Nick and let myself be consumed by someone else's dreams, even after he was dead. I even did it with you because I didn't know I was doing it. It was just what happened. Now I can do anything, be anything. I know where I am, where I have been, for the first time. I need to carry on exploring, discovering new worlds in old places, discovering for myself who I am and what I am here for. So many people go their whole lives and never know who they are and where they are and what they came for; I'm not going to do that. I've woken up now."

The sea boomed softly as the tide began to race in, and Verity twisted the paper again, this time into the shape of a white rose, the paper softened by endless handling. She dropped it gently onto the glowing embers of the bonfire.

David made a move to save it but she waved him back.

"It's all right," she said. "I do have a copy. I just wanted to set it free. By reading it to you and then by burning it."

The paper rose charred at the edges for a second before catching fire properly, flaring up briefly, the fire and the rose becoming one before vanishing in the wind that whipped the ashes up as the first of the waves touched the hearthstones.

"What are you going to do, then?" he asked, as they got to their feet.

Verity let the question settle as she ran through her mind the possibilities that had been appearing miraculously like spring wheat each time she thought about it. She could do a PhD, she might learn a new language, join a gardening club, write up her grandfather's dig notes, maybe learn to fly a glider. The ideas rose up in ranks like dragon's teeth soldiers, some sane, some silly, some downright mad but all shining with potential like the foam-tipped waves that were now licking at the stones of their improvised hearth. She turned as the last scrap of dry wood flared briefly before the water rolled over the edge and dowsed the flames.

"I don't know yet," she said happily as he took her arm in his. "I might just write a book."

Footnotes

When I first wrote the book, I had imagined it would find a traditional publishing deal and any issues regarding quotes would be dealt with by the publishers. Coming back to it when I began self-publishing, I initially believed that as fifty years had elapsed since Eliot's death, I would be able to use the quotations without a problem.

Very close to publication, I discovered I was mistaken and that copyright had been extended to seventy years. Thankfully I had not yet gone ahead and had the chance to go through and remove the quotes rather than seek and pay for permission to use them. I have used footnotes to indicate where a quotation would have been and what that would have included, so that readers can go and consult their well-worn or newly acquired copy of the poems referred to. Given that all the poems I mention are available to read for free online, I hope that this compromise is acceptable. I would urge you to find and read the poem at some point if you can.

All other poetry is my own.

1: *Burnt Norton V.*
2: *The Wasteland: I: The Burial of The Dead*, line 43
3: *Burnt Norton V.*
4: *Little Gidding I*
5: The first words are from Dame Julian of Norwich's shewings but are quoted in the last four lines of *Little Gidding V.*
6: *Little Gidding I*
7: *Burnt Norton I*
8: *Little Gidding I*
9: *Little Gidding I*
10: *Little Gidding I*
11: *Little Gidding I*
12: *Little Gidding I*
13: *Burnt Norton I*
14: *Burnt Norton I*
15: *Burnt Norton I*
16: *Burnt Norton I*
17: *Burnt Norton V*

18: *Burnt Norton V*
19: *East Coker III*
20: *The Dry Salvages III*
21: *The Dry Salvages III*
22: *Little Gidding V*
23: *East Coker V*
24: *Little Gidding V*

Acknowledgements

Thanks go to Jennifer Gloria for her beta reading, and Sarah Lewis-Morgan for her proof-reading skills. I'd especially like to mention Annette Thomson for her brilliant cover art which she came up with after me dithering over what the book was about and how hard it was to find an image to represent the themes of the book; her patience and imagination saved the day and stopped the book going out into the world in its night dress (much as Verity does).

To my family, much gratitude for your support and care during my times of frenetic writing and the times of frustrated non-writing, not to mention the agony and anticipation of a new release.

Final thanks go to Caitlin Matthews for the endorsement on the cover and the blurb and for her support in the final stages of birthing the book. It had become stuck and needed some gentle assistance and encouragement.

If you have enjoyed this book, please consider leaving a review (on Amazon, Goodreads, Facebook or a blog). Reviews help with visibility in a crowded market place as well as helping other potential readers decide if a book is for them or not.

You can find out more at my blog: Zen and the Art of Tight-rope Walking (http//zenandthartofitghtropewalking.wordpress.com)

More books by Vivienne Tuffnell:

Novels:
Square Peg
Away With The Fairies
Strangers and Pilgrims
The Bet

Novella:
The Hedgeway

Short Story collections:
The Wild Hunt and other tales
The Moth's Kiss

Poetry:
Accidental Emeralds
Hallowed Hollow
A Box of Darkness

Non-fiction:
Depression and The Art of Tightrope Walking
Meditating with Aromatics

21981076R00134

Printed in Great Britain
by Amazon